Praise for Paula T. Renfroe

"Hot and steamy, but stirred with subtle nuance, Paula T. Renfroe's debut novel explores the dangers of desire and the complexity of infidelity with care and candor."
>   —Elliott Wilson, co-author of *Ego Trip's Rap List* and
>   *Ego Trip's Big Book of Racism,* and Founder and CEO
>   of rapradar.com

"A fearless depiction of female sexuality, *The Cheating Curve* careens at break-neck speeds while maintaining deft insight into its characters. Paula T. Renfroe cannily layers her heroines with fierce loyalty, unbridled consumerism, occasional hubris and a great deal of heart. This is a thoroughly addictive read."
>   —Mary HK Choi, Features Editor of *Giant* magazine

"If you enjoyed the entertaining exploration of relationships in the movie *Brown Sugar*, you'll love the sexy, captivating, insightful examination of infidelity in *The Cheating Curve*. Renfroe's voice is honest and street smart. With *The Cheating Curve*, Paula T. Renfroe makes a soaring debut as a novelist."
>   —Michael Elliot, screenwriter of *Brown Sugar*

"*The Cheating Curve* accurately depicts the sexual and emotional drama real men and women deal with in relationships. Paula T. Renfroe's writing style is provocative, yet urbane. Who knew cheating could be so titillating?"
>   —Datwon Thomas, COO and Editor in Chief
>   of globalgrind.com

D0050202

The Cheating Curve

PAULA T. RENFROE

KENSINGTON PUBLISHING CORP.

www.kensingtonbooks.com

DAFINA BOOKS are published by

Kensington Publishing Corp.
119 West 40th Street
New York, NY 10018

All Kensington titles, imprints, and distributed lines are available at special quantity discounts for bulk purchases for sales promotion, premiums, fund-raising, educational, or institutional use.

Special book excerpts or customized printings can also be created to fit specific needs. For details, write or phone the office of the Kensington Special Sales Manager: Kensington Publishing Corp., 119 West 40th Street, New York, NY 10018, Attn. Special Sales Department. Phone: 1-800-221-2647.

Dafina and the Dafina logo Reg. U.S. Pat. & TM Off.

ISBN-13: 978-0-7582-3889-4
ISBN-10: 0-7582-3889-4

First Printing: April 2010
10 9 8 7 6 5 4 3 2 1

Printed in the United States of America

For my beloved mother, Julia Belle Renfroe:
grace personified

Acknowledgments

Thank God I didn't travel this writing journey alone—from concept to publication, many a soul helped me along the way. It's such a risky thing to name names, but gratitude must be conveyed. . . .

To my mom, for handing me the blueprint on womanhood. How I miss your counsel. My dad, for making me a daddy's girl.

To my children, Essence and Kaari—my love for you is boundless, my like for you is genuine. Your incredible patience, supreme understanding, and much needed humor made this thing here possible.

To Bonsu, for *everything*.

To my sister, Phyllis, for seeing more in me than I saw in myself at times. Thank you for holding up that mirror. To my brother Kenneth, the very first artist to inspire me. My brother Calvin, for championing Team Paula. And you, Charles, for eternally blurring the line between brother and friend. I'll never be gifted enough to thank you in mere words for all you've done and continue to do.

To my sistergirls: Kathy, no one could ever comprehend the depth and breadth of our friendship. Lisa, you reminded me that I am indeed a warrior. Danielle, for your faith in me through the peaks and valleys. Tee, my go-to-and-get-it-done girl—let's go! Jasmine, for encouraging me to be my best self. Alia and Elaine, for picking up some of my mommy slack. Yvonne, for embracing me and mine. Jackie, Reesie, and Caprice, for your love and support. My phantom editor, Felicia—without your daily morning push-it-through calls, *The Cheating Curve* might still be just a manuscript. Now finish yours. My Akwaaba Book Club sisters for the early support. We can finally do my novel, no need to go easy. Many thank-yous.

To my gem of an agent, Jacqueline Hackett, for taking on this "passion project" in one of the most tumultuous times in publishing and guiding me through with such steadiness—oh, and for making *didactic* my least favorite word in the dictionary. Rakia Clark, for digging *The Cheating Curve* in the first place. My editor, Mercedes Fernandez, for treating me and my manuscript with such gentle care and thoughtfulness. To Kervin, for your selfless guidance and advice. I know. I owe you. I gotchu. To Coffey and Cubannie, my favorite blend of café con leche, thank you for coming through for the boss lady time and time again. To Michael Elliot, Selwyn Hinds, Datwon Thomas, Mary Choi, and Elliott Wilson, for your early blurbs. To Bread Stuy, for the caffeine and conversation and allowing me to take up residence during my entire first draft. Thank you.

To every friend, relative, colleague, stranger, and commuter who has either shared a kind word or trusted me with their personal accounts of infidelity, I thank you. Now the dialogue begins.

The Cheating Curve

Chapter 1

"You are not in Kansas anymore, Dorothy.
You're in Brooklyn."

Langston N. Rogers paced in front of Pretty Inside while she waited for her best friend, Aminah, to arrive. It was Langston's every-other-Sunday-morning ritual. She would read the *Sunday Times* with her husband in bed. Make sweet love on top of the papers. Run five miles either on her treadmill or through Fort Greene Park. Shower. Then meet Aminah for their biweekly Session (Pretty Inside's special name for a mani-pedi). Afterward they'd brunch together somewhere in Brooklyn or occasionally Manhattan.

While Lang was more than anxious to get their Session started, she was in no rush to get off the phone with her new lover. They'd met at the Starbucks around the corner from her office almost three months before, and she hadn't even mentioned him to Aminah yet. It wasn't like them to keep secrets from each other, but she knew Aminah's sensitivity to infidelity all too well. Hell, her name meant "faithful" in Arabic. But it also meant "trustworthy." So if ever there was anyone Langston could share this indiscretion with, it was her best friend since childhood.

Lang whispered into her cell phone despite the fact that At-
lantic Avenue was not bustling with pedestrians. She couldn't help
lowering her voice and glancing behind her.

"I can't do that," she said softly, though not too resolutely. Her
lover had just asked her to take off her panties and touch herself.
"Aminah will be here any minute," she explained. "Plus I'll be sitting for over an hour without any drawers on, leaking and shit. I
don't think so."

Dante Lawrence laughed. The image of the always-stylish,
color-coordinated-even-down-to-her-undergarments Langston getting up from a chair with a wet spot on her designer mini-skirt tickled him initially. But the more he thought about it, the more the
idea of his lover's toes soaking in warm, soapy water, while another
woman sat beneath her washing her feet, pretending to glance up
to ask if the temperature was okay while mesmerized by the sight
of her pretty patron's luscious pearl peaking out from between her
coppery brown thighs turned him on.

"I'm glad you find this so amusing," Lang said, a tad perturbed. "I was beginning to take you seriously."

"You should, because I am," Dante said unwaveringly.

"Come again?" Lang asked, pulling the phone away from her
ear and looking at her tiny Motorola, a bit perplexed.

"They have a bathroom in your nail salon, right?"

"Yeah."

"Go in there and take your panties off," Dante commanded.
"Stick your index and middle finger in your mouth." He paused.
"Lang? You listenin' to me?"

"Uh-huh" escaped from the back of her throat and passed between her lips in a slow, warm breath. Not the cool, exhaling,

puckered-lips kind—the heated type. Like the warm breath you feel when you cup your hands around your mouth to do a fresh-breath check. Lang closed her eyes and leaned back against the building.

"I want you to suck on your fingers like you're sucking on a sticky cherry Blow Pop," he continued. "Then squeeze your nipple really hard with your thumb and your wet fingers."

Lang moaned into the phone with her eyes still closed.

"While you're doin' that, use the fingers on your other hand to rub your clit in a real . . . slow . . . circular . . ."

Just then Aminah Anderson pulled up in her shiny jet-black Range Rover. She stopped her SUV right in front of the parking meter. Aminah immediately pushed the button to lower the passenger's-side window.

"Langston!" she yelled. "Girl, you all right?"

Lang snapped out of her orgasmic trance, whispered to Dante that she had to go, and closed her phone.

Aminah rushed over to Lang, leaving her keys in the ignition, the driver's-side door open, and her fuchsia suede Celine bag on the seat. "You look like you're about to faint or something," she said, putting her arms around Lang's shoulders. "Is it bad news? What's the matter? Sweetie, talk to me."

Lang loved Aminah's nurturing and protective nature. She was a true Cancer to the core, yet at thirty-three she could still be as naive and gullible as an overweight, acne-pocked, out-of-state teenager fresh off the Greyhound with dreams of landing on a billboard above Times Square.

"I'm fine, Minah," she flatly replied. "You, on the other hand, are out of your mind, leaving your keys in the truck, your bag on the seat, and your door open," she said, pointing toward the Range Rover. "You are not in Kansas anymore, Dorothy. You're in Brooklyn."

Aminah sighed with genuine relief. "Well, then, why were you holding on to your cell phone like that, falling against the wall with your eyes closed? You looked like you just received the worst news of your life or something. You scared the crap out of me," she said, playfully punching Lang's shoulder.

"Oh, it was nothing," she lied, twirling a single strand of her #33 auburn, Spanish-wavy, weaved-on ringlets. "Sean called to tell me he was going to play ball at Chelsea Piers and wouldn't have time to straighten up like he promised." Lang couldn't tell Aminah the truth—not now anyway. "I was disappointed, that's all. I mean, damn, you know how much I love a spotless house, especially after a relaxing Sunday. Who wants to go home and clean?"

Aminah eyed her best friend suspiciously. They'd known each other since kindergarten, and after twenty-eight years of friendship, if she knew nothing else about Langston Neale Rogers, she knew when that girl was lying. Besides, hair twirling was always the dead giveaway. Aminah decided to play along anyway.

"Sweetie, I know you love your place clean and all, but you looked like you were on the verge of passing out. You're *that* disappointed?"

Lang hated lying to her best friend and didn't know how much longer she'd be able to do it. She began to tell Aminah the truth but glanced at her watch instead.

"Oh, my God! Minah, grab your keys and bag," she said frantically. "It's two minutes before noon, and you know Erika don't play with her strict-ass 'tough love' lateness policy. I wanted to find a new shade before we soaked."

Aminah put a few quarters in the meter and followed Langston inside, where they were greeted by the fruity smell of mango-scented candles and a huge smile from Richard, the fabulous and friendly receptionist. Rows and rows of scented candles, exotic lotions, and premier hair and skin-care products lined the shelves. Illume. Votivo. Pré de Provence. Archipelago. They passed through the muted gray door that separated the salon area from the beauty boutique out front.

In the nail room Aminah studied every brand of every shade of pink while Langston picked up all the bottles marked with a neon-green NEW sticker. Pink had been Aminah's favorite color since high school. One back-to-school shopping spree to Delancey Street on the lower east side of Manhattan with her father back in the mid eighties started her infatuation that soon blossomed into love and eventually led to her obsession with the color.

On that unseasonably cool late summer day, she'd salivated over racks and racks of cotton-candy-pink leather bombers with fur-trimmed hoods, admired the rose-dyed sheepskins with their matching hats and gloves, and copped her very first pair of high-heeled leather boots in hot pink off of Orchard Street. She was the flyest sophomore girl in Hempstead High School back in '86.

But there was always a science to which hue of the girlish color Aminah decided to wear and when. In her mind, people responded to her color choice accordingly, but in actuality she matched her attitude to the color. When she felt extrafeminine and needed some sensitivity or wanted to be pampered and treated gently— baby pinks. When she anticipated the need to be aggressive and firm, she layered herself in deep pinks with blue and purple under-tones, like magenta, sometimes even cranberry or plum. And when she needed to play up her sexuality and use her feminine mystique to get her way, always something electric—usually fuch-sia did the trick.

Today, however, there were simply too many shades and not nearly enough time. OPI. Dior. M·A·C. Bernadette Thompson. Argenteeny Pinkini. Vanity. Hawaiian Orchid. Jezebel. She went with the glittery Chanel Cry Baby because, quite frankly, she needed both a pick-me-up and some attention. Lang picked YSL's new bloody Red Desire.

The owner, Erika Kirkland, reminded them to turn off their cell phones before their services began. Lang saw that she'd missed three calls in that short time, one from Sean and two from Dante. Aminah barely even looked at her phone as she gladly shut it off and handed Erika her bag to put away.

While their nails soaked in ceramic bowls with aromatherapy stones, their feet in galvanized tins, Langston wondered how she'd tell Aminah about Dante. Aminah had been faithfully married to her high school sweetheart, Aaron "Famous" Anderson, for eleven years now. They'd married one month after she'd graduated from the University of Pennsylvania, and Aminah was loyal to the core. She worked very hard to keep her family happily intact, and in Lang's opinion deserved a medal for it. But then Langston remem-bered that it was just last week that Aminah had admitted that she was getting tired of staying in a marriage with a husband every woman wanted a piece of—literally and figuratively. She'd cried on the phone for almost an hour after hearing yet another "blind item" gossip piece on The Cindy Hunter Hotness radio show on WBLS.

This hip-hop and R&B producer is screwing around yet again on his wife and the mother of his two children. This time he's banging out hip-hop's hottest video chick. Remember the last time he was rumored to be messing with black Hollywood's newest young thing? Will his wife's dumb ass finally leave him? If history gives us any indication, the answer is no. But then again, who are we to judge? How many of you listeners would give up the fabulous homes, the gorgeous jewels, the designer clothes and shoes, the exotic vacations, a generous allowance, and, let's face it, a fine-ass man? If she leaves him, where is she going, and whom is she going to? There's no guarantee that the next man will be faithful. But when is enough enough? When do you put your integrity and pride before material possessions? Listeners, what do you think? Hit me up at 866-CINDYFAX.

In actuality, anyone and everyone who knew Aminah, especially Lang, knew it was neither her vanity nor the pricey baubles and fancy trips that she was putting before her "integrity and pride." It was quite simply her love for her family—her husband, Fame, included. Langston decided not to tell her best friend about her lover. It seemed a little too insensitive at the moment. Instead she ventured into safer waters.

"So how are my godchildren doing?" Lang asked, as the manicurist massaged her feet with Burt's Bees Coconut Foot Creme. Alia was ten going on twenty, and Amir was eight going on forty. Both were gorgeous, intelligent, and wise beyond their years.

"Oh, they're doing just fine," Aminah responded, knowing Lang was avoiding something. She started to pry but decided against it. She had her own issues to grapple with.

"Sean and I were thinking about taking them down to our time-share in Hilton Head when they come stay with us in August," Lang said, enjoying her foot massage.

Langston and her husband took their godchildren away as often as their schedules permitted and babysat them for one weekend every month. Sean had come up with the idea himself almost three years ago when Lang admitted she was too selfish to have children of her own just yet. He thought it was a good way to get her adjusted to the idea and show her how fun and rewarding children could actually be.

Sean was a big kid at heart anyway. He and Amir would play chess and video games till all hours while Alia and Lang hosted mini slumber parties watching DVDs, eating popcorn, and painting each other's nails.

Sean Rogers loved children so much he based his whole profession around having them. He was an English teacher at Boys and Girls High School in the Bedford-Stuyvesant section of Brooklyn. He thought it was the ideal career for a parent. He'd have the exact same vacation time as his children and pretty much the same working hours. And if ever his work schedule conflicted with his family time, he'd be more than happy to be a stay-at-home dad.

He loved his students at Boys and Girls but knew Lang wouldn't even consider giving up her job as the editor-in-chief of the two-year-old *Urban Celebrity Magazine*. And he definitely wasn't raising no latchkey kids. He'd been adamant about that. There were enough disenfranchised black children being cultivated by the streets, receiving their values and morals from awful television programs and their social mores from hip-hop and R&B lyrics. So if the sacrifice had to be made, he was more than willing to make it. Lang promised him that before she turned thirty-five she'd give him a baby, and he was holding her to her word.

"Oh, they'll enjoy that," Aminah said, admiring the color on both her feet and hands. "You know they love the beach, and

Sean's so good at making sand castles, swimming, and barbecuing. Plus he's great with kids, too. I mean, really, Lang, that husband of yours is great at everything."

Not everything, Lang thought as they carefully moved to the drying stations, which were set up with two chairs, two sets of nail dryers on each side—one on the table, the other on the floor—and a flat-screen monitor mounted on the wall between them.

"You're so lucky to have him," Aminah continued. "He not only adores you but respects you."

All true, Lang thought. Sean was beautiful inside and out. He was Hershey-dark-chocolate brown with skin that reminded her of freshly whipped devil's-food cake batter as it was being slowly poured out of a mixing bowl. And he had the softest pair of full lips surrounded by an incredibly sexy, neatly trimmed goatee, with a set of the brightest naturally white teeth on this-here planet Earth. And he smiled so easily with that gorgeous mouth of his—so generously, so effortlessly.

Not to mention, Sean was physically fit. Lean. Ripped in all the right places—chest, back, arms, and abs—but not at all *brolic,* like he'd done seven to ten years upstate. While Sean was good in bed, he wasn't great. He liked it a notch above basic. They did it missionary, doggy, and froggy style. Sure he worked his hips and always put his back into it. He knew when to pull her hair, slap her ass, and ask whose pussy it was. He was especially gifted at the art of making sweet love and had successfully mastered the science of spooning and using his tongue. Sean was incredibly generous between the legs and the sheets. He loved to please more than he liked being pleased. "Your pleasure is my pleasure," he loved to say. But he wasn't imaginative or quite freaky enough for Lang.

"And most importantly, he's faithful," Aminah added, wishing she could say the same about her own man.

Was that the most important thing? Lang wondered.

When they were both seated comfortably, Erika asked which season of *Sex and the City* they'd like to watch while their nails dried.

"Oooo, season six," Aminah responded immediately. "Let's watch the episode where Miranda first meets Blair Underwood. Mmmm, that brother is fine."

Erika laughed as she adjusted the headphones on their ears. "Now, can I get you ladies another lemonade or perhaps some water or ginger tea?"

They both opted for a cool glass of water.

Chapter 2

"I just need to smell you, baby. You can't
be mad at me for that."

"So, where to for brunch today?" Aminah asked as she handed Richard her platinum American Express card to pay for both of their Sessions. Lang and Aminah alternated treating each other to their biweekly outings.

"Ladies, the Er'go candles are ten percent off," Richard announced before swiping Aminah's charge card.

"I'm feeling like some fish and grits today," Lang said, turning her cell phone back on and then sniffing a guava-scented candle. "You up to driving to that soul food spot in Chelsea?"

"Not really," Aminah responded. "Nothing for me today, Richard, thanks. I'm not in a Manhattan mood today. Let's stay local. Night of the Cookers's fried catfish is really good, too."

"Damn, Minah, why'd you ask then?" Lang questioned, placing four candles by the register. "Sean and I just ate at NOC last night. Plus, that Chelsea restaurant has the creamiest grits, and I really have a taste for them with whitings, not catfish. What if I drove?"

"How are you going to drive?" Aminah asked, opening the front door of the salon. "I don't see your car out here."

Richard complimented Lang's nails as he handed her shopping bag to her. She thanked him and carefully reached for one of her candles.

"Sean needed the car," Lang said, walking toward Aminah. "So I grabbed a cab over here. What? You don't trust me with the Range?"

Aminah didn't even hear Lang's last question. The six-five, curly-haired cutie leaning against the diamond white Escalade across the street had captured her attention.

"Lang, come check out this fine brother in front of this Caddy."

"Don't try to change the topic, Minah," Lang said, sniffing one of her candles as she walked toward the door. "You know, for a married woman, you sure have an eye for fine men."

"There's nothing wrong—"

Lang spotted Dante across the street and dropped her candle before Aminah could finish her sentence. The glass surrounding the candle shattered on the sidewalk.

Aminah spun around and looked at Lang with a raised eyebrow. "Sweetie, what's wrong with you today?" she asked, bending down to pick up the glass. Lang just stood there in place, stunned.

"Um, Lang, baby boy across the street looks good. I know. I spotted him. But no one looks good enough for you to be breaking these expensive candles. You better be glad these weren't one of my overpriced Jo Malone votives. You wanna get down here and help me pick up this glass before someone cuts themself?"

Lang squatted down to help Aminah. "I'm sorry, Minah, I—" Before Lang could finish her sentence, she was startled by her vibrating cell phone and cut her finger on a piece of glass. "Shit!"

"Okay, sweetie, calm down. It's not that serious. I was just teasing you anyway. Go back inside, wash your hands, and ask Richard for a Band-Aid. I'll take care of this."

Dante watched Lang rush back inside the nail salon. He dialed her again. This time she picked up.

"Dante, what in the hell are you doing here?"

"I came by to pick up those panties from you, " Dante said very calmly into the phone, watching Aminah go back inside, too.

"You should not have come here."

"You shouldn't have hung up on me."

"I didn't. I told you I had to go."

"I called you back. You didn't pick up."

"I couldn't. I was getting my nails done."

"Listen, Lang, I'm not here to argue with you."

"Then why are you here, Dante?" Lang demanded.

Just then Aminah knocked on the bathroom door and asked her if everything was all right.

"Everything's fine, Minah. Be out there in a second. Um, start up the car and turn up the AC. I'm feeling kinda hot."

"You feelin' sticky, too, baby?" Dante asked, chuckling into the phone.

"Dante, I don't have time for this right now. I will call you later. I hafta go."

"Not before I get those panties."

"Dante, please," Lang pleaded.

"Please what, baby? You in the bathroom now, right?"

"I am, but . . ."

"Good. I just saw Aminah get in her car. I know she's out here waitin' for you and shit, so I won't even bother to ask you to touch yourself again. You can make that up to me later. Just slide on out of those sexy panties you got on, fix your skirt, walk out here, and hand them over to me. It's simple. I just need to smell you, baby. You can't be mad at me for that."

Lang stood in the bathroom, slightly dumbfounded yet completely turned on. She had to be honest with herself—if she had the time, she would've touched herself, cut finger and all. She shook her head.

This is crazy, she thought. There was no way she could just walk outside and hand her panties over to Dante. How in the hell would she explain that to Aminah?

"Dante, I can't," she said. "Aminah doesn't even know about you, about us."

"You're a smart woman. You'll figure something out. Or would you rather I come in there and get them myself? You know what? I think that's what I'm gonna do."

"No, please don't," Lang protested. Dante sounded dead serious, and she knew it would be nothing for him to walk straight into the bathroom, tear her panties right off her cute ass, and not care less about any kind of scene he might create.

"Gimme a second to take care of my cut. I'll be right out there."

Dante hung up the phone and waited inside his truck with all the windows down. Aminah stared at him behind her tinted Stella McCartney sunglasses from across the street. Dante grinned smugly and rested his head on the back of the seat.

Lang tended to her cut, slid out of her panties, and placed them in her shopping bag. She straightened out her mini skirt, took a deep breath, and held it as she walked right past Richard without saying a word, out the door, and across the street. She reached into her bag and handed Dante a pair of black lace La Perla underwear.

Dante held the crotch of her panties right up to his nose and inhaled deeply. Lang finally exhaled. This time it was the cool, puckered-lip kind. He slid the panties onto his rearview mirror as if they were one of those pine-tree air fresheners, winked at Lang, and drove off.

Chapter 3

*"I don't usually approach women, period.
I've never had to."*

"Okay, what the fuck was that, Lang?" Aminah asked as soon as Lang got inside the SUV. She rarely ever used profane language.

Lang, though a bit startled, said nothing.

"We're not going anywhere, Mrs. Rogers, until you tell me why you're sitting here on my pink custom leather seats with no panties on."

Lang pulled down the front of her skirt. She was embarrassed and didn't know where to begin. She had planned on telling Aminah about her affair with Dante eventually, just not today. She cleared her throat.

"Minah, can we drive and talk?" Lang asked as calmly as possible. "I'll try to explain. I promise. I just can't sit here in front of this salon any longer."

Aminah thought about making Lang explain everything to her right then and there. Hell, she questioned whether she'd even be able to drive safely while listening to her best friend offer a valid reason for giving some gorgeous young guy her panties to sniff.

"Only if you promise to tell me the truth this time, Lang."

Lang gazed at Aminah sideways.

"Don't even try it, sweetie," Aminah said, holding up her hand. "You know I know when you're lying, and something tells me that semifainting spell earlier and baby boy displaying your drawers as some kind of interior ornament for his Escalade are somehow connected. You couldn't come up with a better lie than Sean not playing Merry Maid for the day? Girl, please."

Langston was caught. There was no sense even trying to concoct a story at this point. "You're right," Lang admitted. "I promise to come clean. As long as I don't hafta do it here. Please, Minah, can we leave?"

Aminah did a U-turn and headed toward Flatbush Avenue. She asked Lang to choose between Chez Oskar and The Brownstone Lounge for brunch. Lang chose The Brownstone Lounge, hoping there'd be tables available outside.

The two of them listened to India.Arie's first album on their way to the restaurant. Aminah kept her "Sisters of Strength" CDs in heavy rotation inside her SUV—Faith Evans's self-titled debut, *The Essential Nina Simone,* Mary's *My Life, The Miseducation of Lauryn Hill* (sometimes alternated with Norah Jones's first CD), and Lil' Kim's *Hard Core*—which usually threw her passengers for a loop, but the pre-op Kim had always empowered Aminah. She found her unapologetic, in-your-face sexuality inspiring, energizing, and thought provoking. Most of Lil' Kim's lyrics exuded power and control to Aminah. It didn't sound the least bit submissive or degrading. In fact, it sounded like she was grabbing life by the balls, so to speak, living on her own terms, and Aminah couldn't help but respect and admire that. Post-op Kim probably refuted all that, but still.

Now was not the time for Kim though. India.Arie's "Video," "Promises," and "Brown Skin" played in their entirety before either woman uttered a word. Lang was admiring the handsome brownstones in the neighborhood when Aminah finally asked her if the guy in the Escalade was the same person she'd been speaking to on the phone when she'd pulled up earlier. Lang admitted he was.

"Well, who exactly is he, Lang?" Aminah demanded while desperately searching for a place to park. She'd circled around the block three times already. It was a nice, warm, sunny Sunday afternoon in the borough of Brooklyn, and parking was horrendous. Aminah double-parked and waited for someone, anyone, to pull out.

"I don't know where to begin, Aminah," Lang said, twisting her platinum wedding band. She wasn't exactly sure what she wanted to share, nor how much she wanted to reveal. While she had no intention of lying to her best friend again, she wanted to feed Aminah in small doses. Too much information, and her girl was liable to regurgitate right there in the car or, worse, in the restaurant.

"The beginning is always a good place to start, Lang."

Lang nodded in agreement. "Well—"

"Hold that thought," Aminah interrupted. There was a family loading into a Denali up ahead, and she wanted to grab the highly coveted spot before anyone else could. Aminah parallel parked her Range Rover effortlessly, and the two of them walked back toward the restaurant.

They were seated outdoors almost immediately. Live jazz music and an excellent menu kept the popular neighborhood eatery peppered with a mixed blend of ethnicities, though mostly African Americans in their late twenties to early thirties.

The chipper, petite blond waitress happily took their drink orders. Lang, torn between a mimosa and a Ghetto Heaven—aka a watermelon martini—decided on a mimosa. She preferred Veuve Clicquot, but during brunch hours she had to settle for the house sparkling wine, probably Korbel. Lang shuddered at the thought and asked the waitress to go heavy on the orange juice.

Aminah always preceded every meal with a full glass of water. However, The Brownstone Lounge didn't carry any of her preferred brands, so she ordered a pink mimosa and discreetly took sips from the small bottle of Fiji water she always carried with her. Then they served themselves from the all-you-can-eat buffet indoors.

A blessed communion of heavenly breakfast aromas and divine soul-food scents wafted inside the sanctified brownstone-housed restaurant. Cinnamon raisin French toast, old-fashioned pancakes, blueberry waffles, turkey sausage, bacon, home fries, scrambled eggs, fried chicken, barbecue chicken, fried whitings, mixed green salad, collard greens, macaroni and cheese, oven-baked breads, succulent meats, rich sauces and syrups, creamy butters, and heavy creams made every morsel praiseworthy.

Langston and Aminah generously loaded up their plates and walked back toward their table.

"Are you cheating on Sean?" Aminah asked Langston flat out as they took their seats.

Lang took a sip of her mimosa and squinched up her face before answering. "I thought you wanted me to begin at the beginning. That's not the beginning."

"No, it's not," Aminah said curtly, pointing her fork at Langston. "It's the finale. It's the end of your marriage if Sean ever found out. How could you, Lang?" Aminah's voice cracked. She found herself as disappointed in her best friend as she'd been in her husband. She loved them both unconditionally, to a fault even, but hated their abilities to be so self-absorbed, so self-involved that they refused to see or even consider how their egotistical actions affected other people. It went against the very essence of who Aminah was. As far as Aminah was concerned, cheating wasn't some uncontrollable urge like peeing after chugging down a bottle of water. It was a choice, a very conscious and deliberate decision. "You can't do this to him, Lang. Of all men, of all people, Sean doesn't deserve this."

Lang thought that maybe Aminah was more loyal to Sean than she was herself. She wasn't surprised though. Aminah had been more excited than Lang the night Sean had proposed. It was Aminah who had taken complete control over planning Lang and Sean's wedding four years ago. She'd been the proudest, most dutiful, beaming matron of honor in the western hemisphere. Aminah personally oversaw the entire event, from the smallest detail, like whether or not the bridesmaids should wear panty hose (no), to securing either Reverend Al Sharpton or Reverend Run to officiate—the latter was available, the former wasn't. Langston would have been more than happy with city hall, but Sean insisted on having the ultimate Brooklyn wedding, and it was Aminah who made sure he got it.

They'd married on the first Saturday of June 2000 right in the middle of Grand Army Plaza under the Soldiers and Sailors Memorial Arch. Cars zoomed around the busy, traffic-filled circle, honking their horns, congratulating them. The newlyweds took pictures in Prospect Park, at the Brooklyn Botanic Garden, and under the Brooklyn Bridge.

The reception immediately followed at their newly purchased, sparsely furnished brownstone in Stuyvesant Heights. Aminah had hired the renowned floral designer Saundra Parks, the sister who owned Daily Blossom, to adorn each floor of the four-story brownstone with lush floral arrangements.

In the parlor on the first floor, intricately sculpted ceramic pots of plump, majestic purple and soft blue hydrangeas filled every corner. Grammy Award–winning trumpeter Roy Hargrove and his band played familiar jazz standards as well as his own original compositions as guests enjoyed nibbling on appetizers and sipping on cocktails.

Garlands of deep red velvet roses were strewn along the banisters of the glazed mahogany staircases. 'American Beauties' in small, antique, white terra-cotta pots with glints of gold were placed on every other step.

An elegant four-course dinner was served on the second floor where tall vases of white casablancas in delicate glass vases posed as centerpieces.

The hardwood floors on the barren, spacious third level made for the ideal dance space. Aminah's husband mixed current and classic R&B and rap hits with popular and obscure soul records thrown in for good measure and an even better time.

As the festive, yet classy reception evolved into a full-blown, ghetto fabulous affair, it brought Fame back to his high school days of spinning at the local parties and skating rinks. He alternated well-known party songs with their original samples. He played De La Soul's "Breakadawn," Portrait's "Here We Go Again!", Michael Jackson's "I Can't Help It," 3rd Bass's "Gas Face," and Aretha Franklin's "Think."

The well-heeled wedding guests lost all decorum, sweated out their nicely coifed dos, and danced like it was their mama's rent party and last month's rent was way past due.

Mr. and Mrs. Sean Rogers's wedding was a splendid affair, courtesy of Aminah. She adored both of them and wanted their blessed day to reflect both her love for them and theirs for each other.

"What exactly is it you *think* I am doing to him, Aminah?" Lang asked. "You haven't even let me explain myself. You don't even know what's going on. You're presuming an awful lot."

"Are you fucking him?"

Lang hesitated. "Well . . . technically, no."

"I don't believe you, Langston. What the fuck is that supposed to mean?"

"My, my, my, we're just full of profanity today, Mrs. Anderson," Lang said in a poor attempt to lighten the mood.

"Yeah, well, it's been one of those days," Aminah responded, finishing off her pink mimosa. "So how do you technically not fuck someone?"

The truth of the matter was Dante had never entered Lang. His tongue had been inside her, yes. His fingers even—from pinky to thumb in fact—but that was all.

"Okay Aminah. I don't think we should talk about this right now. You're getting upset over something you know nothing about. I would never do anything to jeopardize my marriage with Sean. You know I love him."

"Do you hear yourself, Lang?" Aminah asked, incredulously narrowing her eyes and turning up her lip. "You've already jeopardized your marriage, and for what? For some kid dick?"

Lang laughed nervously.

"I don't see what's so funny."

"Kid dick, Aminah?" Lang asked, giggling a bit still. "That's cause for at least a chuckle, don't you think?"

"No. For the love of God, Lang, I don't. You're taking this way too lightly for me. Do you even understand what's at stake here? What you're risking? What you're throwing away?"

"I'm not throwing my husband away," Lang replied defensively. "I know that much, Aminah. And *you* know more than anyone how much I love Sean. He's my best friend." She paused. "Well, my second-best friend."

Aminah sighed and rested her head in the palm of her right hand. "I just don't want to see you ruin your marriage. How old is this boy anyway, like, twenty-one?"

"Twenty-three," slipped out of Lang's mouth between bites of crispy fried chicken swirled in the thick maple syrup dripping off her waffles.

"Ten years younger, Lang? What could you possibly have in common? Wait." She paused, shaking her head. "Don't even answer that. You're too young to be going through a midlife crisis, so that can't be it."

"Do women even have those?" Lang asked before licking her middle finger and using the wetness to pick up the flavorful crumbs of the chicken.

"Why, Lang?" Aminah asked. "Why risk everything you've built with Sean for some dick on the side?"

"Um, are you sure you want to hear about this?" Lang asked, wiping the corners of her mouth with the cloth napkin.

Aminah nodded her head and ordered another pink mimosa. Lang told Aminah that she'd met Dante at the Starbucks around the corner from her job three months ago, back in April. She was waiting for her unsweetened Venti iced coffee with light ice and heavy cream, and he was standing off to the side next to the napkins and sugar holding his tall soy chai latte just staring at her, looking all young and cocky. She'd tried to ignore him, but he just wouldn't break his stare. She'd headed out the door, and he'd followed.

"Excuse me, miss, what's your name? Can you come hang with me?" he sang, doing his best Jay-Z rendition.

She'd laughed and stopped right in her tracks.

"I know you saw me checking you out, ma," he said, looking down at her. Dante stood about seven inches taller than Lang.

Damn, this young boy is fine, she'd thought.

He pointed to her wedding band and asked if she was happy.

"Very much so," she said.

"Oh, yeah, then why'd you stop?"

Lang had sucked her teeth, rolled her eyes, and resumed her quick pace back to the office. *The nerve,* she thought. He was the one staring at her. The one singing corny-ass songs to her as she walked down the street minding her own damn business trying to enjoy her iced coffee. And then he'd had the audacity, the unmitigated gall, to judge her marriage.

"Slow down, ma!" Dante yelled.

Lang made a sharp right and kept on speed-walking toward Broadway.

"Damn, if you hold up, ma, I can apologize to you correctly."

She turned around and yelled, "What-the-fuck-ever!" back at him.

He laughed. "Wow. Beautiful and feisty, that's a lethal combination. I'm diggin' it though."

Lang had been just about to turn the corner when Dante'd grabbed her arm right in front of Jay-Z's 40/40 Club and swung her around.

Lang looked at Dante like he'd lost his damn mind. But before she could snatch her arm away and curse him the fuck out, she'd melted. Her fleeting anger was no match for that intense stare of his. She had a weakness for dark-skinned men, but unblemished ebony skin with long eyelashes that'd give M·A·C falsies a run for their money, and unruly naturally curly hair, were the equivalent of kryptonite.

Shit, Lang thought.

"Look, ma, I was wrong for what I said back there," he said, still holding on to her arm. "But I saw a spark in your eyes, and for real, I still see it. I'm not gonna front. I even feel it right now."

"I—I—I don't know what you're talking about," Lang stuttered.

He smiled. He knew he had her. Mrs. Composed-in-Designer-Clothes-from-her-Head-to her-Toes was indeed feeling him back. "Look, it's not really my style to approach women in coffee shops," he said, finally releasing her arm. "I don't usually approach women, period. I've never had to. And if I had seen that ring before I'd looked into your eyes and seen what I saw—no offense, ma, but I never woulda stepped to you either. But it's too late for all that now."

"Too late? What is it you think you saw?" Lang asked curiously.

"Oh, I *know* what I saw," Dante responded firmly.

Just then Lang's cell phone had rung. It was her assistant, Merrick. It was production week at *Urban Celebrity,* and they needed her to sign off on some layouts so the files could be sent to the printer that evening.

"I'm right downstairs. I'll be right up," she'd said and hung up her phone.

"Lemme see that," Dante said, taking her Motorola right out of her hands. Dante punched in his number and dialed himself from her phone. When he saw her number show up on his caller ID, he asked for her name and then stored it in his phone.

"Lang," he repeated. "I like that. Well, Lang, I know you gotta get back to work. So I'll give you a call later this evening." He'd turned to walk back in the direction of Starbucks.

"Wait, I don't even know your name."

"Yeah, but you have my number, and I got yours."

Chapter 4

"I can separate sex from love. Though we as women are not socialized to do so, I can and that doesn't make me a bad woman or a bad wife."

Langston and Aminah leisurely nursed steamy cups of mediocre coffee not too long after finishing off their second helpings from the brunch bar. The striking duo looked like an *Essence* summer fashion spread shot on a sidewalk café. Aminah's fuchsia jersey knit halter top and matching skirt couldn't compete with her curves. She had the kind of measurements that commanded a bodacious "Daaamn!" from men and women alike. Though her weight fluctuated with the seasons and the state of her marriage, she was genetically blessed; her waist was usually proportioned twelve inches smaller than her ample D-cup bust and shapely hips, allowing her to maintain an hourglass figure whether she wore a size six or a size ten. This summer she was a healthy 38-26-38. While Fame modestly took credit for making her ass a "hi-C," it was her hundred-squats-per-day regimen that deserved the props for her lifted C-shape booty.

Aminah routinely wore her shiny black hair, slicked back with Aveda's sweet-smelling hair gloss, in a long, sleek ponytail, à la Sade. She missed wearing her thick, long hair natural, but Fame insisted she keep it bone straight. "It's a good look," he'd say. "It complements my image. I don't want anyone mistaking you for some chew-stick, incense-burning bag lady. You're the wife of a successful, self-made millionaire, not the wife of some wannabe poet in the struggle. Look like it."

Langston stood modelesque at five-ten with perky 36Cs, a small waist, nice ass, and long legs that rivaled Naomi Campbell's. Combine all those assets with high cheekbones, pouty lips, and a copper reddish brown complexion, and it was no wonder that most people assumed she actually was some kind of a model. Lang would have considered the modeling profession, but she had absolutely no desire to deal with all the potential rejection and negative energy. She preferred to be complimented, not criticized. And beauty by American standards, though admittedly broader than, say, in her mother's day, was still too reflective of the European aesthetic for Lang's politics.

Lang thought the fashion and beauty industries were still too subjective and, yes, still racist. She'd counted on one hand the number of black models on the catwalk of last season's fashion shows. And magazine covers? Damn near nonexistent if you weren't an A-list celebrity. And while she currently rocked an auburn curly weave by choice and convenience, she had no intention of ever chemically altering the natural texture of her healthy, coarse dark brown hair that fell well past her shoulder blades when blown straight.

"So what's this young boy's name?" Aminah asked more out of annoyance than curiosity as she stirred raw sugar into her coffee.

"Dante," Lang said, relieved to finally share it with her best friend.

"And you haven't had sex with him yet?"

"Not exactly."

Aminah looked at Lang quizzically.

"Hold up," Lang said, putting up her hands in protest. "I'm not saying we haven't done things, but we haven't had actual intercourse yet."

"Done things like what? You mean oral sex?"

"Well, yeah, we've given each other head," Lang admitted. "But it's not just physical with him, Aminah. It's more mental. He's gotten inside my mind sexually. He's invaded a space Sean has no idea even exists." Lang looked visibly starry-eyed as she spoke of her lover. She was definitely smitten, and there was no hiding that.

"Let me get this straight. After three months of seeing pretty boy, you're having only mind sex and head with him?" Aminah asked skeptically.

"No, that's not just it, Minah. Damn."

"Well, do you want to have physical sex with him?" Aminah asked, genuinely confused.

"Of course, of course, what kind of question is that? You're not getting this, are you?"

"Well, not exactly, Lang, and forgive me, but I'm not sure I can."

Lang sighed. "Okay, remember back in high school when we snuck in to see *9 ½ Weeks,* and you thought it was twisted, while I was completely enthralled?"

"Um, yeah, you said you wanted to be turned out like Kim Basinger. How could I ever forget that?"

"Well, I'm still waiting to be turned out, Minah."

"You've got issues, Lang," Aminah said, raising her left eyebrow and taking a sip of her coffee.

Lang rolled her eyes. "What about when we rented that movie *Secretary* two years ago?"

"That weird movie with that Olive Oyl–looking actress who let her boss spank her, put a saddle on her back, and stick a carrot in her mouth?"

"Yes, Aminah, that one," Lang replied, a bit annoyed that she'd reduced one of her favorite films to a horse-and-carriage flick.

"I never got that movie," Aminah said, dismissively flicking her right hand.

"I know, but I did. I actually kinda envied Maggie Gyllenhaal's character," Lang said, smiling mischievously.

"Who?"

" 'Olive Oyl.' "

"Oh." Aminah laughed.

"Anyway, her character finally met someone who intuitively tapped into her secret desires without her having to say a word or even explain herself," Lang said enviously. "Desires that most people viewed as strange and abnormal—and she wasn't letting *that* man get away from her. She bagged him by whatever means necessary."

"That's 'cause they are strange, Lang," Aminah said, throwing up her hands. "You know, you look so normal, so together. It's mind-boggling." She paused to gather her thoughts. "What? You want Sean to make you crawl on all fours while he throws money at you and orders you to pick it up like some kind of hooker?"

"I can't front—that'd be kinda sexy," Lang said, smiling.

"You're one demented sister."

"See, that's the thing. Why can't I be both a together sister and sexually um, um . . . " Lang snapped her fingers, searching for just the right word, ". . . unbound?"

"You absolutely can, but if you want me to attend your pity party because your husband would rather, oh, I don't know, massage your feet after a long day at work than beat your ass with a belt—sorry, but I won't be RSVPing to that affair," Aminah said, shaking her head in disbelief.

Lang finished off her disappointing cup of coffee, slouched down in her seat, and pouted.

"I'm sorry, Lang. I'm trying to follow you, I really am. But after all I've been through with Fame, I just don't get it, and I'm not sure I really want to," Aminah admitted.

"Well, then, let's not do this," Lang said, folding her arms and casually glancing over at the boys playing basketball across the street.

Aminah also looked over at the basketball game and, once again, she found herself hating the actions of someone she loved. It was all so conflicting for her. She gestured for the waitress to bring the check. "Lang, I'm really trying to be your friend here, but you know where I'm coming from," she said, reaching out for Lang's hands and making her unfold her arms.

"I know, Minah," Lang said. "I mean, why do you think I've kept him from you for so long? If Dante hadn't shown up at Pretty Inside, we wouldn't even be talking about this right now. I'm not gonna lie. I know it's selfish. I do. But for some reason it doesn't feel so wrong. It feels perfect for right now."

"Lang, are you catching feelings for this kid?" Aminah asked. "I thought it was just physical—I mean, mental—I mean, sexual." Aminah got flustered.

"It's all those things," Lang admitted. "But, no, there are no feelings involved. I mean, I can't say there's an emotional attachment."

Aminah nodded her head, trying to make sense of what her best friend was saying. She signed the receipt and suggested they walk and talk. Lang grabbed Aminah's hand as they exited the restaurant and swung it like she had when they were little girls in elementary school.

"Aminah, just you trying to understand what it is I'm doing here means the world to me," Lang admitted. "If I were you, I don't think I could stomach listening to a girlfriend justify having an affair. It's all fun and games for me, but you've been on the painful side of it. This is the first time I've ever felt so uncomfortable discussing something with you."

As Langston spoke, tears welled up in Aminah's eyes. "The other side does hurt, Lang," Aminah said, fighting back the tears.

"I know, baby," Lang said, stopping in front of Aminah's car and hugging her best friend tightly. "Let's stop, huh? I mean, really, what's the point in me sharing this with you?"

"You're my best friend. That's the point," Aminah said, pulling from her embrace. "And it's not a game, Lang. It's lives, real lives you're messing with here. And I can't just silently watch you ruin your marriage. It's not worth it, Lang. I promise you it's not worth it."

"But I can't walk away from this, Minah," Lang said, stepping back from Aminah and shaking her head. "Not now anyway. Not yet." Lang gently wiped Aminah's face with her hands and kissed her on the forehead.

"You know, at first I thought I wanted to know everything about this affair," Aminah admitted. "No, no, I'm lying. At first I thought I was gonna be sick when you finally confessed. But then I thought, as crazy as it sounds, I thought maybe, just maybe hearing you explain why you'd cheat on Sean would help me understand Fame's rationale for cheating on me. But now . . ." Aminah shook her head, pacing next to her car. "Now I know I was right. It *is* as crazy as it sounds. Listening to you and this bullshit about not being able to get your freak on with your husband is ludicrous. I'm sorry, Lang, but I just don't get how you could feel even remotely justified entertaining the idea of having sex with a man other than your husband. You have a good man at home."

"Yeah, but you saw him, Minah. The brother is fine," Lang said defiantly.

"Yes, but so is Sean," Aminah countered.

"I know, but it's something about him," Lang said, unsure of how she could explain that "something" to her girlfriend when she hadn't quite nailed it herself. "Minah, he picked up on something within seconds of meeting me that my husband doesn't have a clue about in the six years I've known him."

"What? That you're a freak?" Aminah asked, folding her arms.

Lang detested that word, and Aminah knew it. She'd always thought *freak* held such negative connotations. It denoted something being wrong with you, like you were some kind of a circus spectacle. No, she preferred *sexually liberated.*

"I am *not* a freak, Minah," Lang said, hitting the *T* in *not* so hard that a tiny speckle of spit flew from the little space between her two front teeth.

"I mean, call it what you want, Lang, but I still don't understand why you can't just tell your husband what gets you off."

"What if he's repulsed by it, Minah?" Lang asked sincerely.

"And you know how men's egos are. Sean likes to be either in charge or super-romantic, and I like that, too, some of the time. But, Minah, there's a whole range of sexual expression inside me that doesn't fall into either one of those categories. If I even touch myself while I'm riding him, he's quick to move my hand and do it himself, and that's not always what I want. Sometimes I wanna get myself off with him inside me, and, sure, I may be thinking of something or someone else at the time, but lemme enjoy the experience inside my head."

"You don't think you can share your sexual desires and fantasies with *Sean?*" Aminah asked, still not convinced. "Come on, Lang, you have to come up with something better than that."

"I'm not so sure if Sean would even be my husband if he knew what got me off."

There. She'd said it. Lang knew many a man who'd said they wanted a lady in the streets and a freak in the bed, but in reality she believed there were still certain things, certain acts most men did not want to do with the woman they vowed to honor and cherish.

"Come again, Lang?"

"Listen, Aminah, I think a lot of men practice sexual restraint to some degree with their wives. On the other hand, the sexual possibilities with so-called 'hos' or women they'd never ever consider *wifing* stretch as far as their imaginations will allow them."

"Yeah, but, Lang, we're not talking about most men and hos. We're talking about you and Sean."

"Yeah, and Sean wouldn't want to do anything remotely, I dunno, violent or what other people might perceive as degrading or even humiliating with his respectable wife."

"And that makes him a bad husband?"

"No, not at all, but it leaves me an unsatisfied wife," Lang admitted.

"Unsatisfied? I've never heard you complain about Sean's performance in bed till now. And, honestly, I don't think you would've married Sean if he was a bad lay."

"I never said he was bad. He's actually quite good, but I've got a strong appetite for something more than that. Like, I'd love to have a ménage à trois with Sean and—"

"Another woman?" Aminah asked incredulously. "Really? You actually wanna see another woman doing your husband?"

"Well, that's not where I was going. But if you hadn't cut me off, I was gonna say with Sean, me, and another man."

"Ugh, Lang, that's disgusting. Fuck outta here with that one. Sean's not goin' for that."

"Exactly. And therein lies the problem. We both know plenty of men whose fantasy involves two women. But how many husbands do you know who could even stomach, let alone go through with, the mere idea of a ménage involving themselves, their wives, and another man? And you want me to tell Sean what gets me off? I don't think so, honey. He'd leave me before I could put in my formal request. Hmph. Your boy, Sean, was actually taken aback the first time I gave him head," Lang continued. "I mean, at first he told me it was the best he'd ever had. Then a few minutes later he's asking me how I learned to do it so well and how many men before him had experienced what he just had."

"I just don't get it, Lang. Is it possible to love someone, I mean, really love someone, and still cheat on her—I mean, him?" Aminah questioned.

Langston didn't answer right away. She ran the back of her

hand across the side of her best friend's face. She knew what Aminah was getting at. "Well, Aminah. You know I'm going to say yes, of course. Just because I love my husband doesn't mean I don't find other men desirable."

"Okay, finding them desirable is one thing; fucking them, mentally or physically, is crossing the line," Aminah admitted, removing Lang's hand from her face. "Don't you think it cheapens the love and destroys the trust and weakens the relationship? It's disrespectful to the union, Lang."

"Wait a minute, now, are you asking me about my relationship or yours?"

Aminah didn't answer. She wasn't sure. She was confused her damn self. Lang and Fame were one and the same to her right now.

"Well, no, I don't think it weakens my relationship with my husband," Lang admitted. "If anything it enhances it. I can separate sex from love. Though we as women are not socialized to do so, I can, and that doesn't make me a bad woman or a bad wife."

"Maybe that's true for you, Lang," Aminah said. "But if this is how you want to operate your life, you shouldn't have dragged Sean unknowingly into it. If you knew he wasn't enough for you sexually, you should have declined his marriage proposal. I have never had a problem with your strong, albeit unusual, sex drive. My issue with you right now is your regard—rather, your disregard—for your marriage. I love Sean like a brother, and I can't believe you have been deceiving him these past three months."

While Aminah loved Fame with everything she had, for the first time she thought that maybe she deserved a husband more like Sean, and Fame should have been with a wife like Lang.

"I never thought of you as a liar and a cheat, Lang," Aminah said angrily. She'd had enough of listening to her titillating version of an affair.

"What? I'm not a liar, Aminah."

"Does Sean know about your affair? Has he cosigned it? Given you the green light and a thumbs-up to go fuck another man?"

"Now wait one goddamn minute, Aminah," Lang said, not appreciating her girlfriend's self-righteous questions. "It is not easy for me to stand here and admit to you that I am cheating on my husband who's done nothing but love me. I realize that. Call me stupid. Okay, go ahead. I might give you that. You can even label me a cheater. I've earned that one. But don't call me a liar, Minah. I haven't lied to Sean about anything."

"Lang, you sound so ridiculous right now," Aminah said. "How is it possible to cheat and not lie?"

"Hey, if he doesn't ask, I won't tell," Lang replied, smugly folding her arms.

That stung Aminah. Not only was it a variation of Bill Clinton's gays-in-the-military policy, but it was Fame's marriage philosophy as well. He had told Aminah when they'd gotten engaged that he loved her enough never to lie to her, so before she asked or accused him of anything she should be absolutely certain she could deal with the brutality of an honest answer.

Prior to their engagement, while Aminah was still in college and his success and popularity as a deejay was steadily growing, he'd also suggested she stop looking for the "proof" she didn't really want to find. She'd heeded his advice for the most part. And Fame kept his word. He'd been painfully truthful when questioned. "You stop asking, Minah, and then I won't have to tell," Fame had told her on more than one occasion. "But I respect you too much to lie to your face, baby girl. So why not do us a favor and spare us both the drama and don't bother to question?" Aminah had shaken her head in disbelief.

"How do you lie in bed next to Sean, profess your love for him, and then, hours later, be with another man?" she asked Langston.

"It's selfish, I know. I can admit that," Lang said, shrugging her shoulders. "But I can't help it. I can't just end it. Not now. I'm in too deep. How does Billy Paul sing it? *We both know that it's wrong, but it's much too strong to let it go now.*"

Aminah couldn't stand what seemed to be Lang's cavalier attitude. "And, really, Lang, how could you when you've watched me suffer through all of Fame's mess?"

"Unlike Fame, I'm not that arrogant," Lang responded defiantly. "I have no intention of ever letting Sean find out. I love him too much to be so careless."

"You're already hurting him and your marriage."

"How can I hurt him with something he doesn't know about?" Lang asked.

Aminah didn't respond right away. She gazed at her best friend with tears brimming, waiting to spill over and run down her cheeks, but she wouldn't let them. She batted her eyes and looked away.

"If Fame were more discreet, and you never found out about the other women, would you be hurt, Aminah?" Lang asked more rhetorically than sincerely. "Could you be hurt? No, because you wouldn't know."

"So that's how you see it, huh?" Aminah asked. Lang raised her right eyebrow but said nothing.

Aminah wiped her eyes with the back of her hand, slid her

Stella McCartneys back on, climbed into her car and started it while Lang just stood there. "You want me to drop you off at home?" she asked through the lowered window.

"No, I think—"

Aminah didn't even let Lang finish her sentence. As soon as she heard no, she pulled off, leaving her best friend standing in front of one of the handsome brownstones.

Chapter 5

*"Our bond is strong. Nothing and nobody
can destroy it."*

Aminah was spent. Usually after her Sunday outings with Lang, she'd take herself to the movies before meeting up with Fame and the children for dinner at either her parents' or his mother's home. It was the only day Fame didn't work in "the lab" or make the necessary music-industry party rounds. Sunday was his family day. Every day was family day for Aminah, of course.

This Sunday, Fame, Alia, and Amir were visiting his mother out in Hempstead, Long Island. Aminah really wanted to skip dinner with Fame's mother altogether and drive out farther east to visit her own mother in Sag Harbor, but she knew Fame wouldn't hear of it.

Her parents had owned their summer home out there decades before either P. Diddy or Russell Simmons ever discovered the Hamptons. The Philipses had purchased their beachfront property in Azurest in the early seventies right after Aminah's father had opened his second dental office. He'd been the premier African American dentist serving the Hempstead community and had decided to expand his practice by opening a second office in

St. Albans, Queens, doubling his patient load and tripling his income.

Aminah's dad had been a Howard University freshman rooming with a direct descendent of an 1840s black whaler whose family had owned property in Sag Harbor for almost one hundred years. One incredible summer weekend visit on the beach surrounded by so many prosperous black folks, and the young Nicholas Philips promised himself he'd someday own property in Sag Harbor's historic, affluent African American community. Mission accomplished.

Though Aminah loved her mother-in-law dearly and enjoyed Gloria Anderson's company immensely, she needed guidance from a more mature woman of wisdom. Glo was more like an older sister than a mother-in-law. In fact, Gloria was only fifteen years Aminah's senior. The day Alia was born, Glo became the sexiest thirty-eight-year-old grandmother on Terrace Avenue.

Aminah, though not too optimistic about the outcome, called Fame, hoping to persuade him to let her skip Sunday dinner at his mother's house. She tried his cell, but it went straight to voice mail. She called her mother-in-law.

"Hey, Glo, how are you doing?" Aminah asked, trying to sound as upbeat as possible.

"Fine, girl, you know I always feel good around my grandbabies. You on your way out here, sugar?"

"Um, well, that's what I wanted to talk to Fame about. Is he there?"

"Hold on, sugar, lemme get him for you. He's out on the deck playing with the kids. You know, I never did figure out how to use this intercom you had installed for me throughout the house. That thing gives me the creeps."

Fame tried his hardest to get his mother to leave Hempstead altogether and move to either New Jersey or a nicer part of Long Island, but Gloria simply was not having it. It was bad enough she had let Fame convince her that Terrace Avenue was no longer safe for her. She'd lived there for almost twenty years and knew damn near everyone by their first name. If she didn't know them personally, she usually knew someone who was kin to them. Make no mistake though, everybody knew Miss Glo—"Miss G-L-O," as she liked to be called.

Originally touted as affordable housing for low-income families, Terrace's quality of life had deteriorated slowly and steadily over the years like a neglected cavity in the mouth of a dentalphobe. Drug peddling, random shootings and stabbings, teen pregnancy, and all the other vices that plague inner cities affected Terrace as well. Ironically enough, Aminah's father was currently a member of the zoning committee spearheading the destruction of the low-income projects for the erection of high-income townhomes.

Glo loved her friends on Terrace and didn't want to be too far from them. So much so that she continued to host her Friday-night spades party and fish fry in her Georgian colonial brick home. Fame had eventually succeeded in moving her to a more "appropriate" section of Hempstead, a section that bordered Garden City, a wealthy, overwhelmingly white town that housed Nassau County government officials, Wall Street power brokers, and the actress Susan Lucci, aka the infamous Erica Kane from *All My*

Children. Ironically, though, Glo was still in walking distance—a good walk, but a walk nonetheless—of Terrace.

Glo would slowly stroll down her current too-quiet street listening to all the silence. She thought the manicured, lush lawns looked way better than that expensive, plush, money-green *carpet* her old Terrace next-door neighbor Neesie had laid down just last year right after she'd hit the number. "This grass looks firm enough to deep-sleep on," Glo often thought, laughing to herself. The intimidating yet sculpted lofty hedges of her current neighborhood were a more aesthetically pleasing way than, say, a white picket fence for her current "neighbors" to maintain their privacy and keep their distance.

Unlike on Terrace, Glo knew neither the family on her right nor left. She did say good morning to them nonetheless when she went outside to grab her *Newsday* as Neighbor on the Right slid into her Jaguar and Neighbor on the Left into his Lexus.

"Aaron!" Gloria yelled. "Pick up the phone. It's Minah, and she don't sound too hot. You feel better, sugar, and come see me later this week if you're not up to coming out today, okay?"

"Sure thing, Glo. Thanks for understanding."

"I got it, Ma, hang up the phone!" Fame yelled back. "Hey, baby girl, what's the matter?"

"Um, Fame . . ." Aminah paused.

"What is it, baby girl? Is everything okay?" he asked, genuinely concerned.

"Yes. Well, no, not exactly." Aminah sighed. "Listen, Fame, I really need to visit with *my* mother today. Would you mind if I skipped dinner with you all tonight, and we met at home later?"

"Baby, we're going to see your folks next Sunday," Fame said, walking down the teakwood steps off the deck and away from the children. "You know the deal. My mother's house this Sunday, your parents' home the next. Minah, you know it's the only day I have to spend with my family."

"I understand all that, Fame," Aminah said, clearly agitated. "But it's not about family time for me today. I get plenty of family time every day. What I need is to spend some one-on-one time with my mother. What I really need is to discuss some things with her and—"

"Stop being so selfish, Minah," Fame said. "'What I need, what I need.' Listen to yourself, Minah. What Alia and Amir need is to see us operate as a unit. You know how I feel about this, baby girl. Now, you had your so-called 'me' time earlier today with your girl Lang. So hurry up and bring your fine ass out here and give your husband and your children some of that precious time."

"Selfish?" Aminah couldn't believe what she was hearing. She was so pissed she had to slam on her brakes to prevent herself from running into the back of the Maxima stopped just inches in front of her. "Damn it! Fame, are you fucking kidding me?"

"Whoa, whoa, whoa. Hold up, Aminah. Who do you think you're talking to right now?" Fame asked, glancing back at his children, making sure they were out of earshot.

Aminah paused and took a deep breath. "I'm sorry for cursing at you, Fame," she said, rolling her eyes.

"You better watch your mouth, Aminah," Fame said sternly through clenched teeth. "What's with all the hostility anyway, Minah? I ain't do shit to you."

Fame was getting riled up. Aminah could tell. Whenever he got upset, proper grammar and pronunciation went out the window.

"Listen, Fame, I'm still dealing with that blind item from *Cindy Hunter*—"

"Not that shit again, Minah. Come on now, I'm done talkin' 'bout that."

"Well, I'm not done dealing with it, Fame."

"What? Your girl Lang got you all bent out of shape? Lemme guess, she thinks you should leave me, right? That you can do better? That you're stupid for staying?"

"No, Fame, for your information Langston is the only girl-friend I have who doesn't think I'm stupid for staying."

"Oh, well, that's 'cause Lang got her own good thing goin' on," Fame said, switching his melody rather abruptly. "And by the way he be talkin' at the basketball games, she knows how to treat him right and keep him happy. Them other chicks is just jealous. They'd be the first in line to try and get wit' me if I gave them the opportunity. Take my word for it, Minah, them very same girls that want you to leave me would kill for a chance to get wit' me." Fame chuckled at the memory of one of Aminah's old college roommates propositioning him earlier this month up in Oak Bluffs over the July Fourth weekend. "C'mon, Minah, baby we been through all this. Our bond is strong. Nothing and nobody can de-stroy it."

"Nothing and nobody but you," Aminah said weakly.

"What was that?"

"Nothing, Fame. It's just humiliating for me to walk around as the loyal doting wife of this successful music producer who can't say no to new pussy. Do you ever think about me? How your mess-ing around affects me? How it hurts me, Fame? How it hurts our family?" Despite her conscious effort not to do so, Aminah's eyes watered, and her voice cracked.

"Baby, you crying?" Fame asked, sounding as worried as he felt. The idea of Aminah driving and crying concerned him deeply. He couldn't bear the thought of her getting into a car accident.

"No, I'm not," Aminah lied, wiping her eyes and sniffling. "I think I'm coming down with a summer cold or something."

"Listen, baby, why don't we just talk in person?"

"No, I want to talk now," Aminah whined insistently.

"Okay baby," Fame said softly. "Just be careful driving. I don't want you to get hurt or nothin'."

"That's ironic, Fame, you don't seem to mind hurting me any other time."

"Minah, don't I give you everything you ask for? Huh?"

"Materially, yes, Fame, you do."

While financially Aminah lived a more than comfortable life, internally she did experience some discomfort. She felt as though her life had been a series of television commercials in which she superbly played the principal roles of the compliant wife supporting her husband's career, the patient mother who happily attended all school events and seamlessly transformed into the punctual after-school chauffeur, the obedient daughter, and the ideal daughter-in-law. None of those roles were providing her any comfort right now.

"Materially?" Fame asked in disbelief, sitting down on his mother's teak chaise longue by the pool. "You can't be serious, Minah. You know you're the only woman who's ever gotten everything I have to give. There is no other woman out here who's even worthy of bearing my seeds, never mind sharing my insecurities, my thoughts, my heart, Minah. That's priceless to a man. No one knows me better than you. Haven't I kept my word to you and your father?"

"Which word are you talking about, Fame?" Aminah asked dully, heading eastbound onto the parkway.

"Remember the summer you left for UPenn, and I told your father I was going to marry you when you graduated?" Fame asked. "He laughed and said only if I could provide you with the standard of living you were accustomed to—that was his minimum requirement. He ain't believe I could do it. He thought you'd drop my project ass for one of them corny-ass college dudes. But the day you graduated, what I have waiting for you, baby? Huh? You remember that?"

Aminah said nothing.

"C'mon, baby, reminiscence with me. Just for a minute."

Aminah said nothing again.

"C'mon, baby girl, don't leave me hangin'."

"What's the point, Fame?"

"Minah. Baby. I love you. Even when you're angry with me, I know you know that. You can't question that. Don't be like this, please, Minah. You're too sweet to be cold. You tryin' to tell me you don't remember your graduation day?"

For the first time in a few hours, Aminah smiled. "You know I do," she replied sweetly.

As far as Fame was concerned, those other chicks only got to taste his sex—most of the time anyway. Aminah got his whole body, his most intimate thoughts, his tireless energy, his wallet, his bank account, everything. She was his heart. The mere idea of Aminah leaving him shook him to the core.

Fame just couldn't fathom his life without Aminah, and the idea of another man with his wife was absolutely unbearable. Not to mention that there was no way he was ever going to settle for *visiting* his own children on the weekends and holidays. He already didn't spend enough time with them as it was.

Aminah leaving him simply was not an option. It was not a part of Fame's legendary MAP—his Master Actualization Plan. He'd developed it not too long after he'd graduated from Hempstead High School in 1989. He'd turned down an academic scholarship to pursue his career as a deejay. Glo wasn't the least bit happy, but she told him if he was gonna hike the mountain less climbed, he had to have a plan. It wasn't so much that Fame was forfeiting an education for future success—he just needed present money, "right-now cash," income he could see and use immediately. So in the summer of '89 when most of his boys were kissing their moms on the cheek and either heading off to college or starting their nine-to-five, he had presented Glo with his MAP, a detailed four-year outline of his career and life goals. In the fourth year he planned on having a million dollars after taxes and on proposing to the love of his life if she stood by him the whole time. It was incredibly ambitious, but it had worked.

"I was so proud of you that day, Aminah," Fame said, cradling the cordless phone in the crook of his neck. "Proud and honored."

At the end of Aminah's graduation ceremony, Fame, dressed in a loose-fitting white linen suit, a princess-cut diamond in his left ear, a Rolex on one wrist and an iced-out platinum bracelet on the other, stole her away from her family and friends to walk her over to a campus parking lot. He presented Aminah with eight long-stemmed white roses—one for every year they'd been together—

and a brand-new white CL500 Mercedes-Benz with a big white bow.

After Aminah had finally stopped screaming, Fame had knelt down on one knee.

"You know I don't need a piece of paper to make you my wife, baby girl," he had said, brushing over his low-cut waves with his right hand. "We've been together since we were freshmen in high school. Then you went off to this elite university, got your degree, and stood by your man the whole time. You supported me when my deejaying career took me around the world. Remember when I flew you into Tokyo to spend your spring break with me? You didn't even laugh when I told you I wanted to transition into producing. Instead you bought me my first SP and 950—the equipment I needed to jumpstart my producing career—and I love you for that, baby. That kind of love is rare."

Fame paused to pull out a Harry Winston ring box from his jacket pocket. "Like I said, you've already been my wife for years, and I don't need a legal document to tell me that. But I'm ready to make some babies, and your father's respect is important to me, so I'd like to do this decently and in order. And I know making it legal means a lot to you."

Fame had opened the deep-blue leather box to reveal a five-carat emerald-cut diamond engagement ring.

"I could never forget that day," Aminah admitted on the phone, choking back the tears.

"Me either. Sorry for calling you selfish, baby," Fame said gently. "Listen, you can go on ahead to see your mother if that'll make you feel better. But I'd love it if you could stop by for just a few minutes. You don't have to stay. I really need to see you though. Just for a minute, baby girl."

"Okay, Fame," Aminah said, exiting off the parkway's winding ramp toward Hempstead. She'd already decided to forego her trip to Sag Harbor. Reminiscing with Fame had stirred up an urgent longing to see him.

Aminah enjoyed dinner with her family at Gloria's house that night. After they returned home and put their children to bed, Fame sat at the edge of their oversize, custom-built bed and asked Aminah to stand in front of him.

"You're so fuckin' sexy, you know that, right?"

Aminah blushed.

"I handpicked you, Mrs. Anderson," Fame said, sliding Aminah's skirt off and then kissing her belly button—first circling the outside and then sticking his warm tongue right in the middle. Fame stood up to undo her halter and unfasten her bra.

"Mmmm, mmmm, mmmm, look at all this sweetness, and it all belongs to me," Fame said, sucking gently on Aminah's neck while rolling her nipples back and forth between his fingers. Aminah moaned.

Fame turned his wife around and wrapped his arms around her waist. He knew how much she loved being hugged from behind. She rested the back of her head on his chest. Though Fame was still fully dressed, Aminah could feel his hardness pushing through his denim shorts. They swayed from side to side as if they were slow dancing to their favorite song. "You my baby?" he asked Aminah.

"Yes."

"Yes, who?"

"Mmmm, yes, Daddy, I'm your baby. I'll always be your baby."

Fame sat back down on the bed, turned Aminah around to face him again, and cupped her plump ass. He moved her hot-pink thong to the right and slowly flicked his tongue up and down the hood of her clitoris until Aminah arched her back slightly and moved her pelvis forward. He gently slid two fingers inside his wife and slowly circled them around and around, enjoying the heat of her silkiness. Then he brought his fingers to his mouth. "You taste so sweet, and you're so wet. Feels like you might want something else."

"Mmmm-hmmm," Aminah moaned.

Fame lifted Aminah up off the floor and gently placed her in the middle of their bed. He grabbed the remote from the nightstand, and Anita Baker's sultry voice sang seductively from the ceiling.

Fame undressed and gently slid inside Aminah. She felt like smooth velvet. They made love for three hours straight. Aminah and Fame slept long and hard, Aminah's head tucked right under her husband's chin. The sensation of Fame's warm, steady breath caressing her face was as soothing to her as a relaxing Vichy shower.

It was customary for Fame to buy Aminah an extravagant gift or take her away on a nice little jaunt when their marriage was on shaky ground or when he'd been busted. He strategically distracted her, or at the very least temporarily preoccupied her, with something memorable.

First thing Monday morning, Fame e-mailed his assistant to put in a call to their Louis Vuitton contact and have something exclusive and pink sent to his wife. That afternoon a messenger arrived at the front gate of their home in Jamaica Estates, Queens. The housekeeper, WillieMae, signed for the package addressed to BABY GIRL. Aminah opened the box and found a $14,000 Louis Vuitton stingray art-deco pouch in Galuchat that wouldn't be available until next March. Aminah smiled and subconsciously tucked that "blind item" into the recesses of her brain somewhere.

Chapter 6

"Your skin is like burnished bronze . . . and your hair is like soft wool. You are exquisite."

"*Don't be afraid, don't be afraid, don't be afraid, baby,*" Sean sang loudly and off-key while dust-mopping the upstairs hallway of the Rogers brownstone—the hallway of the black Madonnas. It was lined with various mother-and-child renditions—a pastel water-color by Brenda Joysmith on one wall, an oil-on-canvas by the Harlem-housed painter, TAFA, next to it, and two sepia-toned photographs of Aminah and her children on the opposite wall. One photo was of Aminah cradling a six-week-old Alia, the other was of her snuggling a three-month-old Amir. At the end of the hallway was a Woodrow Nash stoneware Madonna sculpture. Sean could clean only to music. He found it difficult to focus on his Saturday-morning task otherwise.

"Sing it, baby!" Lang yelled out from the bathroom as she vigorously shook mounds of Bon Ami into her dolphin-footed white porcelain tub. A much smaller amount of the cleansing powder was required, but Lang got an inexplicable rush from creating the thick swirls of paste, only to rinse them away with scorching hot water, making her tub sparkle brighter than all the toothy veneers on the celebrity red carpet.

Six days had gone by since Lang had last spoken to Aminah. Next Sunday was her turn to treat for their Session and brunch, but she wasn't exactly certain if they were even still on. She really missed Aminah, but between Sean and work and Dante, it felt as if every second of her time had been tapped. Still, Lang was surprised that Aminah hadn't at least checked to see if she'd made it home after speeding off in such a huff. Lang had picked up the phone several times during the week, intending to call Aminah, but she just kept putting it off.

Lang methodically sprayed and squeegeed the shower door, meticulously wiped down the mirror and tiles—streak-free, of course—conscientiously disinfected the commode, faucets, knobs and door handles, and enthusiastically scrubbed the dark brown tile floor on her hands and knees. It took her exactly fifty-six minutes to tidy up the bathroom to her liking.

Cleaning was a religious act for Lang. Though she practiced it daily, Saturday was her designated day of devotion to her house of worship. She scheduled major cleaning jobs like any other appointment in her BlackBerry. Every first Saturday from nine AM to noon she booked herself to turn over the mattress, clean out the refrigerator, and wipe down her books and bookshelves with a special Scandinavian microfiber cloth. Every twenty-sixth Saturday of the year she sent her drapes out to be dry-cleaned, and at the beginning of every season she had her windows professionally done.

Cleaning gave her chaotic life order. Oddly enough it often gave her a bigger sense of accomplishment than did her career, and she absolutely loved her job at *Urban Celebrity.* She'd successfully conceptualized and launched that magazine, but there was something about the immediate satisfaction of standing in a room she alone was responsible for making mildew-, grime- and dust-free that made her feel like she was unstoppable and that she really could do anything she put her mind to, just like her mother had told her from when Lang had uttered her first word up until their last conversation two nights ago.

Lang wiped the streams of sweat on her forehead with the back of her hot-pink–Water Stop–rubber-gloved hand. Prior to attacking the bathroom, she'd spent over an hour whipping her kitchen back into acceptable shape. She'd Easy-Offed the inside of her stove, Murphy Oiled the wood cabinets, and Swiffered the floor. Her mother taught her always to clean her kitchen and bathroom first. "You never know when someone's going to stop by unexpectedly to ask for a glass of water or to use your bathroom."

"You'll be saying 'Daddy' to meeee," Sean howled.

Lang stepped into the hallway with her hands on her hips. Sean didn't even notice. He was too caught up in the rapture of Aaron Hall. Langston adored Sean's horrible singing, especially when he performed in a white wife beater and baggy Carolina blue basketball shorts. She tapped him on his shoulder.

"Babe, you think Mr. Hall would mind you butchering his song like that?"

"Why should he?" Sean asked, shrugging his shoulders and then turning around to kiss his wife affectionately on her forehead. "He didn't seem to mind R. Kelly snatching up his style and making a better career out of it than he ever did. What is he, like, a dog breeder now or something?"

Lang laughed. "Touché, touché, but, technically, they both kinda borrowed from Charlie Wilson, don't you think?"

"True, true, but at least he wasn't their contemporary," Sean pointed out. "He was more like an elder that they were both clearly influenced by—that's honorable. I don't have a problem with that. I mean, Nas was definitely influenced by Rakim, Michael Jackson by James Brown, Chico DeBarge by Marvin Gaye. Your man R. Kelly jacked Aaron Hall's style. That's dishonorable. There's a difference."

"Babe, you can't be mad at Kells for that," Lang said. "Besides it's not like he solely rested on that particular style anyway. He's gone in all different directions since 'Honey Love' and Public Announcement. He's an incredible songwriter—'I Believe I Can Fly,' babe, and that song with Céline Dion."

" 'I'm Your Angel.' "

"Yeah. Oh, and the 'Ignition' remix? Personally, I think his diversity, not just in performing, but in songwriting is proof positive that he's a musical genius. The brother wrote 'Fortunate' for Maxwell and then 'Bump, Bump, Bump' for B2K. Come on. Give him some kind of credit."

"I'll give you that, I'll give you that," Sean conceded. "But how Aaron Hall abandoned his style and let R. Kelly run with it is still beyond me."

Sean and Lang could talk about music for hours. Jazz. Blues. Pop. Gospel. Hip-hop. Rock. Reggae. World. Soul. R&B. European classical. Hell, television-show tunes. They shared a mutual appreciation for books, fine art, and cinema as well. They'd go on and on with their mostly friendly banter, though sometimes hostile discussions and debates occurred. Intellectual masturbation, Sean called it. "Sometimes there's no other point to our conversation besides the fact that I get off on it, and it just feels so damn good."

Six years ago he'd attempted to interrupt a zealous discussion

Lang was having at a mutual friend's barbecue in South Jersey. She was arguing adamantly that on a purely intellectual level, black folks could not justify the *N* word being acceptable for their use yet deplorable for white folks, when black folks perpetuated its use in the catchy hooks of music that white kids were bigger consumers of.

Just when he was about to interject and co-sign her, something about the unusual sheen of her skin shut down his entire thought process. He was mesmerized by it, drawn to it, he'd say time and time again. Reminded him of a brand-new, shiny copper penny. A reddish brown—no, a brownish red. "Like red clay dirt, if clay had a sheen to it. Like wet clay, then."

At the cookout he'd asked her where her people were from with that uncommonly rich complexion, those high cheekbones, that keen nose, and those pouty, kissable lips. Told her she had to be a direct descendent of Jesus Christ Almighty Himself.

"Okay, that's original," she said, laughing.

He thought she had the cutest laugh he'd ever heard come out of a full-grown woman. It was childlike and infectious. Knew right then and there he'd propose to her. Hoped she'd say yes someday.

"Tell me, Alex Haley, how you figure Jesus and I share the same blood?" she challenged.

"Revelations, chapter one, verses fourteen and fifteen: 'His head and hair were white like wool, as white as snow, and his eyes were like blazing fire. His feet were like bronze glowing in a furnace, and his voice was like the sound of rushing waters.' Your skin is like burnished bronze, your laugh—no, your giggle is like a rippling stream—and your hair is like soft wool," he said, stretching out her thick, shoulder-length, spongy twists. "You are exquisite."

Langston had been both intrigued and skeptical of Sean that day.

"What are you, some kind of religious nut?" she'd asked suspiciously.

Sean had laughed a long, hearty laugh. "Not at all, just a lover of language and a high school English teacher. And you?"

"A manipulator of words of sorts. I'm a magazine editor."

Sean admired Lang's beauty even more today than he did back then. Yet, it was still her mind, her conversation, that stimulated him most. It was what kept him in the house cleaning on a Saturday when he'd much rather be playing basketball.

While the kitchen and the bathroom were strictly off limits to Sean, he was allowed to help Lang clean the living room—the "black love" room. The walls of their living room were covered with various photographs and prints of black couples together. There was an expensively framed poster of William H. Johnson's *Cafe*, Leroy Campbell's *Charmed to the Bone* lithograph, and a series of enlarged black-and-white wedding photographs featuring Sean's parents, Lang's grandparents, and Aminah and Fame, as well as one of Lang and Sean kissing in the Brooklyn Botanic Gardens surrounded by delicate white orchids.

Sean brushed off the espresso-colored linen cushions and fluffed up the creamy off-white cotton pillows as the Ohio Players' "Sweet Sticky Thing" blared from tall, thin, cylinder-shaped speakers in the living room. Upon entering the room, Lang patted and refluffed the very same cushions and pillows.

"You're such a perfectionist. I don't know why I even bother to try to help you," Sean said, flopping down on the couch.

"Sean!" Lang screamed. "I just fixed those. Get your ass up."

"Come here, woman," Sean said, pulling his wife on top of him.

"Stop it. I'm not done with the couch. And I'm all sweaty and funky."

"Forget the couch," Sean said, nuzzling her neck and then smelling her underarms. "And I love your sweat and your funk. Your natural scent turns me on."

Lang playfully tried to wrestle herself out of his clutches, but it was futile. Sean just squeezed her tighter until she stopped struggling. He flicked his tongue up and down her right nipple through her thin T-shirt. Then he circled the outline of her areola. Lang moaned and lifted up her T-shirt. Sean shook his head and pulled it back down. He sucked thirstily on her breast through her light cotton fabric, creating a big wet round spot and leaving her T-shirt translucent. He stopped sucking only to blow his cool breath over her full, ripe breast, causing her nipple to harden even more.

"You still tryna get away from me?" Sean asked.

"Uh-uh," Lang answered with her eyes closed. "But lemme take off my T-shirt, please, baby."

"No," Sean said, now sucking on her left breast and gripping his wife between her legs. With the ball of his hand he rubbed firmly against her clitoris. Lang tried to move his hand inside her shorts, but Sean resisted.

"Be patient," he whispered.

"I can't. This is torture."

Sean stopped fondling her and looked at his wife sideways. "No. Torture would be if I let your hot ass marinate on this couch till I got back from a pickup game."

"Don't even play like that," Lang pleaded in a breathy voice. "I can't take it."

Sean lifted his wife off him and took a seat in one of the dark chocolate leather chairs across from the couch.

"Baby, you can't be serious," Lang said, frustrated. "How you gonna stroke the kitten and leave her purring by her lonesome?"

"Lang, can't you just relax for two minutes and let me do this?" Sean asked, annoyed. "You're in such a rush to get undressed— just take all your damn clothes off then."

Lang lifted her eyebrows, smirked, and did just that.

Try as he might, Sean could only remain so angry with a naked Mrs. Rogers. "Now lie down on the couch," Sean commanded. "If you wanna take charge so badly, I'm gonna sit back and watch you make your own self come."

Langston lay back down on the sofa, fully stretched and spread out. She rubbed up and down her inner thighs. Then she lightly fingered herself, stroking her outer lips, her inner lips, her clitoris, never taking her eyes off her husband.

Next Lang slowly slid her fingers in and out of herself, moaning. She then sucked on her fingers and played with her breasts, squeezing her nipples and lifting each one to meet her moist tongue. The sight of her husband's visibly growing erection excited her. Sean stroked his own hardness as Lang crawled naked on all fours over to him.

"What are you doing, Lang?" Sean asked. "You're not done yet. Why are you so damn hardheaded? Mmmm, and so damn sexy."

"I need to taste you," Lang growled. "I need to taste you right now."

Lang slid her husband's shorts down and swallowed him whole. Sean groaned and palmed the back of her head.

Lang sucked greedily, taking him in inch by inch until her lips pressed up firmly against his base.

"Oh, shit," Sean moaned. The pleasurable sensation of his throbbing piece fitting down his wife's tight throat never ceased to thrill him. Each time was better than the last. She loved to give her all to everything she did. And this was no exception.

Lang slowly slid her husband out of her mouth and straddled him. She gyrated and maneuvered her hips as Sean thrust deeper and deeper inside her until he finally released himself completely. He came, but she didn't, and that was perfectly fine with Lang. The ecstasy of the act itself had been enough for her . . . for now. She got off on the thrill of the buildup. It just meant that the next time she would explode violently. She collapsed on her husband's chest and listened to his heartbeat slow down to its normal, steady thump.

She lay there thinking about the rest of her afternoon. If she hopped into the shower within the next ten minutes, she'd still be able to keep her eyebrow appointment with Guadalupe in Manhattan.

"Sweetheart, when are you getting off the pill?" Sean asked, interrupting her thoughts.

"What? Where'd that come from?" Lang asked, confused.

"I'm ready to start our family, Lang. I know we said when you're thirty-five, but what's a year earlier?"

"Um, baby, I'm only thirty-three—that's two whole years earlier."

"Not really. You're not factoring in the nine months of pregnancy. I want the baby born no later than your thirty-fifth birthday. I don't want to just be getting started at thirty-five."

Lang slid off her husband and back into her shorts. "Wow. I guess I had a different understanding of our timeline."

"Look, Lang, I don't want to wait anymore. You asked me to wait for you to pitch and sell this magazine idea that you had, and I did that. What is it we're waiting for exactly?"

"I dunno, the right time, I guess."

"But what makes thirty-five a better time for you than thirty-three?"

Lang had to carefully consider her answer because she wasn't really sure. One thing she was certain of, though, was that she definitely didn't want to still be messing around with Dante if and when she was finally ready to get pregnant. That was a bit too foul, even for Lang. But she couldn't plan on ending something that hadn't even begun. And now surely wasn't the time to confess to her husband that she was actually reconsidering having children, period.

"Baby, I want to start our family, I really do," Lang said hesitantly, concerned more about appeasing him than admitting the truth. "And you're absolutely right. There really isn't a reason to wait, except I have to know in my heart that I'm ready to be a mother."

"What exactly are you saying, Lang?" Sean asked.

"I'm saying we have to time this pregnancy right. I need to get proactive in naming an executive editor and grooming that person to take my spot so I can take at least a six-week maternity leave."

"Okay, now you're speaking my language," Sean said, reaching inside her shorts.

"Babe, I gotta get ready for my appointment," Lang said, sliding away from her husband's reach. "We don't have time for round two right now, but there's always tonight."

"Keep talking. I like what I'm hearing," Sean said, smiling.

"Oh, really? You think we can take the sequel to the bedroom the next time?"

Sean laughed, grabbing his basketball shorts off the floor, sliding off his wife beater, and heading toward the bathroom in all his naked splendor, leaving Lang alone in the "black love" room to smooth out her cushions and fluff up her pillows again.

Chapter 7

*"You're callin' me, frontin' like everything's lovely,
when really you're pissed to hear that I'm
not available and at your service."*

Sean dropped Lang off at a Starbucks within walking distance of the salon. Her appointment with Guadalupe wasn't until three, so she ordered an unsweetened Venti iced coffee with light ice and heavy cream and then leisurely strolled toward Excellent and Innovative a few blocks away. As she passed a popular seafood restaurant with outdoor seating, she spotted a diamond-white Escalade.

Okay, he doesn't have the only iridescent white Cadillac SUV in New York City, Lang thought, kneading away her brewing anxiety. The mental massage lasted only seconds though. Her black lace thong still hung from his rearview mirror.

"Shit, shit, shit," she muttered. *Okay, this could be just a coincidence,* she thought. But Lang knew better—she'd also seen his vanity plates, UNVME. *Shit, shit, shit, I wonder where he is.*

Lang glanced around, looking out for both Sean and Dante. Did Sean say he was going to watch a game on West Third Street or play in a game at Chelsea Piers? Either way, neither was far enough for her to feel even remotely comfortable right now. As she crossed the street, instinct told her to glance back again. This time she spotted Dante. But he wasn't alone. He was with another woman, and they were both laughing as they sat at one of the Blue Water Grill's outdoor tables. Lang couldn't stop watching as the woman reached over and touched Dante's hand.

"Well, don't they look all cozy and happy," Lang said out loud, flipping open her tiny Motorola. "I should call Aminah right now and tell her what this motherfucker has the nerve to be doing." She paused. "Aw, damn. She's the last person who'd want to hear about this. Damn. Damn. Damn."

She called Dante instead. Lang stood across the street with her arms folded and blatantly stared at the laughing couple from behind her gold-studded Dolce&Gabbana frames.

"Whassup?" he asked, answering the phone in a rather short manner. Lang sensed she was interrupting something.

"Oh. Hey, you sound busy." Lang mustered up all the casualness in her tone that she could fake.

"Actually, I am. Can I call you back later?"

"Yeah, sure, sure. . . ." She paused.

"You all right?" Dante asked, knowing she wasn't.

"Yes, of course, of course, can I ask you something though?"

"Yeah, but make it quick."

"Are you with somebody right now?"

"Yeah," he admitted casually.

"Are you on a date?" Lang asked with more than a little attitude.

"What's with all the questions?" he asked, more amused than annoyed.

Lang sighed. "Fine, Dante, fine."

"You're so full of shit, Lang," Dante said, chuckling.

"How you figure?" she asked.

"You're callin' me, frontin' like everything's lovely, when really you're pissed to hear that I'm not available and at your service. You're heated that I'm with someone else. Admit it."

"What-the-fuck-ever, Dante."

"I know you didn't think you were the only woman—I mean, chick—I was dealing with," he said, correcting himself. "My bad, I used to think I was dealing with a grown-ass woman, but now you got me wondering. Listen, Lang, I'ma talk to you later."

"How are you going to say all that to me and then get off the phone?" Lang asked, perturbed. "What's your rush, Dante?"

"Oh, so you wanna play games?" Dante asked, chuckling. "That's cool. Because like I said, I am with someone right now, and I don't want to be rude."

"So it is a date then?" Lang asked, hoping that maybe he was just showing his cute cousin from out of town around New York or something.

"You know what? I'm not exactly sure. If you wanna know so badly, hold up and lemme me ask my friend."

Dante asked the nice-looking young lady sitting across from him if they were on a date.

"My friend says yes."

"I don't believe you, Dante," Lang said.

"You don't?" Dante responded, deliberately misunderstanding and handing his phone to his date. "Lisa, do me a favor and say hi to my friend Lang."

"Hi, Lang," Lisa purred into the phone.

"Put Dante back on the phone!" Lang barked.

"I don't think she wants to talk me," Lang could hear Lisa say as she handed Dante back his phone.

"Hello."

"Fuck you, Dante," Lang said, snapping the phone shut, turning on her heels, and rushing toward the salon.

"Soon, baby, soon," Dante said, smiling and watching Lang power walk down the street.

Chapter 8

"I think you get off on making me wait."

Lang arrived for her appointment at Excellent and Innovative about seventeen minutes late, aggravated but by no means surprised that the salon was packed. There was no way she could start the workweek off with stray brow hairs. Not to mention she had *The Fabulous Life of Beyoncé* to shoot for VH1 on Monday.

Guadalupe, her favorite Columbian aesthetician, waxed and tweezed her brows into the cleanest natural arch without fail, and she'd been doing so for the past ten years, back when the salon was over on Madison and Thirty-Third.

"Okay, Langston, dear, come on back," Guadalupe said a torturous hour and a half later. She'd skimmed through the July and August issues of *Essence* and studied the latest issues of *Sister 2 Sister*, *Us Weekly*, and *In Touch*, her direct and indirect competition. "So sorry for the delay, my dear."

"I'm the one who should apologize," Lang said. "I got held up in Union Square and lost complete track of time."

"Are we doing your upper lip, too, dear?" Guadalupe asked.

"If it needs to be done, sure, why not."

As Guadalupe spread the hot wax between her brows, it reminded Lang that she needed to schedule a Brazilian with Babbi at
Bliss Soho. Babbi'd been out on maternity leave, and Lang simply
did not trust anyone else to shape up her lust nest. Other salons
and spas had left her completely bald and, quite frankly, humiliated. Other aestheticians at Bliss didn't quite understand exactly
how much hair she wanted to leave on her mound.

Lang required what she called a Brazilian Basic Bikini Combo,
and Babbi understood her vagina vision like no one else. No hairs
between her butt cheeks or her perineum, none between or on her
outer labia either, but please do leave just enough hair for a nice,
even, medium-width (not too thick, not too thin), not-quite-a-
bush, upside-down pyramid (not a landing strip, nor Hitler's mus-
tache)—a nice, full, inverted triangle that came to a precise point
right above her clit. She'd call them on Monday and see if Babbi
was back. Otherwise she'd be rocking a fuzzy-wuzzy for a few
more days.

"Is there anyway you can squeeze me in for a quick manicure or
a polish change?" Lang asked as Guadalupe placed the astringent-
soaked cotton pads on her eyebrows and above her upper lip to
minimize any redness or swelling.

"Sure, dear, but not for another hour or so."

While waiting in the salon, Lang called Sean to see if he was still
in the city, but he was just crossing the Manhattan Bridge at that
very moment.

"Aw, babe, I wish you'd called me ten minutes earlier," he said,
disappointed. "You want me to swing back and get you?"

"No, don't do that, babe. It's not a problem, really. I'm still
waiting to get my nails done."

"What? You're still there?" Sean asked, surprised. "Damn, baby, I thought your appointment was only gonna take fifteen, twenty minutes, tops. It's going on five thirty, and you're still waiting? Maybe you should look for a new salon if E&I runs that far behind schedule."

"No, babe, it's not even their fault. I got here late."

"How'd you do that?" he asked, a little confused. "When I dropped you off you had, like, a whole hour to spare."

"Yeah, I know, babe, but I was so into this *American Legacy* article that I was reading at Starbucks that I lost complete track of time," she lied.

"Really?" Sean asked, more surprised than suspicious. "That's not like you at all. You put the capital *P* in punctuality. Must have been a damn good article."

"Yeah, it was. Oh, she's ready to do my nails now. I gotta go," she lied again.

Lang waited another forty-five minutes for Guadalupe. It was after seven PM when she finally got out of there. A simple eyebrow appointment that should have ended no later than 3:20 became a marathon day of sit-and-wait, thanks to Dante Lawrence. Lang thought about calling her lover before she went home to her husband, but Sean had just called minutes ago to let her know that he was cooking one of her favorite meals—grilled salmon marinated in bourbon on a bed of steamed spinach, drizzled in his special-made honey-sesame soy sauce. And for dessert, spoon-fed fresh strawberries drenched in whipped cream. Yeah, she needed to go straight home. But damnit, it was still annoying her that Dante hadn't called her back.

"Hey, Dante, it's me," Lang said, leaving him a message.

"Look. I just wanted to apologize for spazzing on you earlier. I know it's the weekend, and weekends are suppose to be off-limits for us, but I figured since you broke that rule last Sunday that I could do the same today." She paused. "Anyway, I look forward to seeing you this week. Um, enjoy—" His voice mail interrupted with an abrupt, robotic "good-bye" before she could even finish her lengthy message.

Lang stood on the corner trying to hail a cab back to Brooklyn. It was times like these that she regretted letting Sean convince her that they needed only one car. He thought their BMW 745Ci was indulgent enough already. He reasoned that between her company's car-service account and all the yellow taxis at her disposal, each of which was either tax deductible or work-expense-able, there really was no need to incur yet another liability. Not to mention that the good, old-fashioned subway was often the quickest way between Brooklyn and Manhattan, particularly during rush hour.

For Sean, every single purchase broke down to either an asset or a liability. The Rogers family were by no means hurting for money, and Sean wanted to keep it that way. Plus, the upkeep of their hundred-year-old brownstone was expensive and ongoing, even after all the renovations they'd already had done.

Sean had always lived beneath his means but ultimately had given up on trying to get Lang to do the same. He'd settle for her living within her means. But with Lang's salary alone of $325,000 a year, what that exactly meant still wasn't quite clear to her. At least she'd stopped hiding receipts from her husband. That had to count for something.

After waiting on the corner for more than ten minutes, she finally called for car service. Her cell phone vibrated as she climbed into the backseat of the black Lincoln Navigator.

"Yes?" she answered abruptly. "Take the Manhattan Bridge," she told the driver.

"You with your husband?" Dante asked.

"No, are you with Lisa?" she replied with two parts cynicism and one part curiosity.

Dante laughed. "No, she left over an hour ago."

Lang said nothing.

"Hello? Lang, you still there?"

"Yeah. I'm here," she replied dryly.

"Come see me," he said, more commanding than pleading.

"Oh, so *now* you wanna see me?" Lang asked sarcastically. "Well, I can't. My husband's waiting for me."

"Just for a minute," Dante said, more pleading than commanding. "Stop by real quick."

Lang saw no sense in frontin'. She hadn't stopped thinking about Dante since she'd spied on him earlier.

"Change of plans," Lang informed the driver. "Take the Brooklyn Bridge instead."

Lang met up with Dante at his loft in DUMBO (Down Under the Manhattan Bridge Overpass). Though she'd been to Dante's place several times since they'd met, it was still risky. While none of her people, nor Sean's for that matter, frequented that area too often, it was still Brooklyn. And Brooklyn was always in the house—and on the streets.

"Listen, I can't stay long," Lang said, removing her gold-heeled jeweled thongs as she walked out of the private elevator that opened directly into his loft. Dionne Farris's "Hopeless" off the *Love Jones* soundtrack was playing.

"What was that earlier?" he said, giving her a full-bodied hug, letting his hand linger on her rear end.

"I think that was a little thing called jealousy," Lang said, resting her head on his chest and inhaling the Versace Black Jeans cologne he usually wore. It was one of the sexiest scents she'd ever smelled on a man. She loved it so much she'd bought herself a bottle and sprayed it on her panties from time to time.

"You have a lot of nerve, you know that, right?" he said, kissing her on the cheek.

"Yeah, I know," she said, breaking away from his embrace and walking toward the floor-to-ceiling window, momentarily captivated by the spectacular view of the Manhattan skyline. "Because I'm married I have no right to feel like that or act like that, blah, blah, blah. Yeah, I know."

"No, Langston Neale," he said, walking behind her, hugging her around her waist and kissing her softly on her neck. "I wasn't going to say anything like that. You're entitled to feel the way you feel. I mean I started fucking around with you knowing you were married. I have no right to judge you. But what I started to say was that you had a lot of nerve because I saw you standing across the street from the restaurant lookin' crazy, sexy, and pissed."

"You what?" she said, turning around to face him. Lang was genuinely taken aback.

"You heard me. I saw you, and I know you saw me. And I'm not gonna front," he said, wagging his index finger at her nose as if he were scolding a cute puppy. "I was disappointed in you. You handled yourself like one of these young girls out here. I mean, you showed me some real birdlike tendencies."

"What?" Lang responded, more than a bit perturbed, not appreciating being likened to a tacky 'round-the-way girl always running off at the mouth, always "clucking" so to speak—hence the fowl implication.

"Cursing a brother out. Hanging up the phone. I dunno. I guess I expected more from you."

"What was I supposed to say, Dante?" Lang asked, placing her hands on her hips.

"Let's just say you would have earned more cool points with me if you had just said something to the effect of, 'Listen, D, I know I have a lot of nerve calling you with this bullshit, but I'm standing across the street watching you have lunch with the next chick, and I'm actually feeling a little way about that,'" Dante said, doing his best Langston Neale Rogers imitation. She laughed. "'And I'll admit, I have no idea who she is or what she is to you, but it's bothering me.' I would've expected something more like that from you. I'm supposed to be the younger one in this relationship. Remember?"

"Oh, so we're in a relationship now?" Lang asked, smiling.

"We're relating," Dante responded, smiling back.

"Oh, yeah, and what difference would it have made if I'd said all that?"

"Well, for one, I'd have an even higher regard for you, thinking, 'Now, that's how a grown-ass woman in control of her emotions deals with an uncomfortable situation,'" he said, moving her hands from her hips and wrapping them around his waist. "Then I would have excused myself from Lisa and let her know that I had to go to speak to someone real important to me and that I'd be back shortly. I would've walked across the street, given you the biggest hug and the sweetest kiss and whispered in your ear that you had absolutely nothing to worry about. Oh, and that I found your li'l jealousy thing to be kinda sexy."

"I would not have let you do that. No PDA, remember?" Lang reminded.

"Then I guess I would have lifted up your face up like this," he said, raising her chin. "Then kissed you here." He pressed his lips firmly against her forehead and held it there for a minute. She inhaled his cologne again and slipped out of consciousness for just a few seconds.

Lang sighed. "We're indoors—private displays of affection are allowed. You can kiss me on my lips now."

He lifted her chin again, brought his lips within an inch of hers, closed his eyes, and smiled. Lang stood there with her eyes closed for a full five seconds before she realized he wasn't going to kiss her.

She playfully punched him and pushed him away. "I think you get off on making me wait."

"I do," he admitted, still grinning and then pulling her back into his embrace.

She moved to kiss him on the lips, but he turned his face. She pulled away. He pulled her back into him and sucked on her bottom lip. He gently caressed the top of her lip with his tongue and then finally kissed all of her mouth fully, softly. She moaned. She melted.

She'd underestimated his kissing skills, thinking like a lot of exceptionally good-looking men that he'd be a lazy kisser. She'd melted the very first time this twenty-three-year-old-something-of-a-man-child had kissed her and every single time since. Everything—every muscle, every fiber and tissue—between her legs was fully engorged. The longer he kissed her, the more intense the sensation stirred, the faster her fluids churned, and the warmer the heat between her legs pulsed until her sugar walls came crashing down in a long, rhythmic explosion. A simple kiss—no, a complicated kiss, a very layered kiss—caused her knees to buckle and her sex muscle to throb involuntarily and uncontrollably. Her bottom lip quivered. He lifted up her tank top and then raised her bra and tongue kissed both her breasts.

"I want you, Dante," Lang whined.

"Soon," he replied, still tonguing her erect, sweet brown nipples.

"I'm ready to feel you inside me. I want you so badly," she breathed.

"I know," he said, cupping both of her full breasts in his hands.

"This can't go on forever," she moaned.

"I know that, too," he said, stepping back from her, leaving her tank top raised and admiring her fully exposed breasts. "I'm familiar with that little corny saying about all good things coming to an end."

"Yeah, but we haven't even gotten to the good stuff yet. Let's make that happen tonight, D," she said, stepping toward him and placing her hand on his crotch.

"Nah, not tonight, baby," he said, moving her hand away and pulling her shirt back down.

"Ugh. You're killing me, Dante!" Lang screamed.

"You can take it."

"No, I can't. I want you."

"You can have me."

"No, I want you now," she whined again.

He shook his head.

"I've never had to wait for dick before."

"I know," he said, smiling.

"What? What? What is it? You want me to beg for it?" she asked, clearly frustrated.

He nodded and smiled.

"Fuck that, Dante," Lang said, readjusting her underwire bra and top.

"What? You think you too proud to beg?" he teased.

"Absolutely. I've never had to, and I never will. My name is Langston Neale Rogers, not Lisa what-the-fuck-ever, or did you forget?"

He laughed. "Nah, I didn't forget. How could I? You won't let me."

"Fuck you, Dante."

"You will."

"No, I won't," she said, pouting and walking over to her shoes. "I gotta go anyway. I'm horny, you're not helping, and I'm late for dinner."

Dante nodded.

"Hey, can I ask you a question?" she asked, tilting her head slightly.

"Go for it."

"Did you have sex with Lisa?"

"I did," he admitted, rubbing his chin.

"Damn, Dante. That's fucked up. How long have you known her?"

"She's not married."

"That wasn't the question."

"She wasn't playing hard-to-get. As a matter of fact she was throwing her pussy at me. She even paid for lunch. It was the least I could do."

"What-the-fuck-ever. I'm outta here," she said, sliding back into her thongs and pressing the elevator button.

Dante turned her toward him and kissed her again. Softly. Gently. He sucked her bottom lip and then kissed her lightly.

"Stop playing with me, Dante. You know what you are? You're a clit tease," she said, turning her back to him.

"I like kissing you," he admitted. "I didn't even kiss her, you know?"

"Is that supposed to make a difference to me?" she asked, insulted, pushing the elevator button again.

"It should," he said, blocking the elevator door.

"Oh, really, and why is that?" she asked with her arms folded.

"Because I don't just kiss anybody. I've fucked more females than I've kissed."

"That's sad," she said, shaking her head.

"Nah, not really. I think kissing is way more special, more intimate. Fucking, for me anyway, is mostly recreational."

"Now that's enlightening. That's the problem with you young boys. You're so detached and downright emotionless. I guess I'm supposed to feel special that you kiss me. Well, it still takes one to know one. Remember that."

"You're not detached, and neither am I," Dante said, unfolding her arms.

"I can be," she said, refolding them.

"You are an exceptional lover, though," he said with a slight chuckle.

"You wouldn't know that."

"Yeah, let you tell it. I picked up on your sexual energy the moment we made eye contact."

"What-the-fuck-ever," she said, flicking her hand dismissively.

"You're not emotionless either. In fact, I think you're catching feelings."

"Don't flatter yourself," Lang said, moving Dante out of her way and strutting into the elevator.

"I'm digging you, Lang," Dante said right before the elevator closed. "I'm really digging you."

Langston left Dante's loft fully aroused. Back at home she enjoyed a scrumptious dinner and devoured her husband with a side of strawberries and cream for dessert. They made love in the dining room, had sex in the kitchen, fucked in the bathroom, and collapsed on the bedroom floor. This time she did come, over and over and over again, twice with her husband and just once—the last time, in fact—with her husband inside her but with her lover on her mind.

Chapter 9

*"You have to be either really strong or really weak
just to expect and accept that 'a man's gonna do
what a man's gonna do.'"*

Aminah ordered a large bottle of Ty Nant mineral water as she waited for Rebekkah Morrison to arrive. Water was Aminah's beverage of choice. She enjoyed both flat and sparkling water equally. It irked her when people said water had no taste. Good water had no *aftertaste* whatsoever and was never to be served on the rocks unless the ice cubes were made from the exact same brand of water. Water could be smooth or crisp, effervescent or still. Chilled water served in a frosted glass more than sated Aminah—it delighted her.

No two waters tasted the same to her. She loved Pellegrino but detested Perrier. Found Poland Spring and even Dasani tolerable. Evian deplorable. Favored Lurisia, Fiji, and Panna. Appreciated Voss. Enjoyed smartwater. Detested both Deer Park and Great Bear, and Aquafina quite frankly made her puke.

Though Aminah was not a wedding planner by practice or profession, she had received several requests to do them after creating such a spectacular event for Lang and Sean four years ago. She'd turned them all down. The wife of Aaron "Famous" Anderson did not work. Though she was Ivy League–educated, Fame saw that the best use of all that expensive knowledge was in the rearing and the development of their children.

Initially, Fame even protested Aminah doing Rebekkah's wedding to Imon Alstar, founder and president of All-Stars Records. However, once she reminded him that he'd done a couple lucrative deals with Imon's label and this could possibly lead to more, he happily surrendered. And while she and Rebekkah hadn't been quite chummy in college, they were always cool. In fact, when Rebekkah had relocated from Philadelphia to New York a couple years ago, it was Aminah who'd helped her get acclimated and even brought her to a movie premiere where she'd subsequently met Imon.

Rebekkah sauntered into the restaurant minutes later wearing a dainty white eyelet sundress, white braided leather flip-flops, a straw tote bag trimmed in white leather, large silver hoop earrings, several sterling-silver bangles on her right wrist, and a dainty silver toe ring. She was a natural beauty—the type of woman who was more lip balm than lip gloss, more wedges than stilettos, more Coach than Gucci.

Rebekkah spotted Aminah immediately. She was sipping on her second glass of sparkling water still wearing her Oakley sunglasses with the rose-colored lenses inside the dimly lit restaurant located in the rear of the Tribeca Grand Hotel.

The ladies embraced each other lovingly, ordered their dinner, and fell into a natural rhythm of catch-up conversation.

"I've always loved your locs," Aminah complimented, sliding her pink camouflage frames on top of her head. "That color looks incredible with your complexion. Who does your hair?"

She purposefully complimented sisters with natural hair. She loved to see women embracing their own texture and supported them if not physically at least spiritually. She thought they exuded supreme confidence and a regal beauty that deserved more appreciation and validation by the media and society at large.

"Thanks," Rebekkah said, brushing the back of her intricately twisted updo. "Debra at the Studio in Bed-Stuy. I was literally terrified of cherry plum, but she convinced me to try something new, something different. Before I let her do this, dark brown was more my idea of a risk."

They laughed.

"I know what you mean," Aminah said. "My husband would have a fit if I came home with any other color besides jet black, and heaven help me if I stopped relaxing my hair. . . ." Aminah caught herself. She hated the way she'd just sounded.

Rebekkah raised her eyebrow, took a sip of her pinot grigio, and swiftly changed the subject by asking how Lang was doing. "You know we gave her exclusive coverage of our nuptials in *Urban Celebrity*?"

"I guess she's fine," Aminah replied flatter than her opened bottle of mineral water.

"You guess? Wait. I thought you two spoke practically every day. When'd that change?"

"Last week. We had a little falling out over brunch. Obviously, in the twentysomething years we've been friends we've disagreed before, but this time . . ." Aminah's voice trailed off. "I dunno."

As tempting and maybe even as necessary as it was for Aminah to vent, she didn't quite trust Rebekkah enough to violate Lang's confidence. She'd never done it before and wasn't about to start now, though the irony of feeling conflicted over her double-dipping friend wasn't lost on her.

"Sounds like more than a little fallout? You okay? You wanna talk about it?"

"Well, you know Lang's always been stomping up the career path while I've been gunning down the family lane," Aminah said, attempting to "skirt the issue" just a bit. "And I'll be honest, I just find some of her choices lately to be a little on the selfish side. That's all."

"What choices? Her career choices?"

"Well, not exac—"

"But isn't that the beauty of the time we live in as women?" Rebekkah asked, cutting Aminah off. "We have the freedom to choose our lives and not just deal with some unwanted or forced circumstances. We're our own prime examples. She's a dynamic career woman, you're a happy full-time mother, and I'm a successful single working mom. Oops, correction—newly engaged single working mom. Bam!"

Rebekkah promptly fanned her three-carat conflict-free diamond ring in front of Aminah's salad plate, and they both doubled over with laughter. They quickly regained their composure as the waiter refilled Aminah's water glass and took Rebekkah's order for another glass of pinot grigio.

Aminah cleared her throat. "We have choices. That's great and all. But certain choices come with consequences."

"Okay. I'll give you that. So what's the consequence of Lang's choices?"

God. I wish I could confide in this woman, Aminah thought to herself.

"Well?" Rebekkah asked impatiently.

"Oh, just the repercussions of pissing me off and me putting your butt on timeout."

They both laughed again.

"We'll be fine," Aminah said, waving her hand. "Really. Enough about Lang, we came here to talk about your fabulous day. So what kind of wedding did you have in mind? Are you planning on something really grand with lots of family and friends, or would you prefer something a little more intimate?"

"Well, I heard Lang's wedding was very Brooklyn-centric, so to speak," Rebekkah said, absentmindedly pushing around the mesclun and arugula leaves on her salad plate. "Imon wants the same sort of thing only with a Harlem flair in this sort of winter-wonderland setting with my son as his best man. Of course, he wants everybody who's anybody in the industry to be invited."

Aminah chuckled, taking another sip of her mineral water. "Okay, I think I know what he means, but is that what you'd like as well?"

Rebekkah so desperately wanted to share her insecurities and concerns not only about her wedding day but about her relationship with Imon itself. Their conversation had been so unaffectedly free-flowing that she felt she could fully open up to Aminah.

Rebekkah sighed. "Aminah, I hope I don't sound too nutty, but I've always felt this soothing, really calming energy emanating from you."

Aminah thanked Rebekkah while laughing silently to herself. She recalled telling Lang that she'd kept Rebekkah at a safe distance because she found her to be precisely just that . . . *nutty*.

"I mean it. Listen, I hope I'm not being too forward, but I sort of have a dilemma that I'm hoping you can help me with," Rebekkah confessed.

"Hey, is everything all right?" Aminah asked, placing her hand on top of Rebekkah's.

"Yes. Well, no, not really. I'm not so sure." She paused to take a forkful of her salad and to gather her thoughts. "I love Imon. I really do. And, I mean, I love him with everything, girl." She sighed again. "But the closer it gets to our actual wedding date, the more reservations I have about marrying him."

"Aw, sweetie, wedding jitters are normal," Aminah reassured.

"No. It's not just that," Rebekkah finally admitted. "I mean, I'm really starting to question if I can marry into this whole thing, this whole lifestyle. Being married to someone in the entertainment industry isn't like being married to a normal person."

Aminah nodded as she chewed on her peppery green salad. "Well, you're right about that, but all marriages have their challenges."

"Yeah, I guess so. I don't know." Rebekkah hesitated. She took a sip of her pinot grigio and held it in her mouth for a few seconds, savoring the light, fruity notes before taking another sip. "Please don't take this the wrong way, and I truly, truly mean no harm, but explain to me how you deal with it all. I mean, you seem so happy. I've seen you and Fame out together. You two look so in love. He clearly adores you. Anybody can see that, but I just don't get it, Aminah."

"Deal with what exactly? What is it that you just don't get?" Aminah asked, puzzled.

"I'm sure you've heard all the stories and rumors about Fame. I'm sorry, but I think you have to be either really strong or really weak just to expect and accept that 'a man's gonna do what a man's gonna do.' I don't think I can do that."

Aminah was stunned into silence. She'd expected to talk about tea roses, calla lilies, and color schemes this afternoon, not the pros and cons of being married to an unfaithful spouse in the music business.

"I mean, I think that cheating is the ultimate disrespect," Rebekkah continued. "I don't know how I could be expected to forgive that, never mind forget it."

Aminah stared at Rebekkah in shock and disbelief. It felt as if she were having an allergic reaction to peanuts or shellfish or something, and now her throat was swelling shut rapidly. She subconsciously massaged her throat. She felt in desperate need of a shot of epinephrine to relax her airway—not so much so that she could breath, but just so that she could speak.

"I'm sorry, Aminah. This is so inappropriate," Rebekkah acknowledged. She hadn't intended to offend Aminah. She desperately needed to speak with a woman who could offer her some insight from experience, not just empty sound bites and useless theories.

"That came out all wrong," Rebekkah said apologetically. "I hope I didn't come off judgmental, because I get accused of that all the time. I didn't mean to. Look, I'm genuinely confused myself. I just need some advice."

"Funny, I thought you came here to discuss your wedding," Aminah said, finally finding her voice. Aminah sat up straighter in her chair, elongating her neck and lengthening her spine. She cocked her head slightly. "First of all, let's get one thing straight," she said, punctuating each word with her salad fork pointed directly at Rebekkah. "Fuck what you heard, you don't *really* know me or my husband. I would never discuss private details of my personal life with you. I came here to meet with you as a favor to you. I don't *need* to be here. You understand what I'm saying? Now, I don't know what particular rumors you're referring to, but suffice it to say you can't believe everything you hear. And please, Rebekkah, don't take this the wrong way. I truly, truly mean *you* no harm, but you can take your tacky little wedding plans, your pseudo-*sistah* persona, and kiss my naturally beautiful black ass."

Aminah slid her pink Oakleys back down, tossed five crisp twenty-dollar bills on the table, and strutted out of the Tribeca Grand, leaving her cobalt bottle of Ty Nant only half full.

Chapter 10

"I'm not okay with just good sex. I want great, mind-blowing, turn-me-out sex. And, quite honestly, I want that more than I want kids."

Lang tackled Mondays thoroughly while perpetually caffeinated. It was the only day of the week she arrived in the office before the rest of her staff to professionally and personally prep for her week—materials read, notes jotted, meetings set, e-mails sent, appointments made, and calls returned.

By late afternoon, Lang found herself staring at her phone only to pick it up and place it back down. She rang her assistant to get Aminah on the line.

Lang's phone line buzzed.

"Aminah?"

"No, it's me." Merrick cleared her throat. "Aminah said, and I quote, 'No offense, Merrick, but tell Lang to pick up the phone and call me her damn self. You have yourself a good day.'"

"What a bitch. Fine. And, Merrick, would you please order me a grilled salmon Niçoise salad? Thanks."

Lang released the line and dialed Aminah. Minah picked up on the third ring. "Why must you be so difficult? I just wanted to confirm a spot for brunch next Sunday," Lang said.

"Why, hello to you too, Langston," Aminah said, dropping her keys on the table in her foyer. She'd just returned from bringing Amir home from school. "Are we *still* doing brunch next Sunday?"

"So you wanna cancel?" Lang asked, more disappointed than surprised.

"I've been thinking about it," Aminah replied as she climbed the stairs to her bedroom. "After everything I discovered about you last Sunday, I don't enjoy being in your company."

Lang put Aminah on hold to close her office door. She paced in front of her pewter and glass desk a couple times before picking up the phone again. "So you're judging me now, Minah? You've got nerve. For years—you hear me—not *days*, for years I've watched you stand by Fame while he did his dirt, and not one time have I ever judged you. Disagreed with your decisions, maybe. But judged you? Never. Defended you? Always. And now you're gonna fuckin' judge me?"

"I'm not judging you," Aminah answered calmly. "I just don't agree with you."

"Bullshit. You've already chosen sides. You're on Team Sean."

"I'm siding with what's right," Aminah said firmly.

"See? And there's the judgment."

Merrick knocked on the door to bring in her boss's lunch. Lang motioned with her hand to leave it on her desk and shut the door behind her.

"Not once have I ever said that you forgiving Fame or staying with Fame was wrong or right. I just supported you," Lang continued.

"Wait. You can't possibly expect me to support your decision to cheat on your husband?" Aminah asked, scrunching her face.

"Not my decision, Minah. Damn. Me. I expected my best

friend to support *me* through my shit like I've had *your* back through your shit. Is that asking too much?"

"I . . . I . . . I hadn't thought about it that way," Aminah said, shaking her head.

"'Cause you were so quick to criticize me with no thought of me and my position."

"How could I, Lang? You knew where I'd stand on this. You're asking too much. You know my position."

"The same exact way I thought of you and not my own position when you chose to start your family right away instead of a career after graduating summa cum laude. Shit. You know I'm one hundred percent for women getting their own money first before starting a family they can support on their own, by themselves, married or not. But when folks started saying you were wasting your education, or, better yet, when you yourself asked me if I thought you were crazy not to be a working mom, I said, 'Crazy? No. What a blessing to even have that dilemma.' Do you not remember that, Minah?"

"I do."

"Minah, I've felt like something's been missing in my life for a little while, and I'm trying to figure out what that is. I love Sean, and I love my marriage, but it's not enough to keep me fulfilled. At least I don't think it is, or maybe it's not supposed to be. I dunno. Maybe I'm asking too much from matrimony."

"Listen, Lang, I didn't mean to judge you," Aminah apologized. "But, honey, marriage isn't always gonna be fulfilling. It takes work. The same way you work at your career, you've got to work at marriage, and you're never gonna find the remedy for your relationship outside of it."

"That makes sense, but . . ."

"But nothing, Lang."

"No, hear me out," Lang requested. "I'm not looking for my marriage to fulfill me. I want—no, I crave self-fulfillment. I mean, sue me for wanting it all—a great career, a nice home, a loving husband, and an amazing sex life. I'm not okay with just good sex. I want great, mind-blowing, turn-me-out sex. And, quite honestly, I want that more than I want kids. I work hard, I'm a great catch, and I deserve it. I mean, maybe we can't have it all, but I'm damn sure gonna find out before I give one up for the other."

"Wow, Lang. Did you just say you wanted sex more than you wanted children?"

"Something like that."

"Okay, okay, let's finish this discussion on Sunday," Aminah said, resigned, shaking her head in disbelief.

"See, now you done lost your right to choose," Lang said after chewing her salad. "I'll pick. It's my turn to treat anyway."

"Where to?" Aminah asked Lang as they buckled up inside her immaculate BMW, careful not to smudge their nails. Aminah had left her Range Rover in front of the Rogers' brownstone. Sean had offered to wash and vacuum out her truck while the ladies brunched in Manhattan. They'd just finished spoiling themselves with some especially good pampering at Pretty Inside.

Lang and Aminah had passed up their usual Sunday Sessions for services a bit more indulgent. Lang had treated herself to a luxurious Oatmeal Almond Crunch pedicure, and Aminah to pink rhinestone As encrusted on both her pinkie nails. Soaking in the warm oatmeal batter, being rubbed in an almond/apricot scrub, and then immersed in grape-seed and jojoba oils had Lang's feet feeling not only smoother than Sade's operator (no need to ask), but smelling sweeter than her taboos.

At Pretty Inside they'd discussed the details of Sean and Lang's trip to Hilton Head next week with Alia and Amir, lamented how fast the summer was disappearing, and joked about Lang's cleaning obsession with no mention of the conversation they'd had earlier in the week.

"I've been thinking about fish and grits ever since I mentioned them the last time, so I had Merrick make us a reservation at that li'l spot in Chelsea."

A vocally challenged Langston Rogers drove to Manhattan unhurried, butchering songs from *Epiphany: The Best of Chaka Khan, Volume One* the entire ride. She passed her invisible microphone to Aminah for the powerful notes she couldn't hang with, just like she had in their junior high school days.

Aminah belted out, *"Problem is you ain't been loved like you should. What I got to give will sure 'nuff do you good,"* resuscitating Chaka's "Tell Me Something Good" before Lang mutilated it beyond revival.

"Minah, it makes no sense that you never sang professionally— you know that, right?" Lang said, looking for parking.

"Sure it does. I've never wanted to," Aminah explained. "Lang, we've beaten this topic to death for the past twenty years. See, now that's why I don't like singing around you."

"You've never wanted to, or Master—I mean, Maestro—Fame never wanted you to?" Lang asked playfully.

"Ha-ha, very funny," Aminah said, nodding her head to Chaka's electric "I Know You, I Live You." "Keep playing, Langston Neale Rogers. You don't want me to bring up the fact that at the very premenopausal age of thirty-three, you're still an unpublished author named after not one, but two literary legends and have yet to live up to your namesakes. Correct me if I'm wrong, but I don't believe I've heard any plans from you to write any kind of novel or even so much as develop a short story for that matter. Instead you've chosen to head up a rag—I mean, a tabloid, I mean, a, uh, what do you call that thing you run?" Aminah asked sarcastically while snapping her fingers. "A magazine. Yes, that's it, a glossy ghetto magazine. Now, if that's not fulfilling your destiny, then—"

" 'Nuff said," Lang interrupted.

"Uh-huh, I thought so," Aminah said, smiling as Lang pulled into a parking garage. She knew that would shut Lang right up. Aminah enjoyed singing in the privacy of her shower, her car, and around her house. She'd entertained the idea of being a singer as a teenager, but her parents weren't very supportive. They saw it as a waste of time and intelligence. Plus, Aminah wasn't a big fan of the business side of music either—though she couldn't deny that the business side of music kept her family well dressed, well fed, well heeled, and well housed.

Lang, however, really wanted to write her great American novel someday. She simply was not ready to focus or commit that kind of time and energy just yet. Her mother frequently asked her which should she expect first from her, "a fine piece of literary fiction" or "an adorable specimen of a grandchild."

"And my magazine is *not* ghetto," Lang said, opening the door for Aminah.

Lang and Aminah strolled into the small yet charming restaurant hand in hand, laughing and smiling. It was practically filled to capacity.

Aminah made her way to the table with Lang's hand on the small of her back. They were seated next to another pair of women. The well-dressed duo smiled at them, and they smiled back.

Both Aminah and Lang ordered the extra-flaky-on-the-outside, so-tender-on-the-inside fried whiting with the smooth, not-at-all-grainy, creamy grits. Lang had hers with a Bellini and Aminah a mimosa.

"So how'd that meeting with Rebekkah go?" Lang asked, buttering her visibly steaming-hot piece of cornbread.

"Oh, you're not gonna believe this, Lang," Aminah said. "The real reason she wanted to meet with me was for some premarital counseling. We barely even discussed her wedding."

"You're lying, Minah. Y'all aren't even cool like that," Lang said, taking a sip of her Bellini.

"I know, but apparently she thought so. She basically asked to borrow my manual on coping with a cheating husband in the entertainment industry and then chastised me for writing it. *'I don't know how you deal with all the rumors of your man sleeping around. I know I couldn't, but could you still tell me how just in case I change my mind?' "* Aminah said, imitating Rebekkah.

Langston laughed so loud the woman seated next to her in the black knit tube top and cultured pearls with matching earrings gave her a disapproving look, but Lang ignored her. "No, Minah, what'd you do?"

"I left. And the sad part is before she ripped into me, I was really enjoying her company. But then she had to get all nutty with me."

Lang laughed. "Well, you always said she was."

"Is," Aminah corrected.

"So are you still going to do their wedding?" Lang asked.

"You can't be serious, Lang."

"I so am, Aminah. Business is business."

"Excuse you, this isn't my business. It's barely a hobby," Aminah reminded.

"Girl, please," Lang said, taking another bite of her delicious cornbread. "It could be your business. You and Fame are always on Imon's guest lists anyway. You know you could easily be the urban Preston Bailey."

"Yeah, well, I can't even lie to you," Aminah said after taking a sip of her tangy mimosa. "I was really looking forward to doing it. Though she did kind of throw me for a loop when she said Imon wanted some kind of winter-white-wedding-wonderland extravaganza done up Harlem style, darling," Aminah said, snapping her fingers in the air.

Lang laughed so hard she had to swallow her piece of cornbread whole just to keep from choking on it. "What in the hell is that?" she asked, finishing off her Bellini.

"I'm not quite sure, but I'm seeing this huge wedding at Abyssinian, tons of white and silver or white and gold; the reception at a brownstone on Strivers' Row maybe; and all these fabulous guests decked out in winter white and red velvet, I guess. I don't know, Lang. It all sounds very tasteless. I just know he wanted something flashy with all the A-list people there."

"Oh, goodness, that sounds like Imon Alstar," Lang said. "He must be seen. He's such a media whore. Don't get me wrong, I love media whores, especially the ones who give me exclusive all-access to their wedding. Shit, that brother gets mad when we're *not* talking about him in the magazine. I've met Rebekkah only a couple times, but I pictured her wanting something a bit more, I don't know, Afrocentric, for lack of a better word. You know, more cultural."

"And your picture ain't blurry," Aminah said, laughing at her own corny joke. "She just doesn't know how to tell Imon that."

"Oh, well, it doesn't really matter to me," Lang said, flipping her hand. "You know the deal. *Urban Celebrity* is only interested in her because of who she's marrying. What is she anyway, like, a math teacher or something?"

"No, Lang, damn. The sister is a former sociology professor and a consultant on that new black family drama coming to HBO. Oh, wait a minute," Aminah said, leaning back in her chair and folding her arms. "I finally get it now. So I've only been featured in *Urban Celebrity* because of who I'm married to. Is that how this pseudo-celebrity thing works?"

"Yeah, girl, I thought you knew," Lang said, smiling. "That and who you're best friends with."

They both laughed loud and hard. This time the modish woman in the tortoiseshell Ferragamo eyeglasses gave Langston a disapproving look. She ignored her, too.

"Minah, how is a sociologist-slash-consultant gonna seek advice from a mere acquaintance? That makes absolutely no sense at all."

"No, it sort of does," Aminah explained. "I've gotten better advice in one night from a bartender whose name I never knew than from that marriage counselor we saw once a week for two years straight." Aminah chuckled at her own admission.

"No, thanks, then. I'll pass on the therapist and stick with my favorite bartender up in 40/40. Hey, did I ever tell you I fucked Imon? Well, I tried to anyway."

The lady in pearls cleared her throat. Lang gave her a phony smile, and Aminah gagged on her mimosa. "Lang, shhhh," Aminah managed to get out through a bit of a coughing seizure. "Wait, what do you mean tried to?"

"Girl, his dick was so small I can't really say if we did or didn't. I mean, does it really count if you can't feel a thing? No friction, no nothing, and I was doing my Kegels and everything, Minah." Lang laughed at herself as Aminah dropped her head in her hands. "But you know what he can do, right?"

Aminah hesitated to answer. She knew where Lang was going but was quickly trying to come up with the most tactful way of responding to her question. "Um, go downtown?" Aminah whispered.

"Yes, girl, that flashy Negro can eat him some pussy, you hear me?"

"Excuse me," the dignified woman in the designer eyewear said. "We don't care to hear about your private affairs. Would you mind lowering your voice, please?"

"No problem," Aminah replied, embarrassed. "Pardon us."

Lang rolled her eyes. "Yes, pardon us. Who knew a couple of stuck-up bitches brunching could be so—"

"Lang!" Aminah interrupted. "Must you be so loud and crass? These tables are so tight in here. You know the entire restaurant can hear our conversation even when we're whispering."

Lang rolled her eyes again and ordered a cup of coffee with cream on the side. Aminah ordered apple pie à la mode. The well-dressed female couple was done with their meal and Langston. They didn't even bother to stay for dessert. They left abruptly, shaking their heads, disgusted and offended with Lang's candor.

"You think I was too harsh on Rebekkah?" Aminah asked.

"No, I mean, if she came out her face like you said she did, you did the right thing by checking her," Lang said, lightening her coffee to just the right hue. "She doesn't even know you well enough to be stepping to you with what she's heard about you. C'mon, that's foul by anyone's standards."

Aminah took a healthy bite of the delicious pie, holding the sweet filling and flaky crust in her mouth. As she savored the warm combination of nutmeg, cinnamon, and vanilla, she also reflected on her conversation with Rebekkah. It'd been bothering her all weekend. Bits and pieces of Rebekkah's monologue stuck with her, like lint on her favorite cashmere sweater.

"Lang, why didn't you ever discourage me from marrying Fame?"

Lang took a sip of her freshly brewed coffee before answering. She thought long and hard, though the answer was sitting right in the middle of her mouth, wedged somewhere near the base of her throat, where it'd always been.

"Because I knew you realized what you were marrying into, and I accepted that because you were okay with it," she said. "I knew you were in love with him then, and I know you're still in love with that man now. Minah, you still light up when Fame walks into a room."

Aminah closed her eyes for a couple seconds, visualizing Fame walking through the restaurant, and she smiled. Rebekkah's comments quickly disrupted her daydream though.

"Yeah, but you never thought I was stupid for sticking it out with him?" Aminah asked, almost whining. "Even when I cried and complained about him? And I know I must have cried and complained to you a zillion times over the last ten years."

"Yeah, you have, Minah," Lang said, grinning slightly. "And I don't think you're dumb for staying with Fame. But I can't tell you to leave your husband and the father of your children either. Only you can make that decision. You're many things, but spontaneous isn't one of them. You're very deliberate and intentional. Look, you knew the lifestyle—the women, the late nights, the parties, the afterparties. I mean, why ask all this now? Are you thinking of doing something about it?"

"I dunno. You think I can at this point?" Aminah asked, taking another bite of her pie and feeling particularly vulnerable.

"Of course, Dorothy. You've had the power to go home all along, you didn't need those ruby-red slippers," Lang said, smiling and waving her spoon like a magic wand.

"What are you talking about, Langston?" Aminah asked, dropping her fork.

"Seriously, Minah, it's you who determines how good or bad Fame treats you, not Fame," Lang said, holding Aminah's face and looking at her squarely. "The problem is you've been so accepting of his trifling behavior since our high school days. Not once did you ever really threaten to leave Fame. Sure, you've confronted him, and I'll give Fame extra credit for not lying to you to your face, but you never did anything afterward."

"Did anything like what?" Aminah asked, this time truly whining.

Lang didn't respond right away. Apparently, her best friend's lunch with Rebekkah had awakened a sleeping giant, or at least she'd hoped it had. She'd silently witnessed Aminah endure the embarrassing rumors, but she'd given up on trying to get Aminah to leave Fame a long time ago. When Lang had even suggested to Aminah that she at least try to date other guys while they were away in college, Aminah had thrown a fit and accused her of not being supportive. Aminah made it blatantly clear that she was going to be the wife of Aaron "Famous" Anderson, so there was no need for her to go out with anyone else.

"Listen, Minah," Lang finally said. "You've justified and overlooked Fame's behavior for so long that I've kind of grown used to it. I took your silence and inaction as acceptance. Not doing anything about it is the same as agreeing, as far as I'm concerned."

Aminah rubbed her temples. She knew her girlfriend was right.

"Look, you never demanded that he treat you any better," Lang continued. "And he basically took the Brand Nubian approach—'You gotta love me, or leave me alone'—and you said, with a smile, mind you, 'Fine, I'll love you whether you deserve it or not.'"

"So you're saying you don't think Fame deserves my love?" Aminah asked, even more confused.

"No, Minah, I'm not saying that. I'm saying you've allowed him to get away with so much without any sort of repercussions for his actions, it's not even Fame's fault anymore. Imagine if you raised Alia and Amir like that. They'd be spoiled-rotten brats. For those children to be blessed with so much materially, you've raised them to be very grounded, very level-headed children. Alia's always telling me things like, 'Auntie Lang, no one can treat you any worse than you allow them to.' 'Auntie Lang, never be afraid to shine amongst the lackluster.'"

Aminah smiled with pride. "I got that last one from this motivational speaker at the African-American Women On Tour in Philadelphia years ago. In fact, I went with Rebekkah. Go figure."

"Yeah, well, maybe it's time you shared some of those adages with yourself and whipped your husband into shape," Lang said, finishing up her delicious cup of coffee.

"You don't think it's too late?" Aminah asked, tilting her head slightly like a bewildered puppy.

"It's never too late, sweetie," Lang responded, smoothing Aminah's slicked-back ponytail.

"Yeah, but what am I threatening him with? I'm not leaving Fame so somebody else can have him," Aminah said firmly.

"I never said you had to leave him, but he's gotta relearn how to treat you. Minah, you've made the unwise mistake of accepting his please-forgive-me-I-been-bad gifts and trips. Shit, you should be getting those things regardless," Langston said, waving her right hand as if she were shooing away flies.

"You're right, Lang, you're so right," Aminah admitted. "But I'm scared to change anything now. What if it doesn't go the way I want it to? I'm not raising my children without their father in the house. Maybe I'm just better off leaving things be," Aminah reluctantly admitted, taking the last bite of her pie.

"Scared of what, Minah?" Lang asked, frustrated. "Fame doesn't want to lose you any more than you want to lose him. You think he's trying to let some other man have you? You're a catch by any man's standard. You're beyond platinum, baby—you're diamond status."

Aminah beamed. Lang was great for her ego. She'd championed her causes, rarely failed to be sympathetic, and for the most part withheld her judgment for the last twenty-eight years they'd been friends. It was Lang who'd made sure Aminah didn't "let herself go" after she had her children. Her baby-shower gifts to

Aminah had been beginners African dance classes at Alvin Ailey after she had Alia and a personal trainer not long after Amir was born.

"Yeah," Aminah agreed. "And you're not telling me anything I don't already know." She sighed.

Lang paid the bill, and they strolled over to a furniture store nearby to purchase some office accessories Lang had eyed in their catalog.

"You think I'm crazy for forgiving Fame so many times?" Aminah asked, reaching for Lang's hand.

"Crazy? No," Lang replied, squeezing Aminah's hand. "I think you forgiving him is somewhat divine. Forgiveness and childbirth, I think, are the closest we can get to God. Forget trying to be perfect and righteous. What I'm not so sure about is if forgiveness is warranted or deserved if someone's going to take advantage of it. Like, how often are you supposed to ration that shit out? But maybe that's just the less divine part of me talking. I mean, imagine if we all forgave as much as we wanted to be forgiven."

"That's deep, my sister," Aminah said, nudging her best friend.

"Shhhh, don't tell my readers," Lang said, putting her index finger up to her lips. "They like me for my superficiality, and I'd like to keep it that way. I save the heavy shit for you and my husband."

Aminah laughed and held the door open for Lang. Inside the ultimate organizer's dream store she picked up a few hardwood and chrome hangers for Fame while Lang grabbed a powder-blue leather file box with chocolate contrast stitching. They paid for their goods and walked back to the garage.

"I remember watching this episode of *Angels in America* with

Meryl Streep and Al Pacino," Lang said, opening the passenger's-side door of her car. "Jeffrey Wright—you know, the brother from that George C. Wolfe play *Topdog/Underdog?* He played both a black gay male nurse and an angel. I think he even won an Emmy for those roles, too. Anyway, the male nurse said something like maybe forgiveness is where justice and love meet and that it's not supposed to be easy."

"Now that's a jewel if I ever heard one," Aminah said, fastening her seatbelt.

Lang pressed the 2 button on her CD changer. The Clark Sisters' "You Brought the Sunshine" played as they left Manhattan. While Lang didn't want to come straight out and ask Aminah if she could see herself married to Sean—she was almost certain she could—she did want to play the game of "hypothetical situation" with her. They'd devised it in high school. It allowed each of them to ask any question they wanted without any judgments or repercussions under the guise or the safety net of the question being only hypothetical. The most important rule of the game was that neither one of them could hold a grudge against the other for their response, nor could they bring it up at a later date.

"Minah, hypothetical situation—"

"Wow, we haven't done this in a minute," Aminah said. "Okay, go ahead."

"If we were both single, and we both met Sean at the same time, would you try to bag him for yourself?"

Aminah laughed. "Did you really need a 'hypothetical situation' to ask me that?"

"You're laughing, but I really wanna know, and I don't wanna be mad at you for your answer."

"It depends, Lang, do I know Fame?"

"I dunno. I guess."

"Well, you need to know because my answer depends on that," Aminah explained. "If Fame is in the picture, then absolutely not, but if there's no Fame, then, yes, yes, I would."

"Do you think you'd be better for him than me?"

"Do I or would I?" Aminah asked.

Do had been a slip. Lang allowed silence to take up some space. If the Clark Sisters' "Endow Me" hadn't been playing, the lack of conversation would've filled up the car for at least a good five minutes.

"Lang, if I didn't think you and Sean were good for each other, I would never have gone all out for your wedding," Aminah clarified.

"That's not what I asked you, Minah," Lang replied curtly.

"Okay, fair enough," Aminah conceded. "Yes, yes, I do."

"Do or would?" Lang asked

"I said what I meant, Lang," Aminah said. "And for the record, since this is purely hypothetical, it's do and would."

"Oh, so you think Sean's too good for me now?" Lang asked, glancing at her best friend sideways. She hadn't expected Aminah to be so forthcoming. "What kind of shit is that?"

"No, I never said anything about anybody being good enough," Aminah answered. "You said that. I'm saying I think I'd be better for Sean than you, especially now that you're letting another man lick you."

"Oh, here you go," Lang said, throwing up her right hand. "I thought we had this discussion already."

"We started, but we didn't finish it," Aminah replied, pointing her finger at Lang. "If Sean were my husband, I'd damn sure appreciate him more than you do."

"Oh, so you really wanna get into this again?"

"Looking at Sean walk through Bed-Stuy with his long locs, loafers, and khakis during the week and his jeans and sneakers on the weekends, no one would ever know he had the foresight to invest in Viagra when it first hit the market or Apple when they launched the iPod or JetBlue when they entered the friendly skies," Aminah said.

"Yeah, and I love that about him," Lang said grinning proudly.

"Not always, Lang," Aminah said, reminding her that when Lang had first met him, though she'd loved the way his mind worked and got off on the fact that they both memorized the exact same lines from their mutually favorite movies and books, she was also slightly turned off that he could be a tad bit corny.

Lang nodded at the fond memory of that conversation some five years ago.

"You said you didn't think you could even *date* anyone with any amount of corniness in him, never mind marry him. Remember that?" Aminah asked.

Lang laughed. "Yeah, I sure do."

"No one knows Sean's net worth," Aminah said with obvious admiration. "He doesn't advertise or promote it, and I love that about him, but I think that bothers you sometimes."

"I can't front. It does a little bit," Lang admitted. "Not as much as it used to. I mean, I wouldn't want an Imon, that's for sure. Even Fame can be a little showy, but half a step down from Fame would be just right. I mean, does Sean have to walk around looking *so* regular, so nine-to-five?"

"So what, Lang?" Aminah asked, clearly agitated. "So Sean isn't a walking billboard for consumerism. He learned to make his money work for him at a real early age so he could afford to teach. That makes him hotter than some pussy-hound record exec in a Purple Label suit."

Lang raised her eyebrow, thinking about the last time she'd seen Usher in a RyanKenny button-up and matching cuff links. He looked amazing. She was so distracted by the thought of him, she was missing Aminah's point. Lang shook her head, made a left onto Fulton Street, and tuned back into Aminah.

"But you, you like for people to know you have money."

"Okay. *And.* So do you," Lang said defensively

"I like well-made goods, yes," Aminah clarified. "I like quality products. I can appreciate the craftsmanship of—"

"Bullshit, you're a label whore just like me," Lang said, pointing at Aminah.

They both laughed.

"Okay, but you also like drama," Aminah continued. "You thrive off it. You like tension and friction masked as excitement. That scares me about you, Lang."

"I know, I do like a little tension," Lang admitted, grinning devilishly.

"No, you like a lot of drama," Aminah corrected. "You think a relationship is boring without it. I think that's what that young boy Dante picked up on."

"You think?" Lang asked, surprised that Aminah had even

mentioned his name. "He said he picked up on my radiant sexual energy," she said, winding her hips on the leather car seat, imitating her favorite stripper move.

"Well, that, too."

They both laughed again. Lang made a left turn onto Lewis Avenue. She made a quick stop into Bread Stuy café for a small cup of decaf to go. The aromatic coffee scent and yummy pastry smells lured them directly through the front door. Fortunately, they weren't planning on staying, as all the seats were occupied, including the wooden bench out front and the sprinkling of chairs on the outdoor patio. Some of the patrons appeared to be waiting for a table at the restaurant next door.

Bread Stuy was the ideal place to wait, too. The spirited blend of classic soul, contemporary West African, good R and B, and classic jazz tunes playing in the background, combined with the flavorful conversations, transported you from a late summer afternoon in Stuyvesant Heights to this temporary utopia that magically expunged the mundane act of waiting.

Aminah spotted the divine-looking red-velvet cupcakes behind the glass encasement. She bought six of them for herself, Fame, their children, and her parents to enjoy after a late dinner in Sag Harbor. Lang placed the lid on her small cup of decaf and purchased the remaining two cupcakes for Sean. The sour-cream-frosted pastries were his favorite, and Bread Stuy didn't bake them every day. Sean would be ecstatic.

"Are you ever going to learn to appreciate what you do have, Lang?" Aminah asked as Lang held open the coffee-shop door for her. "I mean, did you have to respond to Dante? He's exceptionally good-looking. I'll give you that. I saw that from across the street. But as far as I'm concerned, the minute you gave him your number, you cheated on Sean."

"First of all, I didn't *give* my number to him," Lang said back inside her BMW. "He took my phone and called his own phone. Remember?"

"But you let him," Aminah said.

"Okay, yeah, I did, but I dunno . . ." Lang paused. "I thought it was cute and clever, and, besides, it turned me on."

"But the minute you let him in, you violated Sean."

"It wasn't that serious, Minah, damn."

"Okay, now you really sound like Fame. *'It was just head. It meant nothing.'* Are you fuckin' kidding me, Lang?"

"All right, all right, Aminah, calm down," Lang said, turning down her tree-lined block. "I thought we were having a nice afternoon. Damn."

"We were, but you know what? It was a mistake. Sunday brunching isn't going to change the fact that what you're doing is deceitful. And that's not a judgment. That's the truth. Cheating on your spouse is undisputedly wrong. And then you wanna know why I'd be a better wife to Sean than you? Between you and Fame, I don't know who's worse. It's all about you. Can't stand either one of you right now. Lemme outta this car. Fucking selfish. That's what you both are."

"Damn, Minah, you act like I don't love my own husband," Lang said, parallel parking three cars behind Aminah's Range Rover. "You know I do."

"I do, huh?" Aminah asked, unbuckling her seatbelt in haste. "Then act like it."

"And I'm ending this thing with Dante," Lang said, grabbing Aminah's arm before she got out of the car.

Aminah looked down at Lang's hand like it was contaminated. Lang released her grip immediately.

"Oh, yeah? Why don't I believe you?" Aminah asked before slamming the door and stomping up the block with her box of cupcakes in tow, speeding off inside her sparkling clean truck.

Chapter 11

"Would you say that Coretta Scott King lacked pride for staying with Dr. King?"

"I really didn't mean to offend you," Rebekkah apologized.

Aminah couldn't believe she was on the phone with this chick. It had been two months since they'd lunched, and already Aminah's autumn routine was in full swing. Every morning she awakened at five AM to alternate between jogging and power walking on her treadmill for forty minutes, followed by twenty minutes of squats and crunches. Usually, by the time she was done showering, Fame would walk through the door from a night in the studio and immediately cook breakfast while Aminah and the children dressed.

The Andersons almost always ate breakfast together. Once Fame got his family out the door, he'd hop in the shower, collapse on their Pratesi sheets, and sleep until it was time to pick up Alia.

Aminah took a sip of her lemon water and then cleared her throat. "Rebekkah, you've apologized enough. I accepted your apology over a month ago. I've got to pick up my son by three o'clock, so . . ."

"Oh, right," Rebekkah said, glancing at her watch. "Aminah, I really need to talk to someone who really understands what I'm about to get into. Everyone around me just sees, you know, the money, the prestige, the award shows. Me? I'm afraid of the post-show." She laughed nervously.

Aminah appreciated Rebekkah's honesty, though she doubted she could offer her any real advice. For reasons unclear to herself, she was willing to offer her some personal insight.

"Being married to a celebrity, whether he's Hollywood or your local friendly neighborhood ghetto celeb, has its challenges," Aminah explained.

Rebekkah let out a soft chuckle.

"No, really, I'm serious," Aminah continued. "Fame loves the accolades. He thrives on the attention. And, I mean, really, girl, you're about to marry someone who renamed himself Imon Alstar—please. You can't tell me you didn't have a clue."

"I hear you," Rebekkah said, nodding.

"So what's the problem then?"

"I don't like the feeling that I'm expected to have this special tolerance of infidelity," Rebekkah admitted.

"Listen, Rebekkah, as difficult as this may be for you to understand, I don't possess some special forbearance for cheating. For rumors, maybe I've developed a thick skin. I'll cop to that."

"Am I crazy for wanting my man to be faithful to me, Aminah?" Rebekkah asked, teetering on sounding hysterical.

"No, not at all," Aminah responded calmly. "This life's not for everybody. It looks very glamorous, and I'm not gonna lie to you, it is, but it comes at a cost."

"But why sell yourself short?" Rebekkah asked, at risk of offending Aminah once again. Rebekkah had to ask—this conversation would tell her whether she could marry Imon. "I don't get that."

"Not that I owe you any sort of explanation, but what is it that you're assuming I'm not getting back?" Aminah asked curiously.

"Loyalty," Rebekkah said bluntly.

Aminah took a deep breath. She was angrier with herself than she was with Rebekkah. She wanted to kick herself for being back in the exact same spot justifying her marriage to some lonely hearted woman who couldn't even properly strut in her Christian Louboutins, let alone walk a good mile in them.

"Fame is loyal to our family," Aminah said confidently. "Divorce is simply not an option for us. We're both committed to that. You know, you said you wanted to speak with me to weigh the pros and cons of marrying Imon, and somehow, once again, we've managed to get back to me and my husband. Listen, Rebekkah, let me make this painfully clear to you: my marital status is not questionable, and my marriage is not in jeopardy. You're the thirty-eight-year-old single mother with only one possible marriage carrot stick dangling in front of her."

Aminah's last little comment had just enough sting in it for Rebekkah to put her own situation in perspective. She'd been approaching this subject with Aminah completely wrong.

"I apologize, Aminah. I have absolutely no right to judge you and your situation."

"It is not a situation, Rebekkah," Aminah corrected. "It's a marriage."

"You're absolutely correct. I'm sorry. Please don't hang up, Aminah. Let me put all my cards on the table."

"Please do and make it quick," Aminah said, reaching for her keys. It was time to pick up Amir.

"I realize the likelihood that he'll cheat on me is really high, and yet I still want to marry this man. There is a lack of sanity in that decision, don't you think? It's like deliberately walking into on-coming traffic and hoping you'll not only survive but not end up a paraplegic," Rebekkah said, tearing.

"Rebekkah, I don't want to misrepresent this life to you. We've had—"

"Where's your pride, girl?" Rebekkah asked. She couldn't ac-cept this loyal-to-family crap Aminah was feeding her. "Your love for yourself?"

"Well, Sade once said love is stronger than pride," Aminah said, shaking her head, quietly admonishing herself. "And my love for myself is definitely strong. It just doesn't keep me warm enough in the midnight hour, on my birthday, on Christmas, or at my children's recitals. Let me ask you something, Rebekkah, would you say that Coretta Scott King lacked pride for staying with Dr. King? Does it make him any less of a great man because he cheated on his wife? He was human, an extraordinary human being, but we're all fallible."

"No, I wouldn't, but Fame is no Dr. King," Rebekkah refuted.

"That's not my point, but are you implying that only men of a certain caliber get a pass? How about Camille Cosby? Does it make her contributions to Spelman any less valuable because Bill had a child outside their marriage? What about Jacqueline Kennedy Onas-sis? I don't know about you, but when I see Camille, Coretta, Jackie O, Hillary even, I see beauty, grace, and poise, not stupidity. I see loyalty, not naïveté. Please don't mistake my kindness for weakness. All these so-called independent women who say they don't need a man, for some reason, seem to want mine," Aminah continued. "What is that about? I love my husband and my family—why am I being persecuted and crucified for doing whatever is necessary to keep my family together? I applaud you and all the other sisters out there for being able to raise your children without fathers in the homes. I'm sure you've had your struggles, but I never wanted that heavy cross or anything remotely resembling it."

For the first time since she'd lunched with Aminah, Rebekkah didn't feel an ounce of pity for her. Clearly, Minah was nobody's fool. Though Rebekkah had mistakenly assumed so, Aminah was nobody's trophy wife either. She was a poised sister determined to keep her family healthy and harmonious at a time when families were about as extinct as a Patrick Kelly original.

"I hear you, Aminah. I'm sorry, I—"

"Rebekkah, I'm not the one with the issues here," Aminah said, interrupting Rebekkah's fourth apology. "I know who I'm married to. *You* sought *me* out, remember?"

"Yeah, I did," Rebekkah admitted sheepishly. "You're right."

Aminah grabbed her Balenciaga bag before heading out her front door. It was almost time to pick up Amir from the School at Columbia University. Fame paid $24,000 a year for their son to attend the elite and progressive elementary school, and Aminah liked to get there early enough to make sure her presence was acknowledged. Plus, Fame wanted to make sure they were getting their money's worth and to reinforce to the school that Amir had proactive parents in his life. He did the same thing for Alia at the UN International School in Jamaica Estates.

"So what's it going to be for you and Imon?" Aminah asked before she hung up the phone. "I do or I don't?"

Rebekkah closed her eyes and sighed heavily. "I do."

Chapter 12

"I want you so bad it hurts. I ache to feel you inside me."

$\mathcal{L}$angston glanced at the glowing clock tower above Madison Square Park outside her office window. It read 10:05 PM, and she'd just put in a full twelve-hour day. While October was just a week away from ending in New York City, at *Urban Celebrity* it was already January, as they'd just finished closing the New Year's issue narrowly on schedule.

In spite of her exhaustingly long day of modifying heds, deks, and captions, clashing with the creative director over the cover, meeting with the publisher about new media kits, and fitting in her custom Brazilian Basic Bikini Combo, Lang was more lusty than tired.

Oddly enough, the intimate hair-removal procedure had been more ecstasy than agony for Lang. Right after she'd wiped herself with the sanitizing towelette, donned the paper thong, and spread her legs wider than her mouth when she said "ah" for her dentist, that small yet powerful muscle between her legs throbbed.

The sensation of the warm wax smoothed on the most intimate parts of her anatomy, followed by the immediate sting of her tiny pubic hairs being ripped from their individual follicles was the ultimate combination of pain and pleasure for Lang. She got off on it.

At the end of the day, after Lang and Merrick said good night to the art director, they made their way to the ladies' room to freshen up. Lang usually treated Merrick to dinner and drinks after a long, hard closing of the magazine, but tonight Lang was using her as arm candy, and since they were skipping their late night meal, she granted Merrick a three-day weekend instead.

Dante had invited Lang to a party at Duvet a couple nights ago, but she wasn't sure she could stand to be around him in a club full of cushy beds, which was why Merrick was her date tonight. It had officially been six months since Lang and Dante had met, and she couldn't believe she hadn't had the satisfaction of feeling all of him inside her yet. She refused to beg and was finally starting to realize that some things just weren't meant to be, and apparently sex with Dante was one of them.

Lang and Merrick strutted to the front of the line at the club. The publicist with the guest list air-kissed Lang on both cheeks, complimented her on her Bottega Veneta bag, and lifted the velvet rope. A burly security guard asked Lang if he could get a free subscription. Lang kissed him on the cheek and told him to give his information to Merrick.

Lang easily maneuvered her way through the packed club to their reserved bed. She kicked off her pumps and swung both of her long legs onto the comfy pillow-covered, white-sheeted bed, careful not to expose her raisin-colored Brazilian panties. She surveyed the room, nodding her head to Doug E. Fresh's classic "All the Way to Heaven."

Lang wanted to be in the ideal position to spot Dante first. Standing exceptionally fine at six-five, he was impossible to miss. She waved Merrick over, and no more than three minutes later two delicate flutes and an ice bucket of Veuve Clicquot were placed in front of them.

"Nice," Merrick said, reaching for her glass. "Who sent this over?"

"He asked to remain anonymous," the leggy blond waitress replied. "Handsome though and an excellent tipper."

"Looks like somebody has an admirer," Merrick said, nudging her boss. "And he knows your favorite champagne, too. Damn, can a single sister get some love?"

"Aw, Merrick," Lang said, giving her a one-hand shoulder hug. She adored Merrick. She especially loved that the twenty-three-year-old trilingual born in Korea and raised in Manhattan referred to herself as a sister. Merrick was as doting as she was driven. She anticipated practically all of Lang's needs both personally and professionally and didn't complain about the strenuous workload or the late hours.

Unbeknownst to Merrick, Lang was grooming her for the executive editor position. Her intention was to promote Merrick to associate editor before the year was out, advance her to senior editor shortly thereafter, and, once she'd proven herself (which she would), the executive editor position was all hers.

"Hey, there's Dante Lawrence," Merrick pointed out to Lang.

Lang gagged on her second glass of Veuve. "Who?" she asked, trying her damnedest not to sound as shocked as she felt.

"Remember? I told you about him," Merrick reminded Lang. "*Black Enterprise* and *The Sun* did a story on him. His parents come from, like, old New England money, and he developed this urban-warfare-game software while still in high school, interned for Electronic Arts during college, and graduated from Stanford with this ridiculous multi-million-dollar developer's deal or something like that."

"Right, right," Lang said, recalling the conversation but not remembering Merrick ever mentioning the young game developer's name. She'd quietly convinced herself that Dante was a basketball player sitting out the season, but more honestly she'd believed he was something a little less legitimate and therefore had no desire whatsoever to know how he got his money. "He looks like a drug dealer."

Merrick laughed. "Oh, Lang, drug dealers are so eighties. Brothers are making big money legitimately nowadays. I sure wouldn't mind being hooked up with him, that's for sure."

"Really?" Lang asked with a devious glint in her eye. "I'll go introduce myself. Then I'll send him over to you, and you can take it from there."

Lang sauntered right up to Dante at the frosty glacieresque bar.

He smiled and leaned his mouth close to her ear. "You coming home with me tonight?" he asked seductively.

Lang took a step back. "Actually, I came over here first to thank you for the bottle, and also because my assistant is attracted to you," she said, pointing over to Merrick.

Merrick lifted her glass and tossed back her long, shiny black hair.

"She's pretty," Dante acknowledged. "But I got my eye on someone else." He scanned Lang from head to toe.

"Really now? Have you had your eye on this someone for a while?"

"I have."

"So you just window shopping or you gonna purchase the merchandise?"

"I wasn't aware the merchandise was available for purchase," he said, raising one eyebrow. "I was told it'd been bought already."

"Yet you still have your eye on it?"

"Not the wisest thing, I know, but I just can't seem to take my eyes off it."

It took all of Lang's self-restraint not to reach out and touch Dante. However, he didn't have a problem rubbing his hand up and down her arm. Lang knew Merrick was watching them, so she asked Dante to join them on their bed. He declined and turned toward his right instead.

"Langston Rogers, this is my boy, Vince Campbell," Dante said, introducing her to the tall honey-brown Allen Iverson–Carmelo Anthony combo standing next to him. "I'm sure he'd love to meet Merrick."

Lang escorted Vince over to Merrick, who smiled immediately. Once they were engaged in a flirtatious banter that excluded her, Lang made her way back over to Dante.

"How come you never told me you were, like, a software developer?"

"How come you never asked?" he replied, taking a small sip of the now very diluted Hennessy he'd been nursing all night.

"I didn't think I wanted to know."

"But I bet you made your own assumptions."

Lang glanced down at the floor sheepishly before shrugging her shoulders.

"Uh-huh, you thought I was a street pharmacist or something."

She nodded her head.

"I think I should be offended," he said, placing his snifter back on the bar. "A black man can't drive an Escalade and own a loft without—"

"I apologize," Lang said, cutting off his sociopolitical monologue before he got his LV loafers scuffed stepping up on his soapbox. She hadn't meant any harm. "I guess the real truth is I just didn't want to get to know you like that."

"Yet you wanna have sex with me like that?"

Lang nodded.

"You never answered my other question," Dante reminded Lang.

"What question was that?" Lang asked, playing dumb.

"Are you leaving here with me?"

"I don't like having my clit teased. It's been six months—"

"I know how long it's been, Lang," Dante interrupted. "You still think you're too proud to beg?"

"What-the-fuck-ever, Dante. My initials aren't TLC," Lang said, walking away.

Dante quickly grabbed her hand and pulled her back. "Come home with me."

"Why should I, Dante, huh? What's in it for me?"

"I'll bet you a case of Cris that you'll be begging before the night's over."

"You know it's gotta be Veuve for me to even consider it worth my time," Lang said, smiling mischievously.

"Veuve for you, Cris for me."

"Bet."

Thirty-five minutes later Merrick called for two cars—one for her, the other for Lang. Dante stayed behind at the bar with Vince.

"See you on Tuesday," Merrick said outside the club, reminding Lang of her three-day weekend.

"Enjoy it," Lang said, hugging her assistant before climbing into the back of the Lincoln Navigator.

"Change of plans," Lang told the driver. "I'm going to DUMBO, not the Stuy."

Twenty minutes later Lang listened to her messages as she waited for Dante in the back of the parked Navigator in front of his loft. She'd missed two calls from Sean.

Sean was used to his wife working late at the magazine, particularly during production, so he had no reason to be suspicious. He also knew she usually took Merrick out after closing an issue, so he knew not to expect her home any time soon.

Hey, baby, I know you're working late and beating yourself up about nailing all the style forecasts and celebrity coupling predictions for the New Year. Um, let me see if I get this right. He laughed. *Beyoncé and Jay will stay together but definitely won't be getting married this year. Wedges are in, and so is the color turquoise. Did I get that right?*

He's such a good listener, Lang thought as she grew tired of waiting for Dante. It'd been twenty-five minutes already.

Sean laughed again.

Anyway, I have a nice surprise for you when you get home. So promise me you'll call me when you're on your way home. Okay, baby? I love you. See you soon.

"What am I doing?" Lang asked out loud as she dialed Dante. "I've got a good man at home, and I'm chasing behind this boy."

His phone went straight to voice mail.

"Listen, Dante. This thing we've been doin' has been, um, fun,

I guess. But I've got too much at stake to risk it all for some half-ass thrills. Once again you've got me waiting for you. And for what? A kiss here. A touch there. Please. I get way more than that, better than that, at home. So I'm out. For good."

Lang tapped the headrest of the driver's seat. "Please take me to Stuyvesant Avenue and . . ."

The piercing xenon headlights from Dante's Escalade interrupted her instructions.

The driver turned on his ignition.

"On second thought . . ."

Dante tapped on the window. Lang rolled it down halfway.

"Listen, I just left you a—"

"Get out the car," Dante instructed.

"No, D, if you would—"

"I'm not gonna repeat myself," Dante said, opening the door. "I'm finally gonna give you what you want. Now we can do it right here, or you can bring your sexy ass upstairs."

An hour and a half later a completely different driver in a black Suburban waited for Langston to wave from the stoop of her brownstone. He nodded his head and pulled off.

Lang unlocked and turned the knob to the front door and then the inside hallway door. She tried to shake from her mind what had just ended less than thirty minutes ago, but it wasn't dissipating that easily. She stood in front of her glazed mahogany staircase, knowing Sean was anxiously awaiting her. He'd told her so when she'd called to let him know she was finally on her way home.

The musky, erotic scent of sandalwood met her at the foot of the steps and escorted her to the top of the staircase where the

renowned Toots Thielemans's legendary harmonica lured her out-
side the door of her bathroom. It sounded to Lang like Toots's
"Obi" had just finished, and now his sexy "Felicia and Bianca"
was just beginning. Next was "O Cantador." "Bluesette" was still
Lang's all-time favorite. She'd have to wait until the very end of
The Brasil Project to hear it though.

She stood.

On the other side of the door, a steamy, hot bubble bath anticipated her arrival. An eager Sean, donned in loose-fitting boxers,
awaited her, too. Carol's Daughter's A Jasmine Evening bath salts
filled the porcelain antique tub. Small white votives lined the floor,
accompanied by sandalwood-scented candles surrounding the
tub. An uncorked, chilled bottle of Veuve sat nearby in a silver
bucket.

She opened the door carefully.

"Happy New Year, baby," Sean said, handing his wife a flute
and then tongue kissing her softly.

Champagne. Damn. She owed Dante a case of Cristal.

Sean lifted off his wife's cashmere sweater and unhooked her
bra. He kissed her gently on her forehead, her cheek, and then lin-
gered at the crook in her neck. He nuzzled her there.

"Please, Dante, please."
"Please what, baby?"

Langston shook her head and moaned for Sean's pleasure, not
her own. She was too numb with memories of Dante to feel present.

Sean traced his warm tongue along his wife's delicate collarbone, softly kissed on her chest, and gently sucked on her right nipple—the more responsive one—and then her left.

"Please take me."
"Take you where? I'm not understanding you, Lang. If there's somewhere you want me to take you, you need to be real specific."

Sean slowly slid his tongue down his wife's taut stomach. He kissed around her belly button as he easily unzipped her skirt and slid off her panties and each of her sheer thigh-highs. He tongued her belly button as he squeezed her ass.

"Please fuck me, Dante."
"Say that again."
"Please fuck me, Dante."

Sean burrowed his nose between his wife's legs, rubbing the hood of her clitoris with the tip of his nose. The strong scent of her sex excited him.

Lang moaned, this time for herself.

Sean slid one finger inside his wife. She was sticky and wet. She instinctively squeezed her muscles, gripping his finger. He slid in another one.

"You sure that's what you want?"
"Yes, I'm sure, Dante."
"Get down on your knees and beg me again."
Lang did as she was told. "Please, Dante, I want you to fuck me. I need you to. Please." *Tears streamed down her face, which was*

pressed against his knees. "I want you so bad it hurts. I ache to feel you inside me."

"Um, Sean," Lang said, choking back tears and bending down slightly to hold his face in her hands. "All this is so sweet. I'm— I'm moved."

"Hey, baby," Sean said, standing up. "Why the tears?"

"I—I—I," she stuttered.

He rested her head on his chest. "Shhhh, you're just tired. Let me bathe you."

Lang stepped into the steamy tub. She stood there for a few seconds, acquainting her lukewarm body with the sweltering temperature before sitting down in jasmine-vanilla-infused water.

Sean lathered the seaweed sponge with Carol's Daughter's hypnotically sweet Almond Dream body cleansing gel and massaged her neck. He took his time gently washing his wife's arms, underarms, her breasts and underneath her breasts, her stomach, and her back. He methodically rubbed and rinsed and rubbed and rinsed.

Lang closed her eyes and moaned. She was perspiring.

"You okay, baby?"

"I'm more than okay. The bath is perfect."

"Should I add some cool water?"

"No, my muscles are a little sore. I need this hot soak. Thank you, baby."

Sean handed his wife a glass of champagne to quench her thirst. Lang sipped slowly. She'd already drunk more than her share of bubbly.

Sean generously soaped the seaweed sponge and gently washed between his wife's legs. Lang closed her eyes.

"Unzip my pants," Dante commanded, looking down at Lang on her knees.

Lang let Dante's pants drop down to his ankles as she moved her mouth toward his crotch.

"I've sampled enough of that already," he said, pushing her face away. "That's not what I want."

He pulled Lang up by her arm and walked her over to his stark-white leather sofa. "Take off your panties and lift up your skirt."

Dante leaned a bare-bottomed Lang over the back of his couch. Dante left Lang exposed as he walked over to get the Magnums from his walnut coffee-table drawer.

Dante stood behind Lang fully erect.

Sean scrubbed down the fronts and backs of his wife's thighs, her calves, and the bottoms of her feet. He carefully washed between each of her toes before helping her stand up.

"This is what you wanted, right?" Dante asked, fiercely ramming himself inside Lang.

"Yes!" Lang screamed.

"You begged for it, didn't you?" he asked, grabbing a handful of her hair.

"Yes!" she screamed again.

"You like it rough, don't you?" he asked, speeding up his rhythm.

"I love it rough," she growled.

Dante smacked Lang's ass.

"Harder!" she yelled.

He smacked her ass so hard his palms stung.

"Hurt me," she pleaded.

Sean filled and refilled a ceramic pitcher with soothing warm water, carefully rinsing off his wife's glistening body.

"You're so gentle with me," Lang said to Sean appreciatively.

"You're my queen," Sean said, tenderly toweling his wife dry. "I wouldn't know how else to treat you."

Chapter 13

"Can't wait to be tasted—see you in a minute."

Thanksgiving was only two weeks away. Fame's goal was not to have any musical projects lingering after December fifteenth so his family and the holiday season would have his undivided attention. Whatever jobs weren't completed by then would just get shelved until the third week of January. Fame always devoted the first two weeks of the year entirely to his family, no exceptions. He believed it brought him good fortune for the year to come.

The S.O.S. Band's "Just Be Good to Me" blared in the *C* room of Fame's recording studio. It was just a little after midnight when Fame pushed the up-and-coming R&B singer's head down in his lap as he slouched down on the black leather couch with his eyes closed. Fame fingered her weave tracks as he thought about sampling the hook and maybe even chopping up other parts of the song.

Friends tell me I am crazy and am wasting time with you . . .

"Faaaame," she whined, lifting up her head and finger combing her hair back into place. "I came over here to sing, not to suck."

"Look, Daisha, I can't work until I release some of this stress," he explained, opening his eyes. "We don't have all night. Come on, now."

I don't care about your other girls. Just be good to me . . .

Daisha was highly infatuated with Fame. He looked good, smelled good, stacked paper, and had the prettiest, brownest penis she'd ever licked. Her secret fantasy wasn't sexual though. It was matrimonial. She envisioned Fame running straight into her welcoming embrace after he divorced his dull and boring wife. In the meantime she was more than willing to settle for being his other woman, his official mistress, something more than just one of his jump-offs. She moved her lips toward his.

"Yo, what's the matter with you?" Fame asked incredulously, wiping his mouth with his hand even though Daisha's lips had only grazed his right cheek. "You know better than that."

Daisha was so quick to give him head their very first night in the studio, he didn't want her lips anywhere near his. There was no telling where her mouth had been or on whom else they'd been.

"What?" Daisha questioned. "My lips are good enough for your dick but not your lips?"

"Not this shit again," Fame said, clearly annoyed and sitting up straight. "Damn, man, can't a brother just get some head without all the chitchat?"

Daisha didn't want to push her luck. Her entire recording career was riding on Fame. She couldn't believe Aaron "Famous" Anderson was working with her in the first place. She didn't even have a record deal, yet he'd agreed to work with her. Her manager would kill her if she blew this opportunity. She moved her head back down toward his lap, but this time Fame snatched it right back up.

"Forget it," he said, standing up, buckling his pants, and walking over to his desk.

"I'm sorry, Fame," she whined, patting the leather couch, gesturing for him to sit back down.

Fame glanced back at her and then over at the phone on his glass desk. He pushed the speaker button and hit one of the speed-dial buttons. A female with a nasally voice answered the phone on the first ring.

"Where you at?" he asked gruffly.

"Up in Santos with my girls," she said, clearly happy to hear from Fame. "Q-Tip is spinnin'. You should come through."

"Nah, I can't, sweetheart," he said, looking over at Daisha, who was pouting on the couch. "I'm workin'. I could use a favor though."

"Oh, really, what kind of a favor?" she asked flirtatiously.

"The mind-blowing kind. How soon can you be here?"

"How soon can you send a car for me?"

"Ten minutes."

"Can I hang with you in the studio, please?" she asked, pleading more than requesting.

"Nah, not tonight, sweetheart. I got too much work to do. Maybe tomorrow night, though," he said, sounding more non-committal than convincing.

"Okay," she said, obviously disappointed. "Well, you gotta

make it quick then. Can you ask the car to wait and make it a round-trip?"

"Not a problem."

"Can't wait to taste you, Fame."

"Can't wait to be tasted. See you in a minute."

During that whole conversation, Daisha never took her eyes off Fame. She couldn't believe he was brazen enough to call the next chick in front of her, and on speakerphone, no less.

"I'm out," she said, standing up and grabbing her knockoff Fendi purse.

"Leave and don't come back," he replied, sliding into the chair behind his desk.

"You can't be serious, Fame;" Daisha asked in disbelief. "You expect me to just sit here while you get head from some other ho? I don't think so."

"Suit yourself," he said, swiveling in his leather chair. "I can't work till I get this nut out. I asked you to take care of me, but you didn't want to, and that's cool 'cause there's nothin' worse than some half-ass head. Shit, that's worse than no head at all."

Daisha was livid. First of all, Fame hadn't *asked* her anything. Secondly, she was more than upset to know that he had this chick on speed dial. She could deal with him having a wife. She reasoned that because they were high school sweethearts, he couldn't walk away from that situation so easily. Daisha now wondered exactly how many other girls on the side there were.

In Fame's mind he didn't have any girls on the side. He didn't take care of any other woman besides his wife and didn't care to invest any time or attention in another woman. What he did have, however, was a couple of Xanaxes. No-hassle stress relievers he could call on in a moment's notice to alleviate his tension.

"I was supposed to work on your stuff tonight, Day, but it's not like I don't have other shit to do," Fame said, typing on his Mac PowerBook. "If you leave now, don't bother ever to come back. It's that simple."

Daisha loved when Famed called her Day. She took it as a pet name, a term of endearment, but really Fame was just being lazy with his tongue, preferring to address her by one syllable instead of two. Daisha sat back down, rolled her eyes, and pouted.

When the other girl strutted in wearing a sequined micro mini dress with a plunging neckline down to her belly button and a faux mink shrug, Fame was still working at his desk. The leggy girl glanced over at Daisha and smirked.

"You want me to do it here?" she purred.

Fame nodded. The other girl unbuckled his jeans and got down on her knees. Fame rested his head on the back of the chair and closed his eyes. Six minutes into her oral exercises, Aminah called.

"Hey, baby," Fame said calmly.

The girl on her knees sucked even harder as Fame maintained his composure, put his index finger to his lips, silencing her, and then placed his hand on top of her head to steady her rhythm.

"You okay?" he asked, concerned.

"Yeah," Aminah said, still sounding groggy. "Can't go back to sleep. You busy?"

"Never too busy for you, baby, you know that."

"You coming home any time soon?" Aminah asked sleepily.

"Lemme just wrap this up," Fame said, gripping the back of the girl's head. "And I'll be there as soon as I can."

"Okay, love you, Fame."

"Love you, too, baby girl."

Fame hung up the phone, and three minutes later the girl on her knees swallowed. Fame grabbed some baby wipes from the bottom file cabinet behind his glass desk, cleaned himself off, and buckled up his pants. He handed his "Xanax" cash to pay the driver.

"Get a bottle of something nice to thank your girls for letting me steal you away," he said, adding three one-hundred dollar bills to her hand.

"Nah, I think I might get me a nice bag or sumthin'," she said stashing the C-notes into her sequined wristlet.

"Really?" Fame asked, surprised. He couldn't recall paying less than one thousand dollars for any of Aminah's bags and was genuinely astonished and shrugged his shoulders.

She hugged him. He hugged her back. Her stilettos clicked out the door, down the elevator, and back into the waiting car.

"All right, shorty, I'm out. Session's canceled," Fame said to Daisha.

"Just like that, Fame?" Daisha asked. "I refuse to suck your dick. I watch you get blown by some stank-club ho on-call, and you're out like that?"

"Yup," he said, shutting down his laptop. "Wifey calls, I gotta answer. You know the deal."

Daisha was pissed. She couldn't wait to get to her day job as an administrative assistant the next morning. She was going to fax Cindy Hunter another blind item.

* * *

What superproducer got brain surgery in his studio last night right before going home early to rock his wife back to sleep? He's so slick he keeps a car waiting to take his jump-off back to the club and then pays in cash so there won't be a paper trail for anyone to follow. Wifey should finally wake up and follow the yellow brick road to divorce court.

Chapter 14

"Baby girl, I came home to take care of you."

Fame made it home to Aminah in almost twenty minutes. He headed straight upstairs to their bedroom. Aminah had dozed back off to sleep. He kissed her neck softly. She rolled over.

"Hey, baby," she said sleepily with her eyes still closed.

Fame kissed her face, her cheeks, the top of her forehead, the bottom of her chin, and then very tenderly on her lips, cupping her face in both of his hands.

"What's the matter?" he asked her gently.

"Just a dream," she said, still groggy. "Just a bad dream."

"Let Daddy make it all better," he said, lifting up her magenta lace-trimmed Fernando Sánchez chemise. Aminah always dressed for bed.

She moaned as her eyes remained shut.

"Baby girl, I came home to take care of you," he said before placing his warm mouth over her ample breast. Aminah had more than a mouthful, so Fame took his time giving proper attention to each one.

She moaned again, still not awakening fully.

He slowly slid his index and middle finger inside her as he lightly circled his tongue around her clitoris, beckoning it to come out and dance with his tongue.

Trying to fake an orgasm with Fame was pointless. He was patient and knew exactly what one felt like. He kept his fingers inside Aminah until he felt her muscles rhythmically contract around his fingers.

Fame was merciless. Up and down, up and down and then around and around with his tongue, all while his two fingers moved in circular motion inside his wife. Not too hard. Not too light. Just the right pressure with a steady, consistent rhythm. Aminah instinctively moved her hips in time with his fingers.

"Mmmm," Aminah moaned.

"Come for Daddy, baby girl."

A millisecond later, Aminah's thighs and her bottom lip quivered.

"You all better?" Fame asked as he kissed his wife gently on her mouth.

Aminah nodded and dozed back off into a deep, restful sleep.

Fame stripped down to his boxers and rested his head between his wife's legs, allowing her tranquilizing scent to lull him to sleep.

Chapter 15

*"I firmly believe that what you put in a relationship,
just like life, is what you get back."*

The next morning as Aminah slowly crept down the congested West Side Highway in her Range Rover, she took a small sip of water from the Fiji bottle that was in her cup holder. She swallowed with relief that it was Friday the twelfth and not the dreaded thirteenth. Though she did not consider herself the least bit superstitious, she also didn't believe in coincidence, and Friday the thirteenth rarely failed to be an unlucky day for Aminah. In fact, just this past August thirteenth she'd caught a flat tire rushing to drop off Alia and Amir at Sean and Lang's the night before their early morning flight to Hilton Head, South Carolina. As she pulled into a parking garage, she silently thanked God and the ancestors that there wouldn't be another one until next May.

Behind New York City's staggeringly tall buildings, the light gray morning sky grew darker and with each minute seemingly more determined to release a chilly November rain on the pavement below. Aminah found dreary days like this one fashionably challenging. She despised lugging around an umbrella. There simply was not enough room in the city for everyone to have their umbrellas opened simultaneously. The one hidden fashion blessing

Aminah counted during times of precipitation was the opportunity to adorn her feet in either her purple corset Marc Jacobs rain boots or her pink Polo ones (their purchase benefited Ralph Lauren's Pink Pony Fund to fight breast cancer). Her pink Polo rubbers did the puddle dance that day.

Aminah arrived ten minutes early for her appointment at Daily Blossom to finalize her floral delivery for Thanksgiving. Each holiday they alternated homes between the Anderson and Philips families. Last year it was at Aminah's aunt's home in Maryland. This year Fame insisted the Anderson clan come over to their "estate" in Jamaica Estates, Queens.

Aminah could have easily luxuriated in the chic floral studio all day long if she didn't have to meet the Benin-born, Cali-based jeweler Chris "The Iceman" Aire for lunch. She left Daily Blossom pleased with her autumn-inspired floral color scheme. Her home would be inundated with hues of peach, coral, orange, burnt orange, pumpkin (both the color and the fruit), and deep, velvety reds for just the right contrast, come the eve of Thanksgiving.

Some thirty or so minutes after Aminah reluctantly tore herself from the fragrant flower spot, she slid into the cushy, sand-colored booth at the back of MoBay. Seated across from her was the jeweler-to-the-stars, Chris Aire. Just seconds prior, the handsome, dark-skinned gentleman had greeted Aminah by kissing her lightly on both cheeks.

The soothing earth tones on the walls and natural wood trim throughout the polished restaurant served as a nice backdrop for her meeting with Chris. Before he made his presentation, they both ordered the spicy jerk chicken salad and, upon Aminah's insistence, MoBay's famously potent Rummy Rum Cake for dessert.

The Andersons had been great customers of Chris's since he'd first opened his custom jewelry company 2Awesome International back in '96. Chris appreciated their loyalty so much so he'd personally greeted and seated them at his spring show just two months ago during New York's Fashion Week.

While Chris could easily have insured and shipped Fame's $95,000 red gold watch smothered in diamonds, he'd almost always rewarded the Andersons, especially Aminah Anderson, with personal delivery service and a substantial discount. Chris smiled confidently as he handed Aminah the exquisite Aire Traveler chronograph. Aminah beamed in awe. Fame would absolutely love it.

Slightly buzzed from the Rummy Rum Cake, Aminah hugged Chris and wished him safe travels. Amir would be getting out of school in exactly thirty minutes.

As Aminah maneuvered her way across 125th Street, she aimlessly pushed the radio control button on her steering wheel. Damn, she thought, way too much money begging on Jazz88, and Aminah'd just donated $1,000 during their last listeners' drive a couple months ago. Switch. Destiny's Child lost their breath for the tenth time that day on Hot 97. Switch. Michael Baisden told black women they needed to take better care of their bodies if they wanted to attract better-quality men on KISS FM. Switch. A commercial on Power 105. Pause. WBLS was the next preset radio station.

Aminah had promised Fame she wouldn't listen during Cindy's time slot, but try as she might she simply couldn't resist. Aminah secretly found her radio show hilarious as long as she wasn't putting her husband on blast. Switch . . .

* * *

Two blocks down from Amir's school, Aminah sat numb for exactly seven minutes before flipping down the driver's-side visor mirror. The reflection of pretty brown eyes strewn with wavy red lines surrounded by smeared black eyeliner startled her. She felt ugly.

Crazy that just some ten hours ago, waking up to Fame's arm wrapped around her thigh with his head resting comfortably between her legs had started Aminah's day off so wonderfully. She'd felt adored. *How quickly things change with the push of a button,* Aminah thought, momentarily captivated by her pathetic reflection.

She reached for the eyedrops and the Pond's facial cloths inside her oversize Marc Jacobs Venetia bag and the tissue box she kept in her glove compartment. She refused to greet Amir with a tear-stained face. He deserved better, and with a couple squeezes of Visine, a few dabs of the Kleenex, some wipes of the cloth, a fresh stroke of eyeliner and mascara behind a pair of Fendi frames—oh, and three deep, cleansing breaths—he got it.

Aminah tuned in and out of her conversation with Amir on their forty-minute congested drive back home to Queens. Friday-afternoon traffic swelled typically and predictably like the transition stage of labor. Exiting off the jam-packed parkway brought the same indescribable relief as finally delivering your first child.

Aminah managed to laugh at Amir's recount of something "mad funny" that had happened in phys ed last period. Exactly what that was, Aminah wasn't sure, but she knew her son's sense of humor well enough to pacify him with just the right chuckle that led to a giggle and then a full-out guffaw. The crescendo of his mother's laughter tickled Amir.

"Hey, Amir, what do you think about spending the night at Grandma Glo's tonight?" she asked, pushing the button above her rearview mirror, opening the tall, wrought-iron, automated, monogrammed driveway gates.

Amir loved the idea. Friday nights at his paternal grandmother's home meant fried fish and coleslaw and cool old ladies cursing and laughing and singing off-key to the sounds of Earth, Wind & Fire, Al Green, and the Stylistics. Grandma Glo might even let him and Alia play out one of her hands in spades.

"Sounds good to me, Mom," Amir said nonchalantly, not wanting to sound too excited and tip off his mom to all the fun he was about to have.

Aminah drove home to pack the children's overnight bags before taking them to their grandmother. She told Gloria she was going out with Lang. Glo didn't require an explanation though. She loved having her grandbabies around, didn't matter that it was "girls night in." She might even let the children take a little swig of her beer after her daughter-in-law was well on her way.

After spending all week in them uptight, fancy private schools, Gloria thought they could benefit from some pure, uneducated fun. Plus, it was the only time her grandbabies got to drink Kool-Aid and soda, as Aminah and Fame kept only one hundred percent fruit juice and triple-filtered water stocked inside their stainless-steel forty-eight-inch side-by-side Viking fridge for them.

Aminah kissed her children and hugged her mother-in-law before climbing back into her Range. She immediately pulled off from Glo's only to pull over just a quarter of a mile down. She sat.

Aminah wasn't sure what she was doing or where she was going. She needed some unconditional loving sans a lecture, which ruled out her own mother for now. She got lost in the mere thought of where to go for almost an hour. It was just about nine o'clock when Aminah rang the doorbell of Lang and Sean's brownstone.

"Hey, gorgeous," Sean greeted Aminah quickly, kissing her cheek and rushing back downstairs. The Sixers were playing the Pacers, and Sean didn't want to miss a minute of the game. "Your girl's not home yet, but I'm expecting her in the next hour or so."

Aminah followed Sean downstairs to his entertainment room, Sean's favorite space in their brownstone. He had complete autonomy over his territory. Lang wasn't even allowed to straighten up downstairs, and Sean maintained it to his liking—clean and comfortable, not sanitized and orderly to the point of trepidation and intimidation. This time of year, Sean ideally started his weekends off with his remote control in hand and NBA League Pass on-screen, giving him a smorgasbord of basketball entertainment viewing options via cable television.

"Help yourself to some water," Sean said, plopping down on his cognac leather sectional in front of his sixty-one-inch plasma. Even with her hook-up, Sean had thought Lang was crazy for spending so much money on the flat screen monitor but had quickly ended his protest the second he'd powered it on.

"I know you like Fiji, but we've got some smartwater down there," he said with eyes fixed on the game.

"Actually, I'm feeling more like a glass of wine," Aminah replied, scanning the well-stocked wine rack behind the bar as well as the freestanding Miele wine cellar unit next to it.

"Gorgeous is turning down water for wine," Sean said, getting up from the couch during a commercial-break time-out. "Uh-oh, tell me all about it." He pulled one bottle from the rack and another from the cellar unit. "Red or white?"

"Red," Aminah replied, taking a seat on the leather and chrome bar stool. Aminah and Sean had been mutually and openly "in like" with each other since they'd met at the same barbecue at which Sean had first encountered Lang some six years ago.

Sean had fallen in like with Aminah from the moment he'd seen her patiently and successfully rocking an overtired two-year-old Amir to sleep while absorbedly listening to a bubbly four-year-old Alia read out loud from a Camille Yarbrough children's book. Sean had felt a tinge of jealousy when the five-carat emerald-cut diamond ring on her left ring finger had nearly blinded him that day. In spite of the fact that Langston had already captured his eyes and mind earlier that day, the maternal vision of Aminah tugged at his heart a bit. Still did.

"I'll take a pinot noir if you have one," Aminah grunted, trying to force off her left rain boot by pushing on its heel with the toe of her right.

"You know, I'll help you get your boots off, Aminah," Sean said, pulling out a California red. "So stop struggling over there before you hurt yourself."

Aminah giggled and stopped battling with her boots. Sean showed her a bottle of Vision Cellars 2002 Chileno Valley Marin County from the African American winery, and Aminah nodded enthusiastically in approval as Sean poured her a glass.

"So, what brings you around these parts on a Friday night, and who's minding my godchildren?" Sean asked, sliding Aminah's boots off effortlessly and then rushing over to the couch. The game was back on.

Aminah took a couple sips and then a big gulp of her pinot noir, barely tasting the delicious fusion of berries and cherries before answering. It was strong, just like she needed; still, Aminah thought she detected hints of something else, rose petals maybe.

"They're out in Hempstead with their grandmother," Aminah said, bringing the bottle and her empty goblet over to the tempered glass coffee table in front of the couch.

"Damn. You're thirsty, huh?" Sean asked with equal parts jest and concern, slightly distracted from his game. "Hey, aren't you driving?"

"Just because I drove here doesn't mean I'm driving home," Aminah replied defensively. "I can always call a cab or a car or, or—"

"Hold up," Sean said, interrupting Aminah. "Now I know something's wrong." Sean muted the surround sound, immediately snatching him out of his "floor seats" atmosphere. He rubbed the side of Aminah's cheek with the back of his hand. "What's wrong, gorgeous?"

Aminah held Sean's hand against her face for a minute. She bit her bottom lip. "I'm just tired, Sean," Aminah finally said as a single tear ran down her cheek.

"You wanna talk about it?" Sean asked, gently brushing the tear away with his thumb.

Aminah shrugged her shoulders.

"What's got you so tired, Aminah?" Sean asked, concerned.

Aminah said nothing as she continued to hold Sean's hand against her face.

"Is it the children?"

Aminah shook her head.

"Is it Fame?"

Aminah didn't respond right away. Fame was more than draining her energy. He was chipping away at her self-esteem, leaving only bits and pieces of her pride intact. Years of wear and tear with only Band-Aid repair left Aminah with a gaping bloody hole in her heart that required trauma surgery at this point. All the years of stuffing bandages just to stop the flow without actually tending to the wound itself left her feeling rather septic.

"I don't wanna talk about it right now, Sean," Aminah finally said, letting go of his hand and resting her head on the armrest of his sofa.

Sean knew better than to push Aminah when it came to Fame. He figured she'd eventually get over whatever he'd done this time, like she always did. The many times Sean questioned Aminah's "proactive surrender," she usually hit him with, "It takes a strong woman to stay and a weak one to leave" or "My marriage is good and worth fighting for" or simply "I love my husband."

"You wanna watch the game then?" Sean asked, flashing his brilliant smile and unmuting the TV. "It's a good one. Philadelphia and Indiana are playing."

Aminah laughed hysterically. She needed that. Sean was truly a basketball fiend. "Only if you pour me another glass."

"All right, but promise me you'll let me or Lang drive you home."

"What if I'm not going home?" Aminah asked with the seriousness of a Barney's warehouse sale.

"Okay, then one of us will drive you out to Hempstead to pick up the kids," Sean said, pouring her a second glass of wine.

Aminah nodded her head in agreement. "What about to the studio? Would you drive me there?"

Sean didn't answer right away. He knew Fame's disdain for

unannounced visitors, particularly his wife. Yet he didn't agree with Fame's stance or Aminah's tolerance of it. Lang had warned him very early on in their relationship not to get caught in the intricate design of Fame and Aminah's marriage. As difficult as it was for Sean to heed Lang's advice, he'd finally learned to abide by it after futile discussions with both of them. Both Aminah and Fame had told him individually and collectively how seriously they took their wedding vows.

He appreciated their honoring of "till death do us part" but deplored their illusion of "forsaking all others."

"Is he expecting you?" Sean asked apprehensively.

He was not in the mood to get caught up in any part of the Anderson family drama, not tonight with such a good game on. Not to mention, Sean and Fame got along like first cousins who acted like brothers 'cause they were raised by the same grandmama.

They shared a mutual love for family and basketball. Sean and Fame not only went to the Garden together regularly to watch the Knicks play but drove out to see the Nets and Sixers whenever they could. It was their schedule conflicts, not their personality differences, that prevented them from hanging out more.

Aminah never answered Sean. She eventually poured herself a third glass of wine instead.

The Sixers beat the Pacers that night by two points. Aminah fell asleep using Sean's lap as her pillow. He was stroking Aminah's head with one hand and flipping channels with the other when Lang arrived home.

The sight of Aminah's head in her husband's lap didn't bother Lang as much as how natural his hand looked, tenderly stroking her best friend's hair. She stood back for a few seconds, trying to decipher the energy she'd walked into. Lang wondered if the strain of juggling two men had made her paranoid. It had already, at the very least, compromised the level of intimacy she and Aminah shared. Lang refused to acknowledge that it was actually her guilt elevating her suspicions.

"Hey, baby," Lang said, pecking her husband on his lips. "What's Minah doing here?"

"Oh, hey, babe, I didn't hear you come in," Sean said, gently lifting Aminah's head like she was a light-sleeping newborn before standing up to stretch. "I'm not exactly sure, but Fame had something to do with it. I know that much."

"Damn it, I was hoping she wasn't listening to BLS this afternoon," Lang said, wrapping her hands affectionately around Sean's neck. "I can't believe she didn't call me. What'd she say?"

"Not much really, just that she was tired," Sean said, hugging Lang around her waist. "What happened on BLS?"

"Not tired enough, I bet," Lang said, glancing down at her best friend suspiciously and rolling her eyes. "Fame had his name all up in Cindy's mouth again. It's been, like, four months since she last spoke his name, but, still, I could just kill him. How is it that his shit is always on full blast?"

Sean dropped his hand from his wife's waist and took a step back from her. "No, the better question is why he keeps taking her for granted like that?" Sean asked, looking at his own wife sideways.

"Babe, I gave up on that answer years ago," Lang said, nonchalantly grabbing her husband by the hand and leading him toward the staircase. "You know those two."

"She deserves better," Sean said, glancing back lovingly at a sleeping Aminah before shutting off the lights.

"Yeah, but she doesn't want Amir and Alia growing up in a broken home," Lang said as they climbed the stairs. "You know they're the main reason she stays. For them and for Fame. Her family is everything to her."

"I've heard all that before," Sean said, extending his arm, gesturing Lang to walk into their bedroom first.

"Then you know better than to even suggest—"

"What about her though?" he asked, sliding out of his sweatpants and tossing them on the white, linen, button-tufted ottoman at the foot of their bed. "Children can be awfully resilient. It's adults who usually don't bounce back too well from shit. Fame's a good father. But let's be honest, he's a shitty husband. That's my dude and all, but he needs to be single if he still wants to be out there like that. Do something once that requires my forgiveness, shame on you. Keep doing that same shit ten, twenty times, and I still forgive you, shame on me."

"So you could forgive one indiscretion?" Lang asked, picking up Sean's sweatpants and placing them in his hamper right next to his closet.

"An indiscretion?" Sean asked quizzically. "You mean cheating? Me? Personally? Yeah, yeah, yeah. Absolutely. *Eventually*."

The thought alone was comforting to Lang, considering a quick after-work tryst with Dante was the reason she was late getting home that evening. She smiled with her back to her husband as she carefully hung up her tailored Tracy Reese skirt suit in her closet.

"I just couldn't stay married to a cheater," Sean expounded from underneath their chocolate faux suede comforter. "I've told you that. I couldn't erase the image of it. It would haunt me, but I'm not judging anyone who could."

"But you'd want me to forgive you for an indiscretion?"

"Of course, but *I* wouldn't cheat. And while I'd *want* you to forgive me, I wouldn't *expect* you to. That's just arrogant," Sean said, reaching for his wife's naked body. "That's why I don't cheat," he continued as he rubbed his wife's stomach. "I'd at least feel guilty if I cheated on you. I think what bothers me most about all of Fame's cheating is his lack of remorse. He has none."

"Yeah, but Aminah's nobody's doormat," Lang said, reaching inside her husband's boxer shorts. "She chooses to stay."

"And Fame takes advantage of that."

"And she allows it," Lang said, annoyed. "Now can we just drop this and talk about something more pleasant?"

"Exactly whose side are you on?" Sean asked weakly as his wife's warm mouth enveloped him.

"I'm on your side," Lang said between oral pulls. "Can't you feel that?"

Chapter 16

"How low must I think of myself to even indulge you and torture myself with this conversation?"

*A*minah woke up at three AM refreshed and determined. She refused to fall apart. She refused to pity herself. And she refused to let Fame slide again. She gazed at her Locman watch. *Good*, she thought. *I can still catch him at the studio.*

Aminah used Sean's bathroom to fix her face, rinse out her mouth, and smooth down her hair. She slid her pink Polo rain boots back on and grabbed her pink Coach umbrella. She disarmed the alarm system and then set it back—Lang had long since given her the code.

The heavy rain was no deterrent for Aminah's will or her Range's all-wheel drive. Aminah sped over the Manhattan Bridge, rushing over to Fame's studio in midtown, hydroplaning a couple times with both Rebekkah's and Lang's words looping in her mind throughout the entire ride.

". . . Cheating is the ultimate disrespect."

It is disrespectful, Aminah thought, agreeing with Rebekkah as she gunned through a yellow light. Aminah struggled with respect. She commanded it so effortlessly from her children and her community yet couldn't buy it at a discount from her husband.

"Doesn't it bother you that he sleeps with other women?"

"I do mind!" Aminah yelled, banging on the steering wheel. "I hate it. It infuriates me. I hate myself for putting up with it. I hate myself!"

The sound of the taxicab's horn snapped Aminah out of her screaming fit. She'd been pounding her fist and ignoring the green light.

". . . Why sell yourself short? I don't get that."

"I don't get it either," Aminah admitted out loud to herself as she blew through several red lights. *Well, no more,* she thought to herself.

". . . You've allowed him to get away with so much without any sort of repercussions for his actions, it's not even Fame's fault anymore."

"Well, I'm more than willing to take full responsibility for my actions or inactions right now," Aminah said as she pulled up in front of the building. Aminah's conversation with herself gave her all the strength and confidence to do what she needed to do. She checked her face and dabbed on a little lip gloss.

Aminah popped open her umbrella and stepped doggedly out into the pouring rain. She pressed the number *12* button.

"Yo!" an intern yelled into the intercom.

"It's Aminah, buzz me in," she commanded.

The intern did as he was told and then frantically ran down the hallway, attempting to alert his boss that his wife was on her way up. However, Daisha was in the middle of recording "I Don't Care 'Bout the Other Girls." So Fame put his hand up, signaling the intern to wait.

Aminah walked out of the elevator and waved for the receptionist to buzz her in.

She did.

"Can I help you?" she asked, full of attitude.

"No, you *may* not," Aminah replied, curtly tossing her wet umbrella in the corner and striding right past her.

She glanced inside the *A* room. No Fame.

He wasn't next door in the *B* room either.

She strolled calmly down the long hallway, staring dead ahead at the *C* room. She could see the back of her husband's head nodding through the glass. She walked right up to the glass and stood with her arms folded.

Daisha's mouth was open, but no lyrics were coming out of it.

"What's wrong with you, girl?" Fame asked, irritated. "You can't just stop midsong."

Daisha pointed toward the glass behind him.

Fame swiveled around and literally jerked backward when he saw his wife glaring directly at him with one raised eyebrow and no smile on her face. She looked good in spite of the rain—hair slicked back in a smooth, long, sleek ponytail, a pair of diamond studs in her ears, and her Fendi frames above her head.

Fame ordered everyone out of the room as he opened the door for Aminah to walk through.

"Minah, baby, what are you doin' here?" Fame asked with a

barely detectable hint of nervousness as he touched his wife's shoulder.

Aminah pushed Fame's hand off her shoulder, pulled her hand back, and slapped Fame clear across his mouth.

Daisha, the intern, and the receptionist standing just outside the door all let out an audible "ooh" simultaneously and grabbed their mouths in shock.

"Have you lost your fuckin' mind?" Fame yelled, slamming the door shut and quickly sliding the blinds down, preventing his staff from witnessing whatever was going to happen next.

"No, have you lost your fuckin' mind!" Aminah asked with her nostrils flaring. "You came home to me, ate me out, and fell asleep between my legs like everything was fine, and me, like your usual dummy, actually thought everything was."

"Calm the fuck down, Minah," Fame said, rubbing his mouth. "You sound like a raving lunatic."

"You have a lot of fuckin' nerve, Aaron *Famous* Anderson," Aminah said, pointing her index finger at his chest. "You have the gall to give me head after getting head from some ho at the club. You're the fuckin' lunatic. I'm just the crazy-ass bitch who has put up with your shit for too long. To soothe my nightmares, Fame? Have you no decency?"

"Minah, what in the hell are you talking about?" he asked with his hands splayed open, genuinely confused.

"Answering a question with a question, huh?" Aminah asked, pacing back and forth. "That means it's true. But you know what? I knew it was true when I heard it on the radio. I'm running around the city trying to make you the perfect home for the perfect Thanksgiving dinner and get you the perfect Christmas gift, and you're getting head from your club jump-off and paying cash for her car service."

Fame was stunned that his wife and Cindy Hunter knew so many details. *How the fuck . . . ?* he wondered to himself.

Suddenly Aminah stopped pacing and stared at the leather sofa, picturing Daisha's head bobbing between her husband's legs. Aminah let out a scream so guttural, so animal-like, it frightened Fame.

"Minah, baby, calm down and listen to me," Fame said soothingly, walking his wife over to his chair and sitting her down. Fame wasn't his usual confident self as he'd been all the other times Aminah had confronted him. While this wasn't unfamiliar territory for him by any means, there was something different about his wife this time that he couldn't quite figure out, and not having a full grasp of the situation had him nervous. He jangled his keys in his pocket. "Most of the time . . ." Fame paused to gather his thoughts. "Look, it was just some head, just oral sex. That's it."

"Why can't you come home and get head from me, Fame, huh?" Aminah whined. "Don't you like the way I do it?" Her voice cracked.

"Come on, baby," Fame said, gently rubbing her back. "You're making me feel bad. It's not even about that. Of course I love the way you do it. You do it best."

Aminah shook her head and leaned forward in the chair.

"My God!" Aminah suddenly screamed, holding her stomach. "How low must I think of myself to even indulge you and torture myself with this conversation?"

"Minah, it meant nothing to me," Fame explained, still unsure of whether to comfort or chastise his wife. "It was just something physical. I've never, ever been involved with any other woman. C'mon, Minah, we've been through all this before."

Aminah glared at Fame in disbelief.

"Okay, so occasionally they get some dick," Fame admitted. "There's so much more to me than dick, Minah, and you get all of it, all of me."

"What about respect, huh?" Aminah asked, wiping her nose. "Do I get that, Fame?"

"Minah, baby, of course," Fame answered, gently stooping down in front of her and holding her face. "I have the highest regard for you. I respect you more than any other woman on the planet. You're the mother of my children, baby. You're my wife."

"How come you're not thinking about the fact that I'm the mother of your children and your wife when you're getting your dick sucked, huh? Are you thinking about me when you make the conscious decision to sleep with another woman? I don't ever not think about you, Fame."

"C'mon, Minah," Fame said, impatiently standing back up. "The two have absolutely nothing to do with each other. Be logical for a second and put your emotions in check."

"Okay, okay, you want logic?" Aminah asked, furiously jumping out of her seat. "Let's try logic *and* reason. How would you feel if I sucked another man's dick? Huh?"

"Aminah, don't play," Fame said, pointing his finger in his wife's face. "Now you really sound crazy."

"*I do it best,*" Aminah said, mocking Fame. "Well, I don't trust you or your fuckin' opinion. I think I need to find out if my head game's tight enough for my damn self."

Fame grabbed Aminah by both her shoulders and shook her violently. "You do some stupid-ass shit like that, and I will break your fuckin' neck."

Aminah jerked herself away. "If you ever put your hands on me again, Fame, as God is my witness, I will blow your fuckin' brains out. I'm *always* strapped with that little twenty-two you bought me. I keep it loaded, and I know how to use it," Aminah said, looking down purposefully at her Marc Jacobs bag.

Fame could not believe that his wife had not only slapped him but threatened his life, and to give another man head all in the same night. *Must be a fuckin' full moon*, Fame thought. The night had definitely gotten out of hand.

"Okay, Minah, baby, you need to calm down," Fame said, walking toward Aminah, feeling more confused than nervous.

"No, Fame," Aminah said, patting her purse with one hand and putting up the other, signaling Fame to stop coming any closer. "I've been too calm for too long. That's the problem."

"Minah, baby," Fame pleaded.

"No more, Fame. You need to start thinking about a life without me. You make me so sick," Aminah snarled and then spat in her husband's face.

She carefully wiped the corners of her mouth and then calmly strutted out of the C room with her chin up and her back straightened.

Daisha, the intern, and the receptionist all pressed themselves against the wall, getting out of her way. Aminah took her time strutting up the platinum-plaque-filled hallway and out the lobby. She pushed the down elevator button, and the doors opened immediately. Aminah drove off in the torrential rain feeling like one of Amir's chessmen, the queen in fact, torn between sacrificing herself on the chessboard to protect the king yet again or forcing the king to be cornered, possibly resulting in checkmate.

"... I can't tell you to leave your husband and the father of your children ... Only you can make that decision."

"What can I live with?" Aminah asked herself as she drove through one of the E-ZPass lanes outside the Midtown Tunnel, recalling a conversation she'd had with Lang.

With spittle dripping down the front of his face, Fame told his staff to go home. He washed his face and called Aminah. No answer. He two-wayed her. No response. Aminah turned off her phone and her Sidekick. This time she didn't care about a lecture. She just wanted to go home.

Chapter 17

"It's yours."

"Baby, you have to see this," Sean said, pulling his wife down the stairs and into his entertainment room. He'd TiVo'd last night's basketball brawl between the Indiana Pacers and the Detroit Pistons. She'd been too tired to watch it the night before, and Sean didn't have the patience to wait for Lang to finish cleaning the entire house.

"Did that guy just throw his drink into that player's face?" Lang asked, holding her rubber cleaning gloves within inches of her mouth. "Oh, that's not right. After he'd calmed down. He was just chillin' on the table like that. I woulda whopped his ass, too."

Sean laughed. "I gotta burn this onto a DVD. That was some historic shit."

"Damn, so, who won the fight—I mean, the game?" Lang asked, laughing and heading back upstairs to finish cleaning, but not before yelling down to Sean to vacuum the runner down the middle of the staircase.

Once their brownstone was clean by Lang's standards, Sean showered and headed over to Basketball City to play in his Saturday-afternoon basketball league. He'd just made a left turn onto Myrtle Avenue when he realized he left his good-luck Nike sports watch on the nightstand. He had just enough time to go back for it. He turned around.

Sean unlocked the front door and then the parlor door. Lang had a hair appointment, so it surprised him to still see her boots by the front door. Before he could bolt up the stairs to retrieve his watch, Lang's moaning slowed him down.

He crept up the stairs quietly and then peered into their slightly cracked bedroom door from the second-to-last step. He rubbed his neatly trimmed goatee and grinned.

Lang was moaning and touching herself. The liquid movement of her sculpted copper body against their dark chocolate faux suede comforter held Sean spellbound. His eyes were fixed on the speed and intensity of her right index and middle fingers circling between her legs.

"Uh, right there," Lang said out loud.

Sean moved up quietly, just outside their bedroom door, not wanting to disturb her groove.

"Right there, right there, right there," Lang panted.

Sean smiled, knowing his wife was about to come.

Then Lang murmured something else that Sean couldn't quite make out, but what he could now see quite clearly was her tiny Motorola cell phone pressed up against her left ear.

"It's yours," she said breathlessly into the phone with her eyes closed. Her long legs collapsed into the folds of the comforter.

Sean felt woozy. His vision blurred as he steadied himself against the wall.

She giggled. Sean couldn't figure out if that was her sexy giggle or the devious one, but at that moment he couldn't decide any-thing. His head hurt too much.

"Can't wait to see you either," she said. Though he couldn't see it, Sean could hear her smile.

His stomach bubbled. Churned. Flipped. He needed air.

Sean swiftly took three steps at a time and hurried out the door with the agility and silence of a cat in heat on a mission, leaving his good-luck watch right there on the nightstand. He didn't need it after all. He'd just lost a game he didn't even know he was playing.

Chapter 18

"There's no such thing as a powerful monogamous man."

Aminah had spent the last seven days resting in her childhood bedroom at her parents' Victorian home in Hempstead. Ever since she'd graduated from high school, Aminah's mother had redecorated her P.I.P. (Pretty in Pink) room every few years. Miss Lenora—as she introduced herself to everyone at least ten years younger than she—wanted the P.I.P. room to mature with Aminah. Three springs ago Miss Lenora had found this elaborate carnation-pink tulle at a fabric shop on Main Street in Sag Harbor and draped it over Aminah's king-size dark Peruvian walnut four-poster bed, creating a billowy cotton-candy canopy. She'd littered the borders around the room with these enormous cocoa-colored floor pillows and scattered satin, fringed magenta pillows on top of them. She'd also had the oak wood floors stained dark espresso and the walls painted in a soft, barely there, hardly detectable pink.

Aminah had wanted to stay at their Sag Harbor summer home, but her mother couldn't tolerate the arctic breeze off the water that time of year. "It's too treacherous for my bones," she'd say whenever Aminah brought up spending the holidays out there.

Aminah's mother was a lady's lady. She dressed for every-thing—bed, gardening, grocery shopping and church. It didn't matter. Rather, it always mattered. Miss Lenora was old-fashioned, so to speak, the type of woman who still wore hat and gloves to Sunday service—winter, spring, summer, and fall—and usually wore her salt-and-pepper hair in a tight chignon at the nape of her neck or in a neat bun on top of her head, always accentuating her high cheekbones. She was a handsome woman. She'd release the pinned-up bun and let her thick, bushy hair free to swell over her shoulders and down her back on holidays and at the request of her husband.

Aminah had inherited her mother's shapely hips and her pater-nal grandmother's full breasts. Where Aminah was an undeniable hourglass, Miss Lenora was a ripe, respectable pear. She didn't understand this new generation's obsession with "working out."

"A lady maintains her figure simply by eating three square meals a day, cleaning her home and tending her garden, never in-dulging anything in excess, taking a nice, leisurely stroll after din-ner, and dancing at least once a week." She was Aminah's role model.

Miss Lenora's homes were neat yet warm and welcoming. Magically, something always seemed to baking in her oven, antici-pating impromptu and expected guests alike. She was the consum-mate hostess. Her houseguests always left with parting gifts—bath soaps and gels, bottles of wine, candles and oils, or freshly baked goods—and a strong desire to return sooner rather than later.

For seven days Miss Lenora fussily nursed her only child back to full emotional health while Aminah's father quietly visited the P.I.P. room daily—pulling down her covers, kissing his baby girl on the cheek, telling her he loved her, reminding her that she and his grandchildren would always have a home to live in and money to burn, and then pulling the covers back over her head, leaving his wife to "woman's work."

Miss Lenora had let Aminah cry for a whole week without any shame, chastisement, or persecution. Made her soak daily in bathwater as hot as she could stand until it was too cold for her to sit in. Seven days of cleansing. Everyone was entitled to that. After that Miss Lenora said the healing process must begin. No wallowing. No self-loathing. Focus on the solution and not the problem. Shift from mourning to healing. Besides, no one had actually died, and her grandchildren needed their mother.

Aminah wasn't quite so sure. While she fully embraced her mother's emotional-cleansing and healing ritual, she thought that perhaps she'd really been grieving because it surely felt like her marriage was dying, if it was not dead already.

Aminah hated ambiguity and indecisiveness, yet she couldn't figure out whether her marriage was worth reviving or resurrecting anymore or if she should just go ahead and arrange its funeral services.

While Aminah refused to speak to Fame, Miss Lenora was in daily contact with him. Every day she'd ask him to put Alia and Amir on the phone and then pass it to Aminah, but not before warning him that if he attempted to speak to Aminah while the children were on the line, Aminah would hang up immediately. Fame couldn't believe it. He hadn't spoken to his wife since the night she'd spat on him in the studio.

Aminah told the children she was out of town helping one of her college girlfriends who'd had some sort of last-minute emergency surgery. Fame reluctantly co-signed her story.

He'd met Lang for dinner at a diner near her office a couple days after the spitting incident, hoping to find some sort of clarity as to his wife's state of mind and being. Lang and Fame frequently wound up hanging and laughing together at various industry functions, though most times they arrived there separately. However, a shared meal together between the childhood friends occurred more often at their respective homes than at popular eateries.

Anticipating Fame's standard twenty-minutes-late arrival, Lang strutted into the crowded diner with her laptop as her companion. But to her genuine surprise, Fame was already seated and apparently on his second Hennessy and Coke.

"What's up, playboy?" Lang asked before giving Fame a concerned hug and kissing him on both cheeks.

"Everything, man. I think I really fucked up this time, Lang," Fame admitted, shaking the four cubes of melting ice in his empty glass. "I know she told you what happened in the studio, and now she won't even talk to me. It's been two days already, and she's still not taking my calls."

"Taking your calls?" Lang asked, confused. "Where the hell is Aminah?"

"Don't act like you don't know that she left me with the children to stay with her parents. C'mon, Lang. You always keep it real with me. That's how we do. Please don't start bullshittin' me now."

Lang explained to Fame that since she and Aminah had had "a little falling out" over her decision not to have a baby right now, they'd been speaking a little less frequently and with a bit less detail.

None of that made sense to Fame. Plus, Lang was twirling her hair, so he knew something was wrong with or missing from her story. Didn't matter though. He needed Lang's advice on getting his wife speaking to him and back home where she belonged.

"Honestly, Fame, Aminah's been fed up for a minute now," Lang said after ordering a turkey cheeseburger and salad. Fame got another Hennessy and Coke. "And your carelessness is beyond ridiculous, man. You've got a leak somewhere, and you need to permanently plug that bitch."

"A leak?"

"Fame, you haven't noticed how more and more detailed the information is about you lately?" Lang asked, wagging her finger in admonishment.

"Nah, I pay that shit no mind," Fame said, rubbing his forehead. "Not till Aminah brings it up, of course."

"Well, you should homey, especially this last one. Why does the entire tristate area know you paid cash for this chick's car service after she gave you head in your studio last week? She must be bragging to her girls or something."

"Nah, nah, she's an old reliable. Plus, she has a man. So it can't be her."

"Who else was it then? Who else was in the studio? Or maybe old reliable was talking about you on her cell phone, and the driver leaked it."

Fame thought about it. He was certain the driver couldn't care less about anything except making his money and getting a good tip, so he immediately eliminated him. He took a sip of his fresh drink, wondering who else besides his wife cared who and where he got head.

"That bitch Daisha," Fame said, slamming down his glass. "Damn. How'd I miss that?"

"You were too busy getting done to notice who was doing you," Lang said before biting into her juicy burger. "That's how."

"She's nothing. I'll handle her. She's dead to me. And if she costs me my wife, I mean that literally. Now tell me how to get my wife home, Lang."

Lang wiped the corner of her mouth before answering. She actually felt bad for him. She missed sharing practically every detail of her life with her best friend. If she and Aminah were on better terms, she'd call Aminah immediately and tell her that Fame was finally showing more vulnerability than ego. But they were on worse terms than they'd ever been. It still hurt her that Aminah had sought Sean out instead of her. Hurt her even more that she still felt a twinge of jealousy just thinking about her husband stroking Aminah's head in his lap.

"Space and time, Fame," Lang said, shaking her head. "That's what I've been giving her."

They parted ways, with Lang heading back to the office and Fame going home. She needed to get work done, and he just couldn't.

Both Fame's mother and mother-in-law told him to just focus on the children and that Aminah would surely come around by Thanksgiving. He'd been patient. She had three more days to get it together, and he was certain of only one thing—his wife had better drive through their monogrammed gates come Thursday morning, or he was gonna lose his damn mind.

Miss Lenora suggested that Fame hire a nanny to help out with Alia and Amir while WillieMae, the housekeeper, focused on getting the home together for the holiday dinner. Glo, however, insisted on staying with her son instead. "Why pay for someone to babysit your kids when they have not one but two grandmothers who don't work?" his mother said. "Boy, please."

Gloria woke Alia and Amir up an hour and a half earlier and made them breakfast, now that Fame was dropping them both off at school. Nights in the studio were becoming a waste of time. Nothing sounded good. No hits were being made. He left the studio early every night. He was exhausted, more emotionally spent than anything else. He missed his wife terribly and sought no solace in other women, found no comfort in his music.

His Master Actualization Plan was not working without his wife. If he'd ever doubted it before, Fame knew now more than ever that Aminah was a core component to his M.A.P.—to his life, period.

On her daughter's eighth day of recovery, Miss Lenora brought Aminah a hot cup of peppermint tea with thick, swirling ribbons of golden honey.

"Let me comb out your hair while you sip on this tea," Miss Lenora said, placing the teacup and saucer on Aminah's vanity table in the dressing area of her walk-in closet.

Aminah took her seat in front of the mirror. Miss Lenora leaned her daughter's head forward and carefully parted her disheveled hair from ear to ear. She gently and methodically brushed out her daughter's matted hair, detangling her thick, long black tresses by working the wooden paddle brush from the ends up to the roots.

"Aminah, sweetheart, sometimes I've wondered if I've set a good or a bad example for you by staying with your father all these years," Miss Lenora admitted.

"Mother, how could you say that?" Aminah questioned, turning her head slightly.

"Now, don't misunderstand me," Miss Lenora replied, adjusting her daughter's head back to face the mirror. "I don't apologize for my choices. There's certainly no shame in standing by your husband and honoring your vows. There's no dishonor in keeping your family intact regardless of whom or what comes before you."

She paused to make another neat part, separating the tangled bales of hair from the smooth, combed-through mane with a plastic butterfly clip.

"But, Aminah, let's be realistic about something," Miss Lenora continued. "There's no such thing as a powerful monogamous man. Simply no such thing. And that I didn't make that blatantly clear to you before you married Aaron is how I think I may have misrepresented the institution of marriage to you."

"Muh-thurrr," Aminah whined like she always did when she respectfully disagreed with Miss Lenora.

"Stop that whining, Aminah," Miss Lenora said, playfully popping her daughter with the parting comb. "In all seriousness, Aminah, just look back through history. No, don't even bother to go that far, look at all the current affairs—"

"I know," Aminah interrupted, touching her mother's arm. "But you, Mother, have set a fine example. You haven't misrepresented anything."

"I don't know, Aminah. I think I made it look a lot easier than it truly is. That's misrepresentation. But I still don't know. At what point does a mother show her daughter . . ." She paused to gather her thoughts and make another neat horizontal part. "At what point does she tell her daughter about the hardships of marriage, about the humiliation of an affair, about the difficulty of choosing to stay, to stand by your husband publicly while despising him privately at times? If I'd had the power to shield you from your father's indiscretions, I would have," Miss Lenora admitted.

"But you couldn't," Aminah replied softly. "The rumors of Daddy's affair followed me all through junior high school, and I played dumb to them for as long as I could, but by the time I reached high school . . ." She paused, remembering.

There was this group of girls from the projects who'd accused Aminah of thinking she was too cute and too good to hang around them because her father was a dentist.

"That's why your daddy is sleeping with his secretary."

"Keep acting stuck-up—see what it got your mother."

"Didn't I see your father coming outta 4B this mornin'? Was Daddy home for breakfast, Ah-Mee-Nuh?"

He wasn't—not that morning anyway.

It was one of the worst days of Aminah's life, her worst childhood memory in fact. She still vividly remembered coming home from school to the smell of burned chocolate-chip cookies and her mother's muffled sobs coming out of her aunt's skirted lap. Miss Lenora never overcooked anything.

Nick Philips was indeed having an affair with his secretary (there was, however, no project chick—but a wheelchair-bound childhood friend he bought groceries for every Monday morning did reside in 4B).

Miss Lenora told her to ignore those little heifers. They were just jealous of Aminah—who she was and what she had. While that may have been true, so was what the project girls and the rest of the village were saying.

Aminah's father was Hempstead's most prominent dentist. He was very popular with everyone, from the street corner and barbershops to the local lodges and town hall. Nicholas Philips—a strong man who met any and all adversity head-on yet laughed so easily in the company of good humor—was difficult not to like. Men and women alike were drawn to him.

The ladies—from the church pews and business associations to the hair salons and day-care centers—particularly adored Dr. Philips. Women discreetly propositioned him in the presence of his wife and openly did so in her absence. He politely yet charmingly declined many more times than he ever accepted. Dr. Philips chalked it up as a hazard of the job.

That afternoon of burned cookies and muffled sobs, Dr. Philip's secretary announced to Miss Lenora on her nineteenth-century Regency style carved-oak canapé that she was pregnant with her husband's child and planned on raising their child, Aminah's half-sibling, right there in Hempstead.

Miss Lenora wanted to pull her daughter out of the public school system, but Nicholas Philips thought it would look poorly to the community if his daughter didn't attend the local public school. How could he prove that he had a personal vested interest if his own child didn't attend? "Besides, the students like Aminah in the talented and gifted programs are receiving a superior education. It's those average kids who are getting gypped."

Aminah had forgotten how painful parts of her childhood were and respected her mother even more for being so emotionally strong through it all. Her mother had kept their family together by undeniable will and remarkable force.

"Yes, and if I could have protected you from all that, I would've."

"Oh, Mother, stop it," Aminah said firmly. "It's not your fault. If anyone should have been trying to protect me more, it should've been my father. I was more confused than hurt. I just didn't understand how my father could step out on you of all women. With such a beautiful, doting, intelligent woman at home who cooked, cleaned, and raised his daughter brilliantly—if I do say so myself. I didn't understand why that wasn't enough for him."

Nick had confessed to only one affair, the one with his secretary, the single time he'd gotten caught, the only time that mattered. He'd fired her immediately with an incredible severance, convinced her to have an abortion (that he was present for at his wife's insistence), and threatened to end her life if she didn't move at least three thousand miles away and forget they'd ever known each other. "I got friends from the ghetto to the White House and in between, and more than one owes me a favor that's just a phone call away."

In front of a Romare Bearden original, Nicholas had stood at the head of his dining room table and apologized to his daughter and wife. He'd promised that nothing like that would ever come to their doorsteps again. Miss Lenora had immediately forgiven him publicly; privately, it had taken quite a few years, but Aminah never could tell.

Miss Lenora rubbed her daughter's back. "I can't answer that question for your father any more than you can for Aaron. If you need those answers, you need to ask him, but more importantly, you need to ask and answer for yourself why you stay. Be clear on those reasons, Aminah."

Yes, clarity. That's what Aminah desired, that and closure and contrition from Fame. All these years of staying with him for the sake of the family didn't seem like enough anymore. His lack of remorse had always pissed Aminah off, but she'd just accepted it as par for the course. Quietly, she'd always felt a bit taken for granted.

"Why did you stay, Mother?" Aminah asked, hoping her mother's answer would offer her some insight into herself.

"Because I wanted to. I loved our relationship, and I still do. Your father loves me, Aminah, and I him."

"Did you ever feel humiliated?"

"Humiliated?" Miss Lenora asked while gathering all of Aminah's hair back into a ponytail. "No, I had absolutely nothing to be ashamed of. Angry at your father enough to want to smother him with a pillow in his sleep, yes, but never humiliated."

"Sometimes I feel like the other women have it better," Aminah admitted. "They don't have to put up with all that we wives have to. It seems like they get to have it all or at least the best of both worlds. The freedom of being single plus the perks of being with a married man."

"Well, that's just nonsense, Aminah," Miss Lenora said, placing the paddle brush on the vanity table. She lifted her daughter's chin and looked her squarely in the eyes. "Understand something, Aminah: the wife is always honored and respected. Back in my day, the mistress was lucky if she got any pity, never mind regard. A wife who stands by her husband can remarry with dignity if she so chooses. Look at Jackie O and Marilyn Monroe—which one was more revered, respected, and honored, while the other died shamefully? God bless the dead, but, well, she did kill herself."

"*Muh-thurrr,*" Aminah whined again, thinking Marilyn Monroe had married—a few times, in fact. True, they were all troubled, but . . .

"Well, it's true. Your generation is perhaps the first to try to make the mistress into something more than what she is. As if being one is something to aspire to. She suffers lonely birthdays and holidays. She bears bastards if she bears children at all. 'Silly girl, you mean nothing to him, now scamper away. There may be dozens of you but only one of me.'"

Aminah thought that maybe that last comment was specifically directed at her father's old secretary.

"Understand something, Aminah; there's value and worth in being an exclusive commodity as opposed to a mass-market item," Miss Lenora continued. "A woman's value depreciates the more her body is used, and I don't care how liberated or self-reliant women get, that piece of fact won't ever change. The day will never come when a woman gains respect for the number of men she's bedded. It's been that way since the beginning of time in practically every culture."

Aminah sighed and wondered if this speech was a part of the healing process.

"You cannot lose your mind because your husband cheats on you," her mother continued. "You cannot fall apart because he has an affair. You cannot destroy your family because of his weaknesses. I'm sorry that the burden falls on us, but there is strength in that, beauty in that. Knowing I can keep my family together by my will and determination is empowering for me. Now, I'll admit to you, Aminah, that Aaron has not been discreet enough for a woman of your caliber. But as you know, your father wasn't always discreet either."

Aminah nodded in agreement. "Do you worry about Dad cheating now?"

Miss Lenora laughed a long, full, hearty laugh. Her eyes actually watered. "Oh, Aminah, baby."

"What's so funny?" Aminah asked, genuinely confused. "I don't get it."

"Your father and I have been married for over thirty-five years, and we *know* each other. Do you know how amazing it is to be with someone who really knows you and you them? We're each other's best friends. I mean that. Not only is it cheaper to keep me, it's easier. But when you get down to it, it's never really been about the other woman. It's always been about him and me. What we have, what we value, our agreement, our commitment. I never had any sort of agreement with that woman. She didn't owe me anything, no allegiance. Nothing. I wanted your father's respect. If being faithful is so hard, at least respect me enough, care about me enough so that it never gets back to me. Don't ever give me a reason to suspect anything. Protect me and my feelings, me and my ego, my pride, my body. Insulate me, if you will."

Aminah realized at that particular moment that she and her mother were indeed kindred spirits. Being insulated would have been enough for Aminah, too.

"I almost left your father," Miss Lenora revealed.

"Are you serious, Mother?" Aminah asked while braiding down her ponytail.

"Yes. I was the one who insisted he fire his secretary and move her out of the state. And if he hadn't done it immediately, I wasn't going to settle for half. Oh, no, I was gonna take it *allll*, and I dared him to stop me. He ain't the only one with connections from the hood to the DC lawn."

Aminah laughed hysterically. She needed that. She hadn't laughed in over a week, and hearing her mother paraphrase one of her father's overused quotes tickled her.

"Yes, I did," Miss Lenora continued. "It's like playing out those last two hands in a good game of spades, and so far nobody's thrown down the high or low joker. So everybody's playing cautiously, but no one suspects you're holding both of them. You gotta know the cards you're holding, baby, when to play which card and when to throw them all down. You've got a good hand, Aminah—you know that, right?"

Aminah nodded and smiled. She'd sleep soundly that night knowing on Thanksgiving morning she'd be checking herself out of the P.I.P. room.

"Now, why don't you give Dorian a call?" Miss Lenora suggested, affectionately smoothing the top of her daughter's head. "I'm afraid your hair requires some professional attention I can't give it."

Chapter 19

"I can't do this without you."

$\mathcal{S}$ean woke up on Thanksgiving morning with absolutely no appetite. Sneaking up on his wife having phone sex with another man had stripped him of his hunger for sex, food, and basketball. He was going through it.

Lang was uneasy. Watching her husband sip on the same can of room-temperature ginger ale from the night before concerned her. His "twenty-four-hour stomach virus" was runnin' one hundred twenty hours straight right about now.

"You think we should just call Fame and cancel, babe?" Lang asked as she slid on her camel suede pants.

"No way," Sean said, rubbing his hand back and forth across his stomach. "I promised Alia and Amir I'd be there, and when *I* make promises, *I* keep them."

Sean couldn't bring himself to flat-out confront Lang just yet. If Aminah hadn't been going through her own thing, he would've been stepped to her about this.

Underneath her sienna cable-knit turtleneck, Lang raised her eyebrow as she pulled the sweater over her head. *Okay, what is that supposed to mean?* she wondered.

On their drive over to Queens, Sean recalled their last baby-making conversation. Weren't they supposed to start planning for their offspring soon? Were all their plans now fucked up over one phone call? *It's not like I actually caught her in bed with another man, just on the phone,* Sean thought to himself. *Right?* His stomach rumbled.

Lang didn't hear the rumbling though. Not only was Dianne Reeves up way too loud, but Lang's mind roamed elsewhere. As their quarter-to-eight—their BMW 745—hugged the curves of the Jackie Robinson Parkway, her thoughts were on trading it in for the new 6 Series.

Even though Lang knew how much Sean absolutely hated carrying a car note, she reasoned that whipping the latest was a necessary element of her job. How was she going to run a magazine that touted itself as the aficionado of what black celebrities were wearing, driving, buying, and applying if she herself didn't live by those very same standards?

"You know you're born with all the eggs you'll ever have, right?" Sean asked, disrupting her mental car-shopping trip.

"What?" Lang asked in confusion, turning down Reeves's soulful "Company."

"These few eggs you have left now are some of your oldest eggs, just hanging on for dear life, hoping to be fertilized."

"What in the hell are you talking about, Sean?" Lang asked, perturbed. Her Thanksgiving was not getting off to a good start.

"That's why it's so much harder for older women to conceive—you're no longer carrying your youngest, strongest, healthiest eggs."

Lang wondered if this stomach thing had traveled up to his head.

"Why the sudden concern for my eggs, Sean, huh? And since when did I become an older woman? 'Cause quite frankly, I'm more worried about *your* stomach."

He knew this stomach thing was merely psychosomatic, but the state of her eggs and the future of their marriage truly did trouble him.

"Do you still want to have my children, Langston?"

Lang didn't answer immediately. Not only would Sean not like what he'd hear, but Thanksgiving Day was not the time to discuss her apprehension about kids, especially when just four months ago they'd discussed her properly planning her maternity leave and proactively grooming her assistant for the transition.

"Sean, honey, I think it's time we got some solid food in your system," Lang said as she parked in the Andersons' driveway. "'Cause the shit that's coming out your mouth has got to be from lack of sustenance."

"No, the shit that's coming out of my mouth is from lack of trust," Sean said, slamming the car door.

"What?"

"You heard."

"What reason have I given you not to trust me?" Lang asked, ringing the doorbell.

"Think about it, Langston," Sean replied.

But she didn't have a chance. Fame answered the door with a look of relief, pulling Sean through the doorway with a heartfelt embrace. Alia followed right behind her father, dragging Lang off in a completely different direction.

Inside the Anderson home it was blatantly apparent that Aminah hadn't been there. For one, all the Daily Blossom arrangements that had arrived the day before were now sitting in a corner of the living room, while all the pumpkins were lined in size order down the middle of the dining room table.

Aminah had bought the orange-skinned fruits to greet her guests at the front doorstep and guide them up the indoor staircase opposite glowing votives; however, Glo had decided they'd work best simply as centerpieces.

The "pumpkin patch" was the first thing Miss Lenora had noticed when she entered the dining room an hour before Lang and Sean arrived.

"Who put these here, and where is Aminah?" she asked to no one in particular, reaching toward the largest pumpkin.

"Isn't she with you?" Fame asked his mother-in-law, sounding all too distressed.

"No Aaron, honey," Miss Lenora replied, concerned as she reached up to touch his shoulder. "She left this morning before Nick and I were even dressed. She said she'd see us later. I assumed she meant here, but clearly, with the pumpkin patch on the table and the flower garden on the floor, she's not here."

Glo leaned against the wall just outside the dining room. She'd strolled in minutes ago from her backyard cigarette break. Normally, Aminah and Fame did not allow smoking in or outside their home. But because Glo had sacrificed "living her life like it's golden" for the past week to care for his children, Fame readily made an exception for his mother.

"*I* put the pumpkins on the table, and I think they look real nice up there," Glo said defensively, strutting over to Lenora.

Miss Lenora had assumed Fame had thrown the pumpkins on the table in haste. She genuinely appreciated Gloria stepping in for

Aminah and wasn't about to belittle her efforts by making Thanksgiving at the Anderson home more uncomfortable than it already was without Aminah there.

"Oh, well, yes, they sure do, Gloria," Miss Lenora lied, turning around to hug Glo, wrinkle up her nose at the lingering smell of cigarette smoke, and ask her how she was doing. To say they liked each other would be an overstatement; to say they didn't would be a lie. They tolerated each other. Of course, Nick and Gloria got along just fine.

"You haven't heard from her?" Nick asked, gripping his son-in-law's right hand, pulling him in for a hug, patting him on the back and whispering, "You need to fix this, son."

"I know. I know. I just don't know how," Fame responded.

The doorbell rang.

"We'll talk later," Nick promised.

Cousins, uncles, aunts, sisters, brothers, nephews, nieces, and friends filled the house by the minute. Everyone inquired about Aminah's whereabouts.

The tristate-area folks informed the out-of-towners of the latest gossip circulating about Fame and Aminah. Some shook their heads, whispered she should leave him, take half his money, all this house, and split the kids. Others murmured she'd be a fool to put a good-looking, hardworking man like Fame back on the market to be snatched up by someone who'd be smart enough to look the other way and never complain while luxuriating in all his wealth before she could even get an appointment with a divorce attorney.

An hour and a half later while Amir was in the middle of impressing Sean and a few of his younger cousins with a card trick, the phone rang.

"Hi, Mom!" Amir shouted into the phone.

"Tell your mother I need to talk to her," Sean whispered into his ear.

Amir nodded at Sean while telling his mother he was fine and, yes, he was co-manning the house with his dad, and that Grandma Glo was fun, but he missed her and wanted to know when she was coming home.

"Well, not today, sweetie," Aminah said.

"Aw, Mom. Your friend's not doing any better?" he asked, concerned.

"She is better, just not fully recovered."

"Well, tell her to hurry up and get better because I need you home in time for Christmas."

Aminah smiled. "I most certainly will. Now tell me a funny story."

He did, and Aminah laughed her signature crescendo laugh. Amir smiled and asked how she was doing.

"Mommy is doing just fine, but she'll be even better when you see her. Now go find your sister and let me speak to Uncle Sean." Amir handed the phone to Sean and ran off to look for his sister.

"Hey, gorgeous, how are you?" Sean asked, smiling for the first time in days.

"I'm *much* better, Sean, thank you."

"Then why aren't you here?"

"Oh, Sean." Aminah sighed. "I'm not ready to be in a house full of people or, for that matter, anywhere near Fame."

"Damn," Sean said, disappointed that he wouldn't get to see her. "Well, where are you spending your Thanksgiving?"

"At the Ritz-Carlton in Battery Park," Aminah said nonchalantly.

Sean could hear her smiling through the phone. He laughed. "That's my girl."

"You know they have a water sommelier here?"

"No, Aminah, only you would know that." Sean laughed again. His stomach was feeling better already.

"I'm sorry I can't be home on Thanksgiving, Sean. I really am. I'm still plotting my next move. You know? Figuring things out. . . ." Her voice trailed off a bit.

"Plotting?" Sean asked, surprised. "You're thinking about leaving Fame?"

"I'm thinking about me and my needs, for a change. Not my husband's, not my children's, *my* future and whether it includes my husband. And if it does, under what clear and concise terms."

"Good for you, Aminah," Sean said, meaning it. "Wish I could be there, too."

"Uh-oh, something's wrong," Aminah detected. "You love holiday gatherings almost as much as basketball. What's going on with you?"

Sean paused to figure out how he should ask Aminah if she had any idea who his wife was phone sexing. Who she was seeing later. Correction—who she couldn't wait to see later.

"Listen, Aminah, I need to ask you something that . . ." He paused again.

"What is it, Sean?"

Sean rubbed his stomach. The nausea was returning, and Alia

was walking toward him with her hand extended. He was running out of time.

"Who is my wife fucking around with?" Sean whispered through clenched teeth.

"Uncle Sean, lemme speak to Mommy. It's my turn."

"Listen, Alia's here to speak with you," Sean said, lowering his voice and turning away from Alia. "But we need to talk in person. Can I see you tomorrow?"

Aminah cleared her throat. "Uh, yeah, sure, sure."

"Where? There?"

"Let me think about that. Maybe we can go somewhere to eat around here. I'll call you on your cell around oneish."

"Cool," Sean said, swiveling around to face his goddaughter with a smile. "Well, here's Alia, and Happy Thanksgiving, gorgeous."

Alia assured her mother that she was being the lady of the house and explained to her that Grandma Glo did a lot of things different from what they were used to—"good different," mostly.

"Has your Grandmother Lenora gotten there yet?" Aminah asked.

"Yes," Alia responded. "Mommy?"

"Yes, sweetie."

"I think it's nice that you're taking care of your friend Nia, but when are you coming home?"

"Real soon. Definitely in time for Christmas. Nia's recovery is coming along nicely, but Daddy is doing a good job filling in for me, right?"

"Um, he's doing a good job for Daddy, just not as good as you."

Alia laughed, recalling her father's "lame" attempt at helping her shop for an outfit for "Dress-Down Day" at school.

Aminah laughed at her daughter's candor. "Okay, well, that's good enough. Would you get him for me, please?"

Fame took the call upstairs in their bedroom.

"Minah, baby, I'm so glad you called," he said, sounding as nervous as he was relieved. "I was getting real worried about you, baby. Where are you? How long before you get here?"

Aminah said nothing.

"Minah, baby, you there?"

"I'm here, Fame," Aminah said flatly.

"Where are you exactly? Everbody's here. We're just waitin' on you."

"Actually, that's why I called." Aminah paused to clear her throat. "I didn't want to be rude and hold up dinner. Listen, I'm not coming home, Fame."

This time Fame said nothing.

"Fame, you there?"

"Yeah, I'm here," Fame said, holding his head down and rubbing his forehead.

Neither said anything for a whole minute. Fame wrestled between feeling angry and being hurt. He settled on frustrated.

"Minah, baby, I can't. I can't do this without you." Fame's voice cracked. "Please, baby, come home. Please. Whatever it is you want me to do, need me to do, I'll do it. Just don't leave me, baby. Don't do that. Please don't do that. Don't make me have to spend Thanksgiving without you. All of our family is here, baby, but it just ain't family without you. Please, baby, I'm begging you. Come home, Minah. I miss you. I miss you more than the children do. Shit, they're fine. I'm the one who's falling apart over here. I can't make music. I can't, Minah. I can't do this without you. You want me to give up the studio, Minah? Huh? I'll do it. I'll do it. Just say you'll come home to me."

Aminah swallowed back the tears but said nothing. She refused to cry. She'd done more than enough of that. *Concentrate on the healing. On the solution . . . on what you want, Aminah.* She replayed her mother's advice.

"You're willing to throw away all that we have, all that we built, over some bullshit, Aminah?"

"I'm not the one putting our marriage in jeopardy time and time again, Fame," Aminah responded, incensed at Fame's audacity. "You did that all by yourself. Don't you dare try to flip this on me."

Fame sighed.

"We barely spent enough time together as a couple or a family," she continued. "How is it that you have the nerve to find time for an affair?"

"Let's be clear on something, Minah," Fame said angrily. "I have never had an affair. Never had a relationship with any other woman. *Relations* in the Clintonian sense of the word, okay, well, yeah. But no affair. No relationship."

"I gotta go, Fame," Aminah said before slamming down the phone.

"Shit. Minah, baby, I'm sorry," Fame said to the dial tone. "Damn it!" Fame threw the cordless phone across the room.

As more family and friends arrived, it eased the tension between the mothers-in-law, but not the curiosity regarding Aminah's whereabouts. Everyone knew how much Aminah loved holidays and family gatherings. But Fame had no answers for them. Neither did Lang. Nor did Miss Lenora.

At the pumpkin table Sean sat next to Amir. Diagonally across from him, Lang sat next to Alia. Sean hadn't uttered as much as a syllable in Lang's direction since they'd arrived, yet no one noticed except, well, Lang. Aminah's absence overshadowed everything. Somehow Fame managed to bless the food, his family, his friends, and his wife, who regrettably couldn't be there. Amen.

Chapter 20

". . . it was so much easier for me to blame the other women because I didn't want to vilify my husband."

*A*minah probably would've slept well past three if it hadn't been for the incessant ringing of her cell phone.

Black Friday found her slumbering through all the early-bird shopping specials. Regardless, Aminah had crossed the last item off her Christmas gift list before the first trick-or-treater had ever buzzed the intercom at her security gate. The only exception this year was Fame's Aire Traveler watch, but receiving his gift hand-delivered from the designer himself was well worth the delay. Though, at this point, Aminah wasn't sure what she was doing with that opulent timepiece. Fame certainly wasn't worthy of it.

She glanced at the caller ID through a half-opened eye.

"Sean?" she answered groggily.

"Hey, gorgeous. You said oneish, so . . ."

"What time is it?" she asked after clearing her throat.

"One-oh-five. I've been redialing your number for the past five minutes straight. You okay over there? I was getting worried."

"Yeah, yeah, I'm fine," Aminah yawned. "Are *you* okay?"

Sean swallowed the lump in his throat. "Uh, nah, not really,

Minah," he admitted. "I think I'm losin' it. Listen, you still wanna grab something to eat? I really need to talk to you. Like, sooner than later."

"Oh, man, Sean, I haven't showered or anything," Aminah revealed, sitting up in the plush bed. She pointed and flexed her toes underneath the soft Egyptian cotton sateen sheets. "You mind coming to the hotel? I'll order room service," she said, swinging her legs over the side of the bed.

"Bet, but don't bother getting me anything. I'm not hungry."

Aminah requested housekeeping to straighten up while she showered, but not before ordering a baby spinach salad with shaved Bosc pears along with the roasted red snapper. She ordered Sean a pot of tea, ginger ale, and the brick-pressed marinated chicken just in case he changed his mind.

As Aminah faced the full blast of hot water from the shower-head and lathered in the Bulgari shower gel, she wondered if her best friend had lied to her about ending her thing with Dante. Lang had been so confident—cocky, in fact—about Sean never finding out, and now here she was about to defend or deny her best friend's affair she had so vehemently and personally deplored.

Great, Aminah thought as she toweled off. *I don't have room in my head or my life for guilt. I won't do it. I'll listen, but I won't lie. Don't need that kind of negative energy circling or hindering me. Nope, not gon' be able to do it.*

Once Sean arrived at the hotel room, they started talking about the dinner the night before and laughed about Amir, Alia, and the pumpkin table.

"All things considered, I have to admit your boy, Fame, han-

dled Thanksgiving dinner pretty damn well," Sean confessed between sips of peppermint tea. The chicken might as well have been
the second runner-up in a beauty pageant.

"Good. Glad to hear it," Aminah said after savoring her pinot
grigio. "I wouldn't've wanted it any other way."

Sean watched Aminah push the yellow corn sauce and red
snapper onto her fork as he wrestled with the sequence of images
replaying in his head. Since last Saturday he'd mentally rewound,
paused, and fast-forwarded the images—so fast that sometimes
they got all distorted, challenging him to decipher which parts he'd
imagined and which had actually occurred. Most times he turned
down the volume till he got to the part where she said she couldn't
wait to see him. He amplified *"CAN'T WAIT TO SEE YOU EI-
THER!"* in surround sound.

This might not just be phone sex, Sean reasoned or unreasoned.
*Clearly, my wife is seeing him. And didn't she say something about
her pussy being his? Hadn't she even called him Daddy?* Sean let out
a soft grunt. It was his stomach again.

He got up from the table and walked over to the window, revealing an impressive view of Lady Liberty. She reminded him of
his wife. Tall. Proud. Alluring. A beacon to guide free men toward
her. . . .

"So tell me, Aminah, who is this dude?" Sean asked, turning
away from the suddenly disturbing view.

"What dude, Sean?" Aminah asked, swallowing a piece of her
tender fish a bit too fast. She coughed a few times and then gulped
down the rest of the pinot in her glass. "I'm not exactly sure what
you're talking about."

"Gorgeous, I know Langston is your absolute best friend in the whole wide world. But you know how much I love that woman. How long I've been waiting to start our family. How I've supported her career in spite of all that." Sean sat back down in his chair next to Aminah and put his face in his hands.

"And I mean, really, when you think about it," he said rubbing his temples, "I mean, really, really think about it, she's probably been using her fucking career as some kind of stalling tactic, some sort of shield to prevent her from giving me my baby, my family."

Aminah pulled Sean's hands down and held them. "Sean, honey, you're confusing me. I'm really trying to follow you. Is this about some dude or about Lang being ready to have children? Because just the other day she told me she was getting Merrick ready to—"

"Lies," Sean spat, releasing her hands. "She's lying, Aminah. The only thing Lang is getting ready to do is get herself killed," he said, pounding on the table, rattling the cold poultry on his plate.

"Okay Sean, calm down," Aminah said, getting up from her seat to rub his back. "First of all, where's all this coming from? Did Langston say something to you specifically about not wanting children or something?"

"She didn't have to, Aminah. She's fucking another man. She's not thinking about me and my kids. She's thinking about the next time she can fuck him. Can you believe that shit?"

How in the hell could Lang be so careless? Aminah wondered as she continued rubbing Sean's back. And exactly when did her best friend start lying to her? Aminah shook her head. She didn't even want to go there right now.

"So this is all speculation," Aminah asked, hoping that it was, believing that it wasn't.

"Fuck, no, this ain't speculation," Sean said, looking at Aminah sideways.

"So how do you know she's sleeping with someone else, Sean?"

"Not you, too, gorgeous?" he asked incredulously, shrugging her hand off his back. "Now *you* tryna play me?"

"No, Sean, not at all. I'm sorry, sweetie. I can't . . ." She paused to stop herself from lying. "I—I just don't want to believe all this."

Sean got up from the table, walked over to the window, glared at Lady Liberty, and then sat down on the couch. He wrung his hands together and reasoned that maybe, just maybe, because Lang had hidden the affair from him, perhaps she hadn't been so forthcoming with Aminah either. After all, Lang did share with him that she and Aminah hadn't been as close lately and that she really missed her.

"You know your girl's a freak, right?" Sean asked Aminah seemingly out of nowhere.

Aminah raised her left eyebrow and then nodded. She braced herself for a detailed description of Dante bending her best friend over in some ghetto Kama Sutra position she'd never even fathomed.

"And I don't have a problem with that," Sean continued. "I love it, in fact. So with my wife being a freak and all, I think nothing of it when I hear her moaning from behind our bedroom door. All I'm thinking is, 'Damn, Lang has got the most insatiable pussy on the planet,' but—"

"Wait," Aminah said, holding up her right hand. "I'm gonna need more wine." She brought both her glass and the bottle over to coffee table in front of the sofa. Sean watched anxiously as she poured another glass and then took a sip.

"Okay, continue."

"Yeah, so as I was saying, Lang's got this insatiable pussy, but that's okay because I put in work. She does tell you I put in work, right?"

Aminah smirked, nodded, and took another sip.

"So last Saturday I'm in such a rush to get to this basketball game that I forget my lucky sports watch. So I turn around to go get it, 'cause, you know, I'm just that superstitious. Anyway, I run up the stairs, get right outside our bedroom door, and I hear Lang moaning and masturbating like she's getting fucked, which, hey, if you know Lang is not surprising. But what is shocking for a man like me, who, you know, puts in work, is finding out that she's not alone in our bedroom."

Aminah spit out her pinot.

"You all right, Minah?" Sean asked, patting her on the back.

"Yeah, I'm fine," she said, wiping her mouth with the back of her hand. "What do you mean she wasn't alone in your bedroom?"

"She was on the phone with another man, Aminah," Sean said, shaking his head in disbelief. He nobly fought back tears. "Moaning for him on our bed. Rubbing my clit for him. Having *his* orgasm on *our* bed, Aminah. Fuck me for loving her!"

Sean dropped his head. It was as unforgettable for him as the day of their wedding. He wept.

It pained Aminah to see Sean agonizing so. She wondered if Fame was hurting. She had hoped he was, though not like this. Tiny pin pricks to his heart? Yes. Tortured mental anguish? Well, no, not quite.

"You're not wrong for loving your wife," Aminah said, wiping his face.

"No? Then why do I feel so stupid?" Sean asked, his voice cracking. "Why do I feel like the last four years have not only been a lie but a waste of my time, my life? Don't you know I coulda had children by now, Aminah? The family I've always wanted, waiting on Langston's ass. And what did all that patience and being a good husband get me, huh? My wife giving my pussy away over the phone."

"Wait, so he wasn't actually there with her in the bedroom?" Aminah clarified.

"Fuck, no, Aminah," Sean said, looking at her like she was certified. "Then you'd be visiting me in jail for a double homicide."

Aminah cleared her throat. "Sean, have you asked Langston about the phone sex?"

He hadn't. He couldn't. He needed information, facts, and ammunition when he confronted Langston. He knew she'd not only deny it, but she'd shred his accusations to ticker tape without physical proof, so he wanted to step to her with facts and reasons, not assumptions and emotions.

But that was only part of it. The first couple of days Sean had struggled, deciding if phone sex was enough of an indiscretion to threaten his marriage. It tore him apart knowing that someone else had gotten inside his wife's head. That she'd allowed another man into the most intimate part of herself, the space she knew he treasured most, and on top of all that, Sean truly believed they'd sexed.

"Aminah, do you know who this motherfucker is? Where she met him? How long they've been seeing each other?"

Aminah didn't know how to answer Sean without selling out Lang.

"You know, it was so much easier for me to blame the other

women because I didn't want to vilify my husband," Aminah explained. "Ultimately, though, I had to realize that my trust wasn't with them. My trust was in him. Those women didn't destroy my trust. Fame did that all by himself. You need to talk to Langston. It really has nothing to do with some guy."

Sean realized at that moment that even if Aminah knew everything, she wasn't going to violate her best friend's confidence. He respected that. And maybe she was right. She certainly had more experience in relationship turmoil than he did. She also had more tolerance for bullshit.

"I know what I gotta do," Sean said, kissing Aminah on her forehead and then brushing the side of her face with the back of his hand. "You are gorgeous, and Fame doesn't deserve you."

He kissed her forehead again. This time he held his cool lips to her warm forehead for a few seconds longer. Aminah closed her eyes and wrapped her arms around his waist. His warm body felt good to her. Sean, reluctant to release her, cupped Aminah's face in his hands before bringing it to his chest. Aminah could feel his heart racing. She placed her hand on his chest. He rested his chin on top of her head and let his hand slide from her waist to her hips to her ass.

"You okay?" she asked in a breathy voice.

"I—I should go," Sean stammered.

He stepped back and thanked Aminah for listening to him. Sean grabbed his peacoat, skully, and scarf off the back of the sofa and headed toward the door.

Aminah followed.

"Wait, Sean, where are you going? We're not done yet."

"Yeah, we are, gorgeous. You're not gonna tell me what I want to know, and I should've known better. You're loyal to her. She doesn't deserve you either. But it's cool. I know what I gotta do."

He kissed her lightly on the lips and then gently closed the door behind him. Aminah stood on the other side, hoping she hadn't betrayed the wrong friend. Praying she'd protected the one who most deserved it.

Chapter 21

*"What is the real point of confession? I think it's
over-rated and self-serving."*

As she mindlessly dodged a couple of familiar potholes on At-
lantic Avenue late Sunday morning, Lang tried to recall the last
time she'd seen Aminah. She'd thought it was two weeks ago when
she found her sleeping on Sean's lap in his entertainment room.
Lang had gotten home late that Friday night after a quickie with
Dante in the back of his Escalade.

I am too grown to be fuckin' in cars. Lang snickered at the memory as she pulled her car directly behind Aminah's.

Aminah had called her two nights ago to apologize for not
speaking to Lang earlier in the day and to reconfirm their Session
and brunch since she'd canceled their last one.

Aminah's intention had been to ask Fame to pass the phone to
Langston after she'd explained to him the reason she wouldn't be
home for Thanksgiving dinner. Instead she had hung up on her
husband before he could finish his lame-ass attempt at an apology,
splurged on four little two-ounce bottles of the insanely expensive
Hawaiian Kona Nigari water at thirty-three dollars a pop, and
soaked in a hot Bulgari bubble bath, forgetting all about wishing
Langston a Happy Turkey Day.

"I've missed you," Lang said, embracing Aminah at Pretty Inside. "You look good, girl. How you feeling?"

Aminah hesitated. While the intimate setting of Pretty Inside wasn't her ideal place to freely vent, she needed to break up the chunks of confusion taking up entirely too much space inside her head.

"I'm feeling kinda torn," Aminah finally said, pulling out of Lang's embrace and walking over to the rainbow wall of designer polishes.

"Really?" Lang asked, following behind her. "Haven't made up your mind yet, huh?"

"Not quite. No," Aminah admitted, comparing a deep metallic-plum polish to a saturated purple one. She wasn't feeling particularly pink these days.

"Life-changing decisions are never easy, sweetie," Lang said, choosing Nars's dark red Metropolis for both her hands and feet. "You know that."

"True," Aminah agreed, placing the purple polish back on the crowded shelf.

Lang and Aminah settled into their cushy seats at the nail stations, both adjusting their hibiscus-print pillows behind them as Natalie Cole sang "This Will Be (An Everlasting Love)" through the ceiling speakers above.

"What's the rush to make a decision anyway?" Lang asked as the manicurist placed her feet in the large porcelain bowl filled with warm water and fresh mint leaves. "You've only been away, what? Two weeks?"

"Because what I'm wrestling with *now* is very time-sensitive."

"*Now*?" Lang asked, confused. "Hold up, Aminah. You're not pregnant, are you?"

Aminah shook her head and chuckled at the irony of that question. There'd been no baby-making action in her bed lately. In fact, she was feeling sort of sexually emaciated. She hadn't had any in two weeks, and she was used to having it damn near every day and at least twice a day on the weekends.

"Well, then, what's so pressing?"

Aminah sipped the cold lemon water Erika had brought over. Denying indiscretions and protecting secrets had left Aminah very frustrated and slightly parched. She needed Lang to be receptive, not deflective, of the truth.

"Well, I'm torn because I had a visitor yesterday," Aminah said, choosing her words cautiously. "And he was in so much pain that he's thinking of walking away from his marriage to put himself out of his misery, and as much as I wanted to help him make a decision, I just couldn't."

"A visitor? Oh, please," Lang said dismissively as the manicurist massaged her right foot. "What's with the cryptic shit, Minah? Fame has a lot of nerve talking about walking away from something. If anybody should be leaving somebody, that body should be you. Hmph. You didn't fall for that bullshit, Aminah, did you?" Lang continued ranting. "Fame is just frontin'. We had dinner. He just wants you back and is trying to pull some sort of ultimatum tactic. He told me. You should have seen your husband's pathetic ass at Thanksgiving. Pumpkins on the table. Flowers on the floor—"

"That *body* is your husband, not mine, damnit!" Aminah snapped, raising her voice, startling both manicurists and stunning Lang.

For a moment, Natalie Cole was the only one saying anything. *"Huggin' and squeezin' and kissin' and pleasin' together forever through rain or whatever . . ."*

"Ladies, I've got a nice red wine in the back," Erika said with a forced smile and stern, reprimanding stare. She had "you two know so much better" written all up in her stance. Erika Kirkland promised her patrons a pleasing pampering experience in a serene setting, hence the ginger-lei-scented Er'go candles and the no-cell-phone policy. "I'll be back in two seconds with a nice *full* glass for each of you."

As they sipped on their Bordeaux, Lang reluctantly agreed to finish their discussion outside of Pretty Inside. She didn't know what the hell Aminah was talking about, but every time she initiated conversation—demanding clarification—Aminah held up her hand and closed her eyes. She was embarrassed for causing a mini-scene and refused to indulge Lang. She needed some time to get recentered.

Why would Sean want out of our marriage? Lang wondered as she carefully slid her hands and feet under the nail driers. *And exactly when did he go see Aminah yesterday?*

Lang felt a tinge of guilt as she recalled leaving the house early yesterday to go for a run in Fort Greene Park. She'd showered at Dante's after her run. She'd sexed Dante after her shower. Not once had she given any thought to Sean's whereabouts. She'd gotten careless.

An hour and a half later Lang and Aminah pulled into a parking garage a couple blocks down from Bubby's in DUMBO. Lang had picked the waterfront eatery for its child-friendly atmosphere in case things got heated again. No argument of theirs could compete with the sounds of bored and hungry toddlers. Plus, the great view of Manhattan couldn't make Aminah's mood any worse.

On their quick, chilly walk to the restaurant, Lang expressed to Aminah that she found it hard to believe Sean would just want to divorce her out of nowhere. He'd given her no indication at all that anything was wrong. And on top of all that, she couldn't understand why he'd talk to Aminah about it instead of coming to his own wife.

"So let me get this straight," Lang said after ordering Bubby's popular sour-cream pancakes, "Sean came to visit you at your hotel yesterday and told you he wanted out of our marriage?"

"You said you were ending your affair with Dante. I knew you were lying."

"I wasn't lying. I just never said exactly when. And what does that have to do with Sean trying to leave me?"

"Everything," Aminah said, picking through the fresh bread in front of her, passing on the sourdough, selecting the pumpernickel. "Play with semantics all you want, Langston, but don't play with your husband's life."

Lang had a sudden epiphany. "Oh, my God, you told him."

Aminah rolled her eyes and finished off her mimosa. "No, Langston, you and your arrogant ass, swearing you'd never get caught, gloating about the fact that you were so much slicker, when really you're just more deceptive than Fame. *You. Your* sorry ass told him."

"Whatever, Aminah. Save the theatrics. I can't believe you'd use your own relationship problems as an excuse to blow up my spot. So much for loyalty."

"Fuck you, Langston," Aminah said, ignoring the Peasant French Toast the waiter had just placed in front of her and then standing up suddenly to leave. "And to think I protected you and your lies instead of telling Sean what he wanted and deserved to know. Your husband came crying to *me*. Not you. And *I* was there to comfort him—"

"Well, why the hell would he need comforting if you didn't tell him anything?"

"Because he heard you having phone sex, you dumbass!" Aminah yelled, causing the diners at nearby tables, including the bored and hungry toddlers, to turn around and stare. "Langston Neale Rogers," Aminah said, lowering her voice and leaning across the table, "your husband watched you finger fuck yourself last Saturday on the phone with another man on top of the same bed he makes love to you on. He listened to you tell Dante you couldn't wait to see him. *You* told him everything. I told him nothing."

For the second time that day, Lang was silenced.

Aminah glared down at her. She was done. Done with Langston. Done with other people's problems. Done.

"You got the bill, right?" Aminah asked, putting on her coat.

"Don't go," Lang said weakly. "I'm sorry, Aminah."

"Yeah, you are."

"Okay, I deserved that."

"It's the truth."

"Sit down, Minah, please," Lang begged pathetically.

Aminah stood for a few more seconds and shook her head before reluctantly sitting back down. She rubbed her temples over her lukewarm French toast. "Come clean, Langston. Sean's in agony, and you're responsible for putting him there."

"That wasn't my intention."

"Your intention, Lang?" Aminah asked incredulously. "Unbelievable. I am so pissed off that you've got me in the middle of your mess when I'm dealing with my own damn marriage. And that's all you can say. I'm outta here."

"I'm sorry, Minah," Lang said, grabbing Aminah's wrist.

"Stop apologizing and repair what you've done, Lang," Aminah said before the waiter interrupted to ask if they needed anything else. Aminah requested the check.

Lang didn't know how Aminah expected her to fix this. She needed time to think. Clearly, her best friend wasn't the right person to talk to. She saw confession as the only solution. Lang wondered if Dante would make a good listener.

"Well, if he already knows, what would be the purpose of me admitting to anything?" Lang questioned. "I mean, really, Minah, think about it. What is the real point of confession? I think it's over-rated and self-serving. What purpose does it serve? To rid yourself of some guilt and in the process inflict pain on someone you love? That's selfish. Why would I voluntarily do that?"

"You're unreal," Aminah said, standing back up.

"And phone sex isn't even a good enough reason to throw away a marriage after four whole years," Lang said, quickly signing the receipt.

Aminah walked away.

Lang grabbed her jacket and followed.

"You're not just guilty of phone sex, Langston," Aminah said, glancing back at her as she exited the restaurant.

"But the phone sex is all he knows about, right?"

"Yes, as far as I know," Aminah said, power walking back to the garage.

"Listen, Aminah—"

"No, I am done listening, Lang," Aminah said, stopping abruptly.

"You wanna throw your marriage away over some pubescent sex? Go right ahead. But I guarantee you, Lang, if you don't tell Sean the truth now, your marriage is really over. You betrayed your husband. He knows it. I know it. And you did it."

"But why would I admit to anything, Minah?" Lang asked, pacing the sidewalk. "He's known for, what, two weeks now and hasn't said a word? I can't see myself doing that."

"Because it's the right thing to do," Aminah said, exasperated. "Admit you're wrong, beg for forgiveness, and work this out."

"Forgiveness for phone sex?"

"No, forgiveness for cheating on your husband."

"Is that really cheating?" Lang questioned, quickening her pace to keep up with Aminah. "I mean, if that's all he knows, I'm not copping to that. He's just gonna have to confront me or get over it. Maybe he's pretending it didn't happen."

"Sean knows it's not just phone sex, Lang," Aminah said right before handing the valet her parking ticket. "He heard everything you said to Dante that day. You're not listening to me."

Lang was listening, she just wasn't accepting. She was more than willing to give up Dante. She'd miss the hot sex, his youthful energy, his unpredictably and spontaneity, sure, but all that was minor compared to losing the man she believed was her soul mate. She refused to let him just dispose of their marriage like some cheap BIC razor.

"I won't do it, Minah," Lang said defiantly. "I'll give up Dante, but I won't confront Sean. If he hasn't said anything by now, maybe he's just dealing with it."

"Fine," Aminah said, climbing into her truck. "Live your life, girl."

Lang watched as Aminah drove off, figuring she was probably going back to the hotel to drink some more designer water and soak in another fragrant bubble bath. Lang wasn't ready to go home yet either. She told the valet to keep her car a little while longer.

Lang thought about Sean's moods and actions over the last few days on her cold, brisk walk through DUMBO. *On Thanksgiving, Sean's stomach was still acting up,* she recalled. *And he made a big deal about being able to keep his word. I didn't know what the hell he was getting at.*

Lang remembered cleaning on Saturday without Sean, figuring maybe he'd had an early game or something. Saturday night she'd tried to make love to him, but he wasn't in the mood. Said he was too tired. She assumed it was his stomach and suggested he see his doctor. He'd said it was fine and that in fact his appetite was on the rebound.

Don't worry, Sean, Lang thought as Dante buzzed her into his building. *I'm gonna fix it. I just gotta do this my way, baby. Just hold tight.*

Lang exited Dante's private elevator. He'd keyed her up and rushed back over to his waiting sofa. The Philadelphia Eagles were putting a hurting on the New York Giants, and he didn't want to miss a single snap.

Lang unzipped her Etu Evans leather boots and propped them on the bamboo mat to the left of the elevator. She slid off her trouser socks and removed the plastic Saran Wrap she'd asked the manicurist to put on for extra anti-smudge protection.

"D, my husband knows about us," Lang said, collapsing into Dante's chest.

"Word, how?" Dante asked, rubbing Lang's back as she lay between his legs.

"He overheard me talking to you on the phone."

"When?" Dante asked, sitting up.

"Last Saturday. I was masturbating in our bedroom with you on the phone, and apparently, he just stood there listening and watching."

"Oh, yeah, you were extra nasty that day," Dante recalled, smiling.

Lang pinched Dante's arm.

"Ow. Damn. Sorry, Lang. That's fucked up. I know I wouldn't ever wanna be him. Wait, so he's just now confronting you with all this?"

"No, Aminah just did," Lang said meekly. "He told her everything. I don't really understand why he hasn't said anything to me yet."

Dante wasn't used to seeing Lang unsure of herself, so vulnerable, and while he hadn't treated her with much tenderness, still, he was no cad.

"She wants me to confess, come clean, and ask him to forgive me, but that just doesn't make sense to me."

"Then don't do it."

"But I'm not really sure what to do."

"Well, I don't know either, but, man, if you were my wife . . ."

"But I am *not* your wife."

"You got that right," Dante said smugly. "'Cause if you were, you damn sure wouldn't be at another man's house giving him head while I'm home making a nice meal for you, playing the perfect husband. It's not only humiliating—shit's emasculating. A real man would know how to keep his horny wife home and satisfied."

"You know nothing about me or my husband."

"I know he's not enough man for you."

"Fuck you, Dante."

"You already have, sweetheart. That's exactly why you're in the mess you're in."

Lang slapped Dante across his face.

Dante smirked and rubbed the side of his cheek. He flicked off the television. The Giants lost.

"Your shit's all fucked up, so I'm gonna let that slide. But your husband is too pedestrian for you, Langston. He's not imaginative enough for you, and you're not comfortable revealing all sides of yourself to him. Your marriage is a lie, and what you have with me is real, if nothing else. I know it, and you know it. It's over. Trust me."

Lang left Dante's loft furious. *How dare he,* she fumed, walking back to the garage. *Judge my husband and our marriage. He doesn't know shit about who we are and what we have.*

On her drive home it dawned on Lang that Dante's haughty, preconceived notions about her husband and their marriage were probably based on her representation of their relationship. He'd witnessed Lang lie to Sean about her whereabouts over the phone while he was still inside her.

Langston sat in front her brownstone prepping her defense. *Deny. Deny. Deny. That's my new mantra,* Lang thought as she walked through the front door.

She was surprised to find Sean eating a full plate of fried chicken, collard greens, candied yams, black-eyed peas, and cornbread while reading *The New York Times Magazine* at their kitchen table. Soul-food Sundays. Sean insisted on having them. He'd grown up on them.

"How was brunch?" Sean asked between bites of crispy chicken.

"It was cool," Lang said, moving in to kiss Sean's lips. He turned his head.

"Damn, babe, you see I'm eating. How's Aminah doing?"

"She's fine," Lang replied suspiciously. "I see your stomach's better."

"Oh, yeah, appetite's back and in full effect," he said, patting his full yet ripped stomach. "I feel like a new man."

"A new man, huh?"

"Yup. A new and improved Sean."

Langston peaked inside the pots and pans Sean had left on the stove. Everything looked delicious. Smelled even better.

I don't want to give all this up, Lang thought as she nibbled on a piece of cornbread. *I'd be a fool to trade certainty for unpredictability.*

"No need to pick," Sean said without turning around to face his wife. "You know I made you a plate. It's in the fridge where it always is."

Chapter 22

"... instincts don't lie."

As she crept past all the double-parked cars lined up two-by-two like kindergarteners holding hands on a school trip, Aminah cursed the little New York City gnomes responsible for alternate-side-of-the-street parking. While the opposite side of the street was completely void of cars, antiquated parking rules forbade her to park over there for another two hours.

Nearly a month had passed since Miss Lenora had suggested her daughter make an appointment with Dorian at G's Urban Hairstyles. He was the premier hairstylist at the Aveda concept salon, Brooklyn's own Louis Vuitton Don and Aminah's mane keeper for the last five years.

After Aminah fed a meter on Flatbush Avenue, she glanced at her watch and smiled to herself. She quickly crossed over the street and strolled into G's, relieved that she was at least still eleven minutes early.

Aminah was Dorian's first client the morning before Christmas Eve, though he didn't strut in till twenty minutes after she did, sporting a short, curly mohawk, a Louis man bag, belt, watch, sunglasses, and neck-to-ankle fitted black Prada. After carefully hanging up his *"fripperies,"* he beckoned Aminah to his chair.

"Where have you been, girl?" Dorian asked, loosening her thick ponytail. "You know better than to stay away from me this long."

"I only missed a couple appointments," Aminah replied lamely, knowing she'd stood Dorian up for the last six or seven Friday mornings. "Needed time to hibernate."

"Mmmm-hmmmm. No excuse," Dorian reprimanded.

"But, I . . ."

"And please tell me you're not *really* tryna leave Fame, girl. Say it ain't so, girl. Say it ain't so!"

Aminah laughed hysterically. God, she missed Dorian. She wasn't the least bit surprised that he and the rest of the trendy salon were well informed of her separation from Fame.

"Well, I'll tell you this," Aminah said.

"Do tell."

"I've made my decision."

"Uh-huh."

"And while I love you like a sister, Dorian . . ."

"This I know."

"Fame deserves to hear it first."

The front of the salon seemed to let out a collective sigh as Aminah smiled to herself. Dorian reluctantly agreed to respect her wishes after futile attempts at prying for hints while he touched up, washed, conditioned, and trimmed Aminah's locks. An hour later he slicked on Aveda's finishing gloss, preparing to pull her hair back in her signature sleek ponytail.

"I want my hair down," Aminah said, stopping Dorian mid brushstroke.

"Excuse you?"

"You heard me, Dorian. I want some curls, some layers, something sexy, something fresh."

"Well, all right, Miss Minah," Dorian said, clapping his hands excitedly. "It'll be a minute though. I didn't exactly schedule you for an extreme makeover."

"Whoa, whoa, whoa, no one said anything about a makeover," Aminah said, holding up her left hand still bearing her emerald-cut wedding ring. "And extreme . . . ?"

"Oh, just stop it, Mrs. Pretty Famous. Lemme just get my next client prepped, and I will hook you up something fierce."

Aminah mindlessly flipped through *Essence, Sophisticate's Black Hair, Redbook,* and *Cosmopolitan* as she waited for Dorian. She returned a couple e-mails on her Sidekick and checked her voice mail. Miss Lenora had left a message firmly stating that she expected to see her grandchildren at her Kwanzaa celebration next week with or without their father.

"Yeah, so, I really admire my client," Dorian said as he sliced into Aminah's hair with his thousand-dollar sapphire titanium shears.

Aminah kept her eyes shut.

"She's paying her own way through Barnard by dancing on the side."

"By on-the-side dancing, you mean stripping?" Aminah asked, refusing to acknowledge the hair piling up in her lap.

Dorian laughed. "Well, yes, she is an *exotic* dancer, but a real bright girl, Aminah. Four-point-oh student. Determined. You'd never know she danced. Rocks conservative gear. Performs exclusively for high-profile clients. Like, just the other night she did Imon Alstar's bachelor party, and he handpicked her to service him."

Aminah had completely forgotten about Rebekkah's New Year's Eve wedding to Imon. She wondered if Fame had even bothered to RSVP, not that she'd planned on attending.

"You can open your eyes, Aminah."

She refused.

"Don't worry, honey, this ain't *Waiting to Exhale*. You're no Angela Bassett, and I'm definitely not Loretta Devine," Dorian said, putting down his straightedge and picking up his shears to create a dramatic, sweeping bang.

"So, by service, you mean a private dance?"

Dorian chuckled. "No, hon, service meaning performing a job, if you know what I mean. Think blow, not hand. And let's just say they know each very well now, in the biblical sense."

"Isn't his wedding next week?" Aminah asked, peering through her long, slanted bang.

"Yup, she only did his bachelor party. So technically, he didn't break any vows. I mean, really, what's a boy to do anyway?"

Aminah didn't answer. She shut her eyes and contemplated calling Rebekkah, though they hadn't spoken in a couple months.

"Now, Aminah, honey, I'm just giving you some shape so your hair sashays like Sting and The Police with every step you take and every breath you take. Okay, you've still got most of your length, baby girl. Now open your eyes again."

Aminah loved it. She shook her head from side to side, admiring the layered movement. She stood up to hug Dorian. Customers in nearby chairs nodded approvingly.

"Hold the applause," Dorian said, taking a bow. "I'm not done yet. If it looks this good bone straight, imagine what it's gonna look like once I'm done curling the hell out of it."

As Dorian magically maneuvered his flatiron like a curling iron, Aminah questioned whether it was even her place to tell the bride a week before her wedding that her fiancé had indulged in a tryst. Besides, homegirl had insulted her marriage to Fame. Still, she felt this nagging sense of obligation. Perhaps because the last couple times they'd spoken, their main topic of conversation had been trust and mistrust, loyalty and disloyalty.

Aminah felt as incredible as she looked. She had flips that rivaled Farrah's and layers Mary would envy. She doubled Dorian's usual tip and called Rebekkah on her walk to her car.

Rebekkah was genuinely happy to hear from Aminah and readily agreed to meet Aminah to "catchup."

Aminah was delighted to find Rebekkah already seated with a wooden tray of appetizers, a glass of wine, and a tall bottle of Voss water in the cozy lounge area of the modish bistro. Rebekkah embraced Aminah fully, complimented her hair, and insisted she try the delicious spring rolls.

"I was so happy to hear from you," Rebekkah said, smiling. "How have you been?"

"Really, really good. You?"

"I've been marvelous," Rebekkah beamed. "After we last spoke, I decided to release all my fears and love like I've never been hurt, as that saying goes. I'm still a little nervous about the wedding, but that's to be expected."

Aminah nodded in agreement. On the drive over, she had wrestled with her decision to tell or not to tell. She still hadn't resolved if Rebekkah's very personal matters were really any of her business.

"I'm just going on and on about my wedding—how are you and Fame doing?" Rebekkah asked, touching Aminah's thigh. "I've been hearing all these nasty rumors about you two splitting up."

"Yeah, rumors seem to follow our marriage," Aminah responded casually, flipping back her new do. "I can't really change that."

"I take my hat off to you, Aminah," Rebekkah said after finishing off her second glass of wine. "How you stand by your husband. I admire that. I really do."

"Well, you're about to get married and make that commitment for better or for worse, right?" Aminah questioned as the waitress refilled her water glass.

"Yeah, we're writing our own vows."

"Really?" Aminah asked, raising her eyebrow.

"I confronted Imon about the whole infidelity thing. He said it was time for him to settle down, and he'd had enough of empty sexual relationships, and that was all I needed."

"His word?"

"Yup, it's enough for me. I'm happy. He's happy. My son's happy."

Great, Aminah thought, nibbling on another spring roll. *How do I? Do I even . . . ?*

"I would be devastated if Imon cheated on me, on us," Rebekkah admitted, interrupting Aminah's cross-examination of herself.

Rebbekah had opened up the lane for Aminah to ask her—hypothetically, of course—if she'd consider working things out if she found out Imon had cheated. She emphasized to Rebekkah that it wasn't only her feelings but her son's well-being and stability to consider as well.

"No. Absolutely not," Rebekkah answered, firmly sitting her glass down.

"Let's say Imon were unfaithful before you even got married. Would you want to know?"

"Yes, of course."

"But would you still go through with it?"

Rebekkah paused. She picked up her wineglass and eyed Aminah suspiciously. "What are you getting at? If there's something you're trying to tell me, just say it."

While Aminah took no pleasure in revealing Imon's indiscretions, the irony of the situation hadn't escaped her. Rebekkah had all but called Aminah an idiot for staying married to Fame all these years, and now she had information that could potentially have Rebekkah looking rather foolish.

"Look, Rebekkah, I need to be honest with you. I overheard something about Imon."

"Overheard something?"

Aminah cleared her throat. "At the salon today someone was talking about Imon's bachelor party and how this exotic-dancer friend of theirs had worked it. And, well . . ."

Aminah struggled with the most tactful way to say *"Your future husband just got a blow job from a stripper."*

"Tell me, Aminah," Rebekkah demanded.

"Well, allegedly, she performed oral sex on him."

Rebekkah shook her head in disbelief. "He got head from a stripper before our wedding?"

"Well, that's not all. I mean, supposedly he had sex with her, too."

"Oh, my God," Rebekkah said, dropping her glass of wine. "We made love the morning of his bachelor party and, and every morning since."

A busboy rushed over to sweep up the shattered glass, but Rebekkah was oblivious to him. "I'm gonna be sick," she said, holding her stomach.

Aminah rubbed her back.

"You don't understand. I also gave him . . . Ugh, I'm gonna be sick."

Aminah gently wiped the beads of sweat forming on Rebekkah's forehead.

"My mouth was at the same place as some nasty stripper's!"

Before Aminah could utter another comforting word, Rebekkah threw up all over the polished ebony lacquer floors. She wiped her mouth with the back of her hand. "I need to get tested. I need some air. I need to get out of here."

"Okay, Rebekkah, slow down a minute. Just calm down."

Rebekkah's stomach tightened in continuous knots. She closed her eyes.

Aminah wetted a cloth napkin and wiped Rebekkah's mouth and hands.

"I'm sorry, Rebekkah, that I had to come to you with this. My conscience just wouldn't let me ignore what I heard without letting you know your instincts were right all along. You know if anybody understands what you're goin' through right now, it's me."

"For once I wish I were wrong," Rebekkah said, sniffling.

"I don't know how much good wishing does, sweetie, but I do know that instincts don't lie."

Aminah took Rebekkah to the bathroom and apologized again for being the bearer of bad news. She offered to drive Rebekkah home, but she insisted on walking.

By the time Aminah swiped the key to her hotel room later that evening, she'd received an e-mail blast on her Sidekick informing all the invited guests that the wedding of Imon Alstar and Rebekkah Morrison had been officially called off due to *unforeseen circumstances*.

Chapter 23

"What you whisper will be proclaimed from the roofs."

Sean woke up just after dawn on Christmas Eve, thankful that it was a Friday. He was anxious to get his holiday started. He had been even more anxious than his students to exit Boys and Girls High School yesterday afternoon. So much, in fact, he had stepped on one kid's foot rushing out the door.

"Yo, Mr. Rogers, watch the Timbs, son."

"My bad, Marcus, I'm rushin' home to wifey," Sean lied. "You know how it is?"

Marcus didn't but nodded his head anyway, thinking if his Shawna looked anything like that dime Mr. Rogers was married to, he'd fuck up fifty pairs of new Timberlands to get to her, too.

Usually, Sean slept late on Christmas Eve. He'd take the day off whether it was an official school holiday or not.

He and Langston typically spent December twenty-fifth house hopping, gift delivering, and food sampling. In direct contrast, the twenty-fourth was an all-day, indoor love fest reserved exclusively for the two of them.

On the afternoon of their very first Christmas Eve together,

Lang had stacked all her gifts on Sean's dining room table while he'd prepared Belgian waffles in the small kitchen of his co-op.

"What are you doing over there, Langston?" Sean had asked, topping the waffles with fresh strawberries and powdered sugar. "You know Christmas isn't till tomorrow, young lady."

"Oh, I don't wanna wait, Sean," Lang had whined, shaking a weighty box. "Let's open them today, please." They did and had every Christmas Eve thereafter.

Breaking tradition was never easy, but this year it simply couldn't be helped. Sean had promised himself peace and some solitude on Jesus' birthday.

He showered and dressed quickly as Lang slept soundly that Friday morning. Before loading up the BMW with gifts for his parents, Alia, and Amir, he slowly scanned their bedecked living room.

Lang loved trimming their home for the holiday season. A stunning arrangement of three dozen dark red calla lilies in a crystal Baccarat vase that Fame and Aminah had given them last year for their third wedding anniversary stood in the center of their coffee table. Fresh mistletoe and pepperberry sprays hung over the arches, cream poinsettias with gold-splashed leaves topped every other stair step, and a spicy blend of cinnamon and something citrusy faintly cologned the air. Sean could never figure out how Langston kept that scent perpetually lingering. He made a mental note to light the fireplace when he returned.

Sean picked up a present from Langston more out of instinct than out of curiosity. Whoever had said Christmas was for the kids never got good shit. Say what you wanted about Lang, but that girl had impeccable taste and gave as good as she got. Sean counted seven gifts from his wife. He'd gotten her only two this year.

On the drive down to his parents' in Moorestown, New Jersey, Sean thought about all the fun holidays he and Lang had shared together—all the laughter, good memories, all the joy. They outnumbered the bad (because really there was only one). A couple blemishes here and there, sure (but only one scar). Did it make sense to abandon all that? Today he'd confront his wife.

"You know, I wasn't expecting you till tomorrow," Sean's mother said an hour and a half later, placing a plate of salmon cakes, home fries, and scrambled eggs in front of him.

"I may still drive back down," Sean said, breaking off a piece of the hot, flaky salmon cake.

His mother immediately popped him with her dishcloth. "Boy, you know better than to partake without giving thanks first."

Sean rubbed his upper arm, said a quick grace, and shoveled a huge scoop of home fries into his mouth.

"And what do you mean *may* drive back down?" Mrs. Rogers asked indignantly.

"Aw, Ma, don't be offended," Sean said, one-arm hugging his mother around her waist. "I'm just switching things up this holiday, that's all. I'd rather do all my running around today and relax in my own home on Christmas. Makes more sense."

"Now hold on one minute. Is something going on between you and Langston?" Mrs. Rogers asked suspiciously.

"Ma, why would you ask me something like that?"

"Mmmm-hmmm. I knew it."

"Knew what?"

"Sean Sekou Rogers, you act like I didn't know you before you knew yourself. First of all, you show up here on Christmas Eve *without* your wife, and I'm not supposed to notice? And how many times have you told me, 'Do not disturb us on Christmas Eve? You can call us the twenty-third, and you'll see us on the twenty-fifth, but do not, I repeat, do not disturb us on Christmas Eve lock-down,'" Mrs. Rogers said, mocking her son.

"Don't even respond to that, son," Mr. Rogers said, strolling into their spacious country kitchen.

Sean stood up to embrace his father. He strongly favored him, not only in appearance, but in demeanor as well.

"Let the boy eat in peace," Mr. Rogers said, kissing his wife on the cheek and discreetly squeezing her rear end.

Mrs. Rogers swatted her husband's hand away. "Lee, you're not the least bit concerned that our son drives down from New York *alone* on Christmas Eve, the day of their festive love shut-in?"

Lee Rogers shook his head as he washed his hands at the kitchen sink. He joined his son at the table and waited for his plate.

"You look good, Sean."

"Thanks, Pops. I feel good too."

"Well, there you go, Leatrice," Mr. Rogers said to his wife. "Our one and only son looks and feels good—now, what better gift is there, huh?"

"Hmph," Mrs. Rogers uttered under her breath, placing a hot plate of food in front of her husband and then turning abruptly, walking toward the kitchen sink. "A grandchild or two—now that would make a great gift."

Sean ignored her last comment. He and his dad were having too much fun predicting the outcome of tomorrow night's game between the Lakers and the Heat to let his mother ruin it. Shaq and Kobe going head-to-head as opponents would make for an exciting game.

* * *

Sean outsang Donell Jones crossing over the Verrazano Bridge back into Brooklyn. He flowed easily to "U Know What's Up" and "Shorty (Got Her Eyes on Me)." He reflected on how much he'd enjoyed his father's company and his mother's meal. Actually, he'd enjoyed his time with her as well until she'd mumbled something about not having grandchildren.

Sean came from a pair of only children—he was the only child of two only children. Both his maternal and paternal grandparents came from extremely large families and had vowed to have small ones. In fact, Lee Rogers's mother had instilled so deeply in Lee that the rich got richer while the poor had babies that after Sean was born, he'd had a vasectomy.

While Leatrice Rogers didn't mind having just one child—it afforded a very nice life replete with plenty of vacations, weekend getaways, and a historic landmark home in one of the nation's top school districts for her only child—she did look forward to spoiling at least a couple of grandchildren. Her best friend's bumper sticker read: IF I'D KNOWN GRANDCHILDREN WERE GONNA BE THIS MUCH FUN, I WOULD'VE HAD THEM FIRST. Leatrice was envious.

Sean ejected Donell Jones and loaded Stevie Wonder. Felt like Donell had more insight into his wife's straying on "Where I Wanna Be," like he was justifying Lang cheating on him—*"She doesn't fully understand me. That I'd rather leave than to cheat."* He'd felt many things over the last few weeks; however, empathy wasn't one of them. "Superwoman (Where Were You When I Needed You)" echoed his mind state precisely: *"Very well, wish that you knew me too. Very well, and I think I can cope with everything going through your head."*

Sean drove through the monogrammed Anderson gates a little after one in the afternoon. It was still very strange for him to be greeted by Fame instead of Aminah.

"How's it going, man?" Sean asked Fame sincerely.

"Oh, you know how it's going," Fame said, patting him on the back.

Fame missed Aminah terribly. He'd spoken to her nightly. And while their conversations were more civil, he couldn't say they were necessarily more loving. The children had recently gotten his hopes up though. Both Alia and Amir had reassured him that their mother would be home for Christmas. It was only Christmas Eve, but still . . .

"Don't look so happy to see me, man," Sean joked.

"No offense, Sean, man, but you ain't my wife," Fame said, relieving him of his packages. "Hold up, whatchu doing out the house on Christmas Eve anyway?"

Sean laughed. "Damn, I just left my parents, and my mom asked me the same exact thing."

"And where's Lang?"

Sean laughed again.

Actually, Lang had been blowing up Sean's phone since ten o'clock that morning. He'd told her he had some errands to run and that he'd be home before five. Since Thanksgiving weekend, he'd been telling her everything and asking her nothing. Lang didn't protest, especially since last week had left her feeling like a victim of sodomy. She confronted a Sean who was somewhat criminal—physically hostile and emotionally vacant.

Last night had been the extreme opposite though. It was the first time they'd even cuddled since Sean's bout with that stomach virus last month. The tenderness of the moment had caught Lang off guard—Sean, too. Lang had attempted to straddle him, but he had gently slid her off him and held her through the night, inhaling her lavender-scented, smooth skin. She fell asleep appreciating the return of her husband.

Prior to that, there'd been no tender love-making in the Rogers' home. No sex whatsoever in their bed either—rough sex on the granite kitchen counter, the mahogany staircase, and bent over their espresso linen sofa, but not the bed. Lang had ruined the appeal of sex in bed; it was simply a resting place for Sean now.

While this new aggressive creature had initially excited the hell out of Lang—especially since she'd given up Dante—she found herself missing, longing even, for his gentle, naturally sensual self.

When Lang woke up Christmas Eve morning and discovered that Sean was already out of bed, she'd hoped to find him downstairs brewing coffee and preparing their traditional Christmas breakfast of homemade Belgian waffles topped with strawberries and confectioners' sugar. Instead she found a few gifts missing from under their tree. She no longer knew how to interpret Sean's actions. Hated that she even needed to. He'd used to be so transparent to her.

"Lang's at home," Sean finally replied. "Where are my godchildren?"

"They're wrapping gifts in front of the tree," Fame said, leading Sean toward the living room.

After conversing with Fame for a while and playing with Alia and Amir most of the afternoon, Sean mulled over exactly how he'd confront his wife on his drive home. He was firm on his decision though. Had been since that afternoon with Aminah up at the Ritz-Carlton. His emotions, however, were ping-ponging again. The only consistent feeling that afternoon was jealousy. He not only admired and desired what his parents had, he envied it. And even without Aminah, Fame had his children. He was jealous of him, too.

Lang was just finishing up dinner when Sean arrived a little before five. She'd made waffles.

"Merry Christmas, baby," Lang said, handing Sean a peppermint martini.

"Thanks."

"You hungry?"

"Not really. Maybe later. You go ahead and eat though."

"No. That's okay," Lang said, a bit disappointed. "I'd much rather open presents."

Sean placed his martini on the coffee table and tended to the logs in the fireplace as Lang went for the largest box as usual. He watched her tear off the wrapping paper.

"Oh, my God, Sean," Lang exclaimed. "Is this what I think it is?"

He'd gotten her the rare Kopi Luwak coffee beans. The few coffeehouses that occasionally served it charged somewhere in the range of fifty dollars a cup and two hundred dollars per pound.

The luwak, a cousin of the mongoose in southeast Asia, ate "coffee cherries" off the tree. The undigested coffee beans were manually retrieved from its feces, and supposedly the fermentation process in the luwak's digestive tract made for a distinctive, flavorful cup of coffee.

Yeah, Langston, Sean thought, squinting his eyes and nodding slightly. *I wanted you to have something really shitty.*

"Yummy. Do you know how hard this is to find? I can't wait to drink it."

"I knew you'd appreciate it," Sean said, smiling.

"Okay, you next," Lang said, handing Sean one of his boxes. Inside was a Burberry trench coat. He'd wanted one for as long as Lang could remember, but never could bring himself to spend a thousand dollars on a raincoat. Lang admired how distinctive her husband looked in it.

Lang picked up the Tiffany box and sat back down on the sofa to open it.

"Oh, Sean honey, these sterling-silver napkin rings are so nice," Lang said after pulling back the tissue paper. "Oooo, these aren't napkins inside the rings though," Lang said, smiling and pulling out the sheets of paper, expecting to read a travel itinerary to Anguilla or St. Barths. She'd been hinting to Sean all year long that it was time they returned to the Caribbean.

"There is nothing concealed that will not be disclosed, or hidden that will not be made known," Sean recited from the Gospel of Luke.

"Huh? Sean, baby, what'd you say?" Lang said, distracted by the rolled-up document.

"What you have said in the dark will be heard in the daylight, and what you have whispered in the ear in the inner rooms will be proclaimed from the roofs."

Lang unrolled the piece of paper. "A petition for divorce?" Lang asked, confused. "What in the hell . . . ?"

"I waited, Lang," Sean said calmly. "I waited to see if you were ever gonna tell me. Confess to me."

"Tell you what, Sean?"

"And even now you continue to insult me. I know about your

affair, Langston. Just tell me who he is, Lang. Somebody in the industry?"

"There's nobody else, Sean. I don't know what you think . . ."

Sean raised his arm, as if to slap Lang, but she stopped him.

"Are you crazy?" Lang asked, holding Sean's arm.

"Lying by omission is still lying." Sean's voice cracked. He blinked back the tears.

"I don't know what the fuck has gotten into you lately, but—"

"No, the question is *who* the fuck has gotten into you lately, Lang, huh?" Sean asked, grabbing her by the throat and lifting her off the couch.

"Sean!" Lang gagged as she feebly tried to claw his hands from around her neck.

"I swear to God I could kill you," he said just before releasing her.

Lang coughed.

"Was he worth it?"

Lang shook her head, sobbing hysterically. She couldn't believe what was happening.

"How long have you been seeing him?"

"Not long," Lang said between gasps. " I swear. It's over. I—I—I made a mistake."

"A mistake?" Sean laughed.

"I'm sorry, Sean. I'm so sorry. I can't lose you. You can't leave me. We can get through this."

"It's too late, Langston. You lost me the minute you opened yourself up to him."

Sean grabbed his new trench coat off the sofa. "I'll be back later tonight, and I want you out of this house, or as God is my witness, Langston, I swear I might actually kill you."

"Sean, please . . ."

"Merry fuckin' Christmas, Langston," Sean said and slammed the door.

Chapter 24

". . . plans are just that. . . . Plans."

$\mathcal{A}$minah woke up Christmas morning next to a snoring, puffy-eyed Langston. She'd never in her whole life witnessed any human being—colicky babies included—cry as much as Langston had the night before. Lang had sobbed over the phone all the way to the Ritz, on the parking ticket stub the valet had handed her in front of the luxury hotel, and on a shared elevator ride with a couple of nondescript European tourists.

She'd collapsed into Aminah's arms as soon as she'd opened the door and bawled some more on her shoulder.

Aminah never thought to utter an *I told you so*. Instead she carefully guided Langston over to the sofa and slowly undressed her.

Lang allowed her head to fall backward on the couch after Aminah had taken off her ski jacket. Her body lay limp as Aminah easily slid off her sneakers and socks, though she seemed to stiffen a bit as Aminah struggled to raise her hips and pull down her cashmere sweatpants and cotton thong.

Lang made no attempt to help Aminah pull the long-sleeved

thermal shirt over her head or her arms through the armholes. Aminah let out a soft grunt when she finally got the top completely off and wasn't the least bit surprised to find Lang's perky nipples saluting her braless.

Aminah thought that at that particular moment her usually strikingly attractive girlfriend—with her toned, naked brown body sort of slouched down on the coach with her head leaned all the way back and her legs spread somewhere between slight and wide—favored a chic model strung out on heroine.

Aminah shook her head in pity as she quickly slid out of her own bathrobe and filled the shower stall with blistering hot water. She adjusted the temperature to a notch above tepid before leading Lang into the makeshift, glass-enclosed sauna.

"Breathe," Aminah said as she stood naked holding up Lang under the steady stream of warm water. "You're holding your breath. I need you to release it. Let it out. Let it go, Lang."

Lang lifted her head to face the showerhead and let out the air she'd been unconsciously constricting. It wasn't exactly a deep, cleansing breath, but at least now she was aware of her breathing—sort of.

"You're gonna be okay," Aminah said before kissing Lang on the forehead and tenderly bathing her body.

Lang wailed as Aminah washed. She wanted to fold up into the fetal position in the corner of the stall, but Aminah wouldn't let her. "Let it out, baby," Aminah said. "Let it all out. You can cry all you want, Lang, but I won't let you fall."

Aminah toweled her dry.

Lang whimpered.

Aminah oiled her down, dressed her for bed, and forced her to sip chamomile tea.

Langston finally fell asleep with a headache worthy of ten Percocets. She made due with three extra-strength Advils.

In the morning Aminah felt Lang's forehead, worried that she'd cried herself sick the night before. She was cool. Relieved, Aminah jotted a quick note, asking Lang to call her when she woke up, along with instructions for her to order some herbal tea bags as well as cucumber slices and to alternate between the two to reduce the puffiness around her eyes. She hated to leave her all alone on Christmas, but, well, it was Christmas, and she wasn't denying her children for anyone.

Aminah belted her crimson blouson dress, admiring how the red satin ribbon accentuated her waistline while the V-neck did the same for her cleavage. She inspected her eyelashes for Great Lash Mascara clumps. None. Checked the edges of her lips for any excess M•A•C Lipgelée goo. Negative. She nodded approvingly at her reflection.

Before exiting the sumptuous suite that had served as her plush little safe haven, Aminah requested the concierge to send a bellhop for all her bags, the valet to bring around her Range Rover, informed the front desk that while she wouldn't be returning, her guest would be staying indefinitely, and prepaid Lang's room and incidentals for the week. The manager cordially applied the same generous discount they'd given Aminah for staying so long and being such a delightful guest.

Aminah smoothed Lang's hair out of her face and kissed her lovingly on the cheek before exiting the suite.

Inside her truck Aminah loaded the six CDs she'd purchased the day before—Anthony Hamilton's *Comin' from Where I'm From*, Usher's *Confessions*, Maxwell's *Urban Hang Suite*, Outkast's *Speakerboxxx/The Love Below* (though she only inserted

The Love Below), Maroon 5's *Songs About Jane,* and Kanye's *The College Dropout.* Her "Sisters of Strength" rotation—India, Mary, Faith, Lauryn (sometimes alternated with Norah), Kim, and Nina Simone—would always be fingertips away, but Aminah craved some masculine vulnerability.

She found no early morning Christmas traffic surprising her through the Battery Tunnel, nor down the streets of Brooklyn. She enjoyed her solitude on the road almost as much as Anthony Hamilton's soulful "Since I Seen't You." She ended her rousing "Charlene" duet with Mr. Hamilton right before pulling up to the Rogers' brownstone.

Aminah rang Sean's doorbell a little after seven AM, not the least bit concerned about awakening him. She'd taken care of that a few minutes ago after exiting the tunnel and informing him to expect her shortly.

He answered the door in a wife beater, baggy sweats, and a little bit of sleep in the corner of his right eye.

"Oh, my God, Sean!" Aminah screamed, startling him into full alertness.

"Quiet girl," Sean playfully reprimanded, pulling her through the front door. "You'll wake up the whole block."

Aminah rubbed Sean's head before he led her to the couch and offered her something to drink.

The eighteen-inch locs he'd been growing for the past ten years were no more. He'd trimmed them over the years when they'd gotten either too long or too heavy to play ball, but after coming home to an empty house last night he felt compelled to cut them completely off.

He believed his hair and his home held energy. So he'd burned sage in every room, grabbed his scissors and then his clippers, and rid his head and his universe of all the old forces, making way for some new, more positive ones.

"Yeah, I got rid of 'em late last night," he said, slowly dragging his hand across his wavy, low-cut Caesar. "The plan was to cut them off the day my first child was born, but, you know, plans are just that . . ." He paused. "Plans."

"I can't believe it," Aminah said, shaking her head. "You've got a nice-shaped noggin though."

They both laughed.

"You okay?" Aminah asked, concerned, touching his thigh.

"I'm maintaining, under the circumstances," Sean responded, placing his hand on top of hers. "But man, Aminah, I was so out of sorts, I think I might actually owe Lang an apology."

"I seriously doubt that," Aminah said. "But why would you even think so?"

"Well, without going into too much detail, those last few weeks I was so rough with her—sexually, I mean—that I didn't recognize myself."

"Now, Sean, we both know my girl is actually a bit of a masochist," Aminah said dismissively. "I wouldn't concern your pretty new head with that."

"No, this was different. I wasn't trying to please her or turn her on. I intentionally did my best to physically hurt her and make her feel the pain she caused me. She brought out the monster in me, Aminah. I did things to my wife I never thought I'd do," Sean admitted, shaking his head before lowering it.

Aminah was silent for a minute. While she certainly understood Sean's remorse, she wasn't convinced that Lang still hadn't managed to derive some sort of pleasure from her husband's attempt to inflict pain.

"You both did things you wish you hadn't," Aminah finally said, lifting his head. "What's done is done. Besides, you already cut your hair. And I'm sure you've burned sage in every room. You're starting fresh, right? How's it feel?"

"Feels good to have the place to myself. I know that much," Sean said, relieved that Aminah hadn't judged him.

"It doesn't feel strange at all? Being in this big house all by yourself?"

"Strange, no. Different, yes."

Aminah nodded.

"Listen, Aminah, about that kiss."

Aminah put her fingers up to Sean's mouth to silence him. He pulled them down, folded them, and kissed the back of her hand. She didn't want to talk about the kiss. She felt guilty enough just thinking about it. The kiss was special. The kiss felt good. Aminah shook her head.

"Aminah, sweet Aminah, I definitely owe you an apology."

"No, you don't."

"Yes, I do," Sean insisted. "I was vulnerable. You were vulnerable. And I acted on an attraction I've had for years. And we're both married—hell, you're my wife's, well, soon-to-be ex-wife's best friend—and for that I was wrong, and I apologize. I just don't get down like that."

"Apology accepted," Aminah said, smiling at Sean lovingly. "You don't have to be sorry though. You've got great lips."

"Oh, I didn't say I was sorry," Sean clarified, laughing. "I said I apologize. Big damn difference. So we cool?"

"Without a doubt," Aminah answered, giggling.

"Good. 'Cause I don't want any awkwardness between us. So what brings you out so early on Christmas morning anyway, young lady?"

"Well, my babies will be getting up soon, and I wouldn't miss spending this day with them for anything in the world."

Sean nodded and silently vowed to have a child of his own to spend the holidays with in the next couple years.

"So you came over to check on me first, huh?"

"Actually, I have a gift for you," Aminah said, reaching inside of her oversize leather Cavalli satchel and handing Sean an elegantly wrapped, palm-sized box.

"You know you shouldn't've gotten me anything," Sean said, tearing off the giftwrap immediately.

"Clearly." Aminah laughed. She studied his face, trying to discern his reaction.

"I know it's not your style, but I thought . . . I dunno." She paused. "I thought that maybe, right now more than anything, you could use some time."

"Nah, it's incredible," Sean said, admiring the diamond-encrusted red gold watch that was so obviously intended for Fame. "You sure you want me to have this?"

"Absolutely," Aminah said assuredly. She wasn't having the first thought of regret, never mind a second one.

"I don't know, gorgeous," Sean said, reluctant to remove the watch from its case. While it didn't feel quite right to accept a gift that was meant for another man, it didn't feel like the worst sin in the world to Sean either. He held the box, contemplating whether he should hand it back and just thank Aminah for the thought alone.

"Here, lemme get that for you," Aminah said, taking out the watch, ignoring Sean's hesitancy.

"Okay," Sean said, nodding his head as Aminah fastened the watch on his wrist. The rich red gold complemented his smooth, dark skin. "'Cause I'm changing some things about myself, gorgeous, and one of them is my style. So thank you. Really. This may be just what I need to set things off properly."

Aminah felt even more confident about giving away Fame's gift, particularly after seeing it on Sean. She treasured their unique relationship.

"You're going back to him, aren't you?" Sean asked, getting used to the weight of the watch on his wrist.

"I know you think he doesn't deserve me, but—"

"I know I said that a few weeks ago," Sean interrupted. "But seeing him yesterday with Alia and Amir and without you, it just didn't look right. Didn't feel right either. I can't front."

"Thank you," Aminah said, hugging Sean.

"For what?"

"For being you," she said before getting up from the couch and walking toward the door.

Sean thanked Aminah again for the watch. And as much as he wanted to know how much it had cost her, he resisted. While he definitely wouldn't wear it to school, especially after lecturing his students about delayed gratification and excessive spending all year long, he couldn't wait to show it off to his boys when they went out for New Year's Eve. It would be the first one he'd celebrate without Lang in over six years.

Aminah told Sean to call her if he needed anything, including company. He agreed but told her he needed time with himself more than anything else. They embraced each other lovingly yet platonically before Aminah headed home.

*   *   *

Aminah punched in the security code at her monogrammed gates a little before nine AM. It felt good driving up her winding driveway. She grinned at the Christmas décor. She'd given Fame the number of the holiday landscaping company that she'd hired every year, but he insisted on doing it himself.

He'd been spending more time at home since Aminah'd left and had actually enjoyed hanging up all the lights with Alia and Amir. They'd begged him to get the fifteen-foot-tall inflatable snow globe for the front lawn. The humongous, illuminated snowman with the white faux snow swirling all around tickled Aminah to tears. Clearly the children were having their way with their father, mostly because they were the closest he could get to his wife.

Aminah unlocked her front door and disarmed the security system. She panned the front foyer. Fame had remembered to call Daily Blossom. Lush red and deep burgundy floral arrangements filled the living room, dining room, and hallway. Roses, gloriosa lilies, and anthuriums were set about.

Aminah smiled, inhaling the wonderful scent of the fresh bay, eucalyptus, and chinaberry garlands. She blinked back tears.

Home.

She'd missed it.

Before his wife left him, Fame wouldn't have heard the DEA busting down his front door if he was sleeping. Since then, however, he'd slept much lighter and woke up earlier. He'd actually been staring down at Aminah coming up the driveway from her window seat in their bedroom. He'd observed her from the top of the staircase reaching for the mistletoe above the doorway and covering her mouth in awe of all the flowers.

Fame took one deliberate and quiet step at a time. He hadn't wanted to disturb Aminah's moment, but she'd heard him step off the bottom step and quickly spun around.

They both stood motionless for a few seconds.

Fame moved first.

He scooped Aminah up, cradling her head with one arm and wrapping the other tightly around her waist while burying his head into the crook of her neck. He shut his eyes and inhaled her scent. She caressed the back of his neck.

He wept.

They stood there holding each other for only a minute or two, though it felt more like an hour.

"God, I've missed you," Fame said, touching her new hairstyle. "You look breathtaking."

"You like it?" Aminah asked, wiping his face.

"I love it, Minah. You look beautiful, baby."

He finally released her. He scanned the foyer, walked along the edge of the living and dining room, and then opened the front door. "Where are your bags, baby?" Fame asked, concerned. "You're here to stay, right, Aminah?"

Aminah cleared her throat.

"Let's sit down," Aminah said, leading him into their living room. "We need to talk."

"Please, Minah, baby. I can't take it. As God is my witness, my heart can't take it."

"Wait a minute, Fame. Hear me out."

Fame sighed heavily and dropped his head in disbelief, shaking it from side to side.

"Look at me, Fame."

Fame kept his head low.

"I can't talk to you if don't look at me."

Fame shook his head again. He was emotionally spent. "Minah, baby, I think I've finally reached my breaking point." Fame's voice cracked. "I'm not sure I can take what you have to say, Minah. I've been really goin' through it. I can't. I'm tellin' you. I can't."

"You think I haven't been going through it, too, Fame?"

He finally looked up at his wife. As difficult as it was to look at her and not cry again, he swallowed a couple times, forcing back the tears. And as hard as it was not to physically drag her up the stairs and permanently lock her in their bedroom, he restrained himself.

"I can no longer be in a relationship, in a marriage, where I am blatantly disrespected and my feelings are disregarded," Aminah said, looking at her husband squarely. "I can no longer excuse and ignore unacceptable behavior from my spouse and my partner in life. I never, ever wanted . . ." She paused to keep her own emotions in check. "Never imagined raising my children without their father in the home. But . . ."

"Aminah. Baby, please don't . . ."

"No, Fame, I can't, and I won't. I am not the same woman, Fame. I am not the same wife. Hell, I'm not even the same mother. No one's needs, not yours, not even Alia's and Amir's, are coming before my own. And quite frankly, I don't know if you'll like the me I'm becoming, and so—"

"I'll like her," Fame interrupted, grabbing Aminah's face and kissing her. "I'll love her, I'll adore her, just don't leave me again, baby, please—"

"No, Fame, listen to me," Aminah said, taking his hands off her face and holding them in her own. "I am not staying—"

"Please don't leave me, Minah," Fame begged, getting down on his knees in front of her. "Please, baby."

He laid his head in her lap and wept again.

Aminah rubbed the back of his head. She blinked back tears.

"I am not staying in a marriage with a cheating husband. I deserve better."

She lifted his head off her lap.

"I can get better, Fame," she stated, staring him directly into his eyes. "Are you still a cheating husband, Aaron 'Famous' Anderson?"

Fame kissed Aminah softly on her lips.

"I love you, Minah," he said, grabbing her face. "You're the only woman I've ever loved, and I want you to know that, to really know that, to feel that."

Aminah looked away, but Fame turned her head to face him again. He held her chin.

"I hate myself for jeopardizing what I value most. You. Us. Our family. I hate that I'm responsible for you not feeling completely secure in our marriage. But as God is my witness, Minah, I promise, if you give me another chance, I'll make it up to you. Please forgive me, baby."

She looked away again. He turned her toward him again.

"And, no, I'm not *still* a cheating husband. I'm your dedicated husband committed to making you unbelievably happy. Come back to me, Aminah. Please, baby, please come back to me."

A tear slid down her cheek. He kissed it away. He kissed her neck, her chin, and then her forehead.

"I came home to stay," Aminah finally said.

Fame lifted Aminah off the couch and spun her around. Aminah giggled and screamed, pleading with Fame to put her down. He finally did and asked Aminah where all her bags were if she'd planned on staying all along.

"In the Range, babe," she said, smiling. "I just needed you to carry them in."

Alia and Amir woke up twenty minutes later, pleasantly yet awkwardly surprised to find their mother smoothing down the front of her red dress and their father straightening out the waistband of his sweatpants in front of the Christmas tree.

"Mommy's home!" Amir yelled, running into her arms. "Told you, Daddy."

"You sure did, 'Mir."

"Mommy!" Alia yelled, joining in for a group hug.

Fame broke out the DVD camcorder to film Aminah and the children opening up all their presents. Aminah told Fame she'd gotten him something months ago but changed her mind about giving it to him. He didn't care. Her return home had been the only gift he'd desired and prayed for.

After making breakfast for the family, Fame told Alia and Amir to keep themselves occupied for the next hour or two with their new iPods, video games, clothes, and books while he made up for some lost time with their mother.

Fame swept Aminah up in his arms and carried her up to their bedroom. She playfully squirmed in a weak protest. He'd wanted her to hear this classic Angela Bofill song he'd fallen asleep to practically every night since she'd left him.

Fame gently placed his wife down on their twelve-foot-wide, ten-foot-long, pillow-topped bed and then cued up "This Time

I'll Be Sweeter." He sang softly in Aminah's ear while the late, great Ms. Bofill sang sweetly above from the ceiling speakers.

Fame lifted Aminah's dress above her head.

Darling, can't you see what losing you has done to me.

He slid off her bra and panties.

He pulled her up to stand naked in front of him as he blindfolded her with her satin belt and then lightly fingered her from the top of her scalp to the tips of her toes.

He slowly ran his warm tongue from the back of her knees to the nape of her neck.

Aminah removed her blindfold and then her husband's clothes.

I won't mess around. I won't let you down.

They made love, slowly and tenderly. It took all of Fame's stamina and willpower not to come inside his wife as soon as he entered her. He hadn't gone that long without sex since he'd started having it, not counting the quickie they'd just had right before their children had awakened.

Aminah's body convulsed. She relaxed her thighs' tight grip from around Fame's waist as he moaned in satisfaction, finally releasing himself inside his wife.

Chapter 25

*"There is in fact a cheating curve, rules of fidelity that
we bend depending on the caliber of the man, how much
we have vested, and, quite frankly, exactly how much
bullshit we're willing to put up with. . . ."*

"I gotta get him back, Aminah."

"Really? And in whose best interest would that be? Yours or his?"

"Would you like the same color on your feet?" the manicurist asked Aminah before Lang answered her.

"Ours," Lang stated with the resolution of a chubby chick on her first day at Jenny Craig.

The ladies were enjoying their first Sessions of the year at Pretty Inside. It'd been a little over a week since Aminah had left a broken-hearted Lang snoring at the Ritz. They'd spoken daily, and Aminah knew headstrong Lang would rebound quickly, just not this quickly. In fact, it was actually Lang who had insisted they keep their biweekly appointment at Pretty Inside when Aminah'd offered to cancel it.

"I don't lose," Lang continued. "I win. I'm a winner. You went back to Fame. I can go back to Sean. You took Fame back. Sean can take me back."

Aminah shook her head in disbelief as Erika refilled their flutes with Lang's favorite champagne. She was hosting her New Year's pamper celebration for her favorite clients.

"It's different, Lang," Aminah said, admiring the cotton-candy color on her fingers and toes. She was feeling pink again. "Different situations. Different people. Besides, you should be focusing more on you, not him."

"Yeah, right," Lang responded, twisting her mouth in complete disagreement. "That's exactly the kind of thinking that got me into this situation."

Lang had awakened Christmas afternoon headache-free, mind clear. One night of torrential wailing was more than enough for her. Crying simply wasn't her style.

She had listened to all the new messages on her cell phone before making her way to the bathroom. Most of the calls had been holiday wishes from friends and family, including Aminah and the Anderson clan. Four were from her mother—"Where are you?" "Please call me." "I'm worried." "Sean told me." None were from him though.

Lang had reached toward the mirror above the bathroom sink and outlined her face, marveling a bit at the new shape and texture of her eyelids. She had favored a one-round Mike Tyson opponent circa 1988. She'd gently caressed her face with both hands the same sort of way models do in those facial cleanser commercials. She massaged her temples before carefully stroking her eyelids.

"This is not you, Langston Neale Rogers," she said to her reflection. "I don't know who this is staring back at me, but it's not you."

Lang applied warm compresses to her face, ordered the tea bags and cucumbers per Aminah's instructions, and then called her mother to let her know she was staying at the Ritz and to reassure her that she was okay—not fine, but okay.

Mrs. Burgess had begged Lang to come home. "You don't owe me an explanation, though I mean, of course, I'd like one."

Lang didn't want to be around family, hers or anyone else's. And she especially didn't want to talk about Sean and her marriage or lack thereof.

"You know your sister and the twins flew in from California," Mrs. Burgess continued. "It'd be a shame if—"

"How long are they here?" Lang interrupted. She'd forgotten her big sis was in town.

"Their flight leaves early in the morning on the thirty-first. I think she and Keith are flying to Vegas for some New Year's Eve party, and the kids are goin'—"

"Excellent," Lang interrupted again. "So I'll see them way before they leave. In fact, I'll take the twins ice-skating in Rockefeller Center—no, Prospect Park, maybe—um, tomorrow. And I'll get my hands on some front-row seats to *A Raisin in the Sun* for all of us. You'll love Phylicia Rashad, Mom. Diddy's actually pretty good, too. Sanaa Lathan's impressive of course. We can all go. It'll be my family gift."

Her thoughts careened through her mind and tumbled out of her mouth with no sense of connection. Somehow she had to get them working together. Her head was making way too much noise. Running always helped. And Lang felt like running, but not inside some fancy hotel gym either. Outside. By the water. She some needed air, the cold, crisp kind.

"Langston, you don't sound like yourself, honey. We're worried about you. Is what Sean said true? Are you really getting a divorce?"

Lang didn't answer right away.

"Langston."

"God, I hope not, Mom," Lang finally said as she slid on her sweats from the night before. She'd need to get the rest of her things. No, she'd send Aminah. At least she'd packed enough clothes to get her through the week.

"But what happened to make Sean—"

"I cheated on him, Mom," Lang whispered. Her voice cracked. She cleared her throat and laced up her sneakers.

Mrs. Burgess said nothing.

"And I got caught," Lang continued. "And I lied about it. And I got caught in the lie. And I can't face anyone today. Maybe tomorrow, but—"

"Come home, Langston," Mrs. Burgess interrupted. "Stop punishing yourself and come home."

Lang declined her mother's offer. She spoke to her sister, Cullen, who understood her need to be alone. She wished her brother-in-law and the twins a Merry Christmas and promised to join them all tomorrow for Kwanzaa brunch.

Then Lang ran—what felt like for her life—through Battery Park. The cold mist from the water stung her face, but no more than the tears had the night before. She felt alive. Her cheeks tingled. Her chest hurt. No, it was her heart. Her lungs were on fire, but at least she was breathing. And her head had finally stopped making so much noise.

Lang enjoyed breakfast with her family out in Hempstead the following morning. No one brought up Sean except her niece and nephew. They adored their uncle Sean. She apologized for disappointing them and explained that while he wouldn't be able to make it over to see them this visit, she'd make it up to them by taking them ice-skating.

Later Lang asked her mother and Cullen to join her in the kitchen to help with the dishes and to explain the breakup and the affair and the aftermath thus far.

Cullen rinsed the last dish, hugged her little sister, and told her everything would be okay. "You're strong, Langston. I know this won't break you, but, man, you really know how to mess up a good thing when you want to, don't you?"

"I know," Lang agreed, still holding on to her sister with wet rubber gloves. "But I'm hoping I can fix it somehow."

Mrs. Burgess continued to dry and put away the dishes as she listened to her girls. She wasn't quite ready to console Lang—saw no point in chastising her either. She was worried though, more for her daughter's marriage than her daughter. She'd spoken to Sean. And had heard him so clearly. Her son-in-law had already checked out of their union. Her child was in denial if she thought she could get her husband back. He was already gone.

"I hope you can, too," Cullen said, rubbing her sister's back before releasing her embrace and grabbing the broom. "I don't know how you went out like that. A man like Sean, a *brother* like Sean . . . I mean, he's so attentive, so giving, so rare. . . . You get someone like that . . ." Cullen paused, shaking her head.

Lang bit her bottom lip, bracing herself for her sister's admonishment. But Cullen wasn't used to seeing her sister so emotionally exposed and wasn't about to exploit her vulnerability.

Lang bent down with the dustpan, anticipating Cullen's reproval.

"Here's the thing, Langston. When you get what you had with

Sean, you're supposed to treasure that as the sacred gift it is," Cullen said, stooping down to put her arm around her little sister. "You understand me?"

Lang nodded before dropping her head.

"Now, I know you get off on constant stimulation and finding that next thing to turn you on," Cullen said, lifting her sister's chin.

Lang rolled her eyes.

"You always have, Langston. But I gotta ask, was it worth the risk of losing your husband? I mean, you guys were talking children. What was your plan—to keep chasing the rush and the kids?"

Lang shrugged her shoulders and put away the dustpan. No one said a word, which was fine by Lang. Even if she had a plan per se, her sister, with her *Cosby Show*-type marriage, wouldn't understand it. Stimulation was vital to Lang's existence. Her plan had been simply not to get caught.

Lang pulled three coffee mugs out of the cabinet and then scanned her mother's coffee-bean selection.

"Give Sean some time, some space," Cullen finally said, sighing a bit and taking a seat on one of the stools in front of the kitchen island. "He may come around. Lord knows he adored the hell outta you."

"Yeah, but I'm afraid if I give him too much space, he'll get used to life without me in it," Lang admitted, eyeing her quiet mother suspiciously before handing her Dean & DeLuca's Ethiopian Yirgacheffe blend.

Gail Burgess was long on advice and full of opinions. Her silence wasn't lost on either of her daughters.

"Get comfortable not having me around," Lang continued as she took a seat next to her sister.

"Well, nothing beats a failure but a try," Cullen said, repeating what their deceased father had used to say to them whenever his girls were discouraged. Mr. Burgess had died in a tragic car accident when Lang and Cullen were both teenagers.

Lang smiled and hugged her sister again. She felt hopeful.

"Men don't forgive, Langston," Mrs. Burgess finally said after filling the grinder with the coffee beans. "And on that rare occasion that they do, they never forget," she added sadly.

While Gail Burgess pitied her daughter, she also felt a certain level of personal guilt. She had known her youngest wasn't ready for marriage some four years ago and had told her so a few days after her engagement party.

She'd not only witnessed her newly engaged daughter flirting too intently with one of her church member's married sons, but more importantly she understood the very essence of who and what her daughter was. And Langston Neale Rogers, just like Zora Neale Hurston and Langston Hughes, was a free spirit. Nothing and no one held Lang's attention too long. Never had.

Mrs. Burgess had envisioned her bright little girl traveling the world, accomplishing great things, bearing gifts from exotic places, but never really settling down. Langston and conformity had just never gotten along too well. Particularly after her father had died. According to Lang, life, no matter how long it was, was too short for it not to be a blast. And her mother not only respected that but also embraced it. *Free woman,* as the author Pearl Cleage deemed—Gail Burgess was one and had raised a pair of 'em.

However, Lang was also determined and defiant. And to everyone around her, including her mother, blissfully married. She insisted that Sean understood and even appreciated her flirtatious nature and in fact was secure enough not to feel threatened by it. She'd convinced her mother that her commitment to Sean was more compromise than conformity.

And Mrs. Burgess subscribed to it all. She frequently asked Lang if she should expect the great American novel or an adorable grandchild first, all the while ignoring that slight sense that something about her daughter's marriage still wasn't *quite right*.

"Oh, Langston," Mrs. Burgess said, rubbing her youngest child's shoulder before sitting on the stool right next to her. "I just want you to be happy. That's all I've ever wanted for my girls."

The Burgess women sipped on their coffee as their mother recounted the afternoon Sean had tearfully asked Lang's hand in marriage. He'd openly professed his love for her daughter and vowed to take care of her mind, body, and soul. She'd prayed that it'd be enough to sustain her maverick of a daughter.

Lang promised herself she wouldn't cry anymore, but reliving Sean's proposal had been emotional for all three women. Cullen and Mrs. Burgess comforted Lang. And Lang allowed them. Mrs. Burgess even succeeded in convincing Langston to stay in her old room, once she checked out of the hotel, at least until she found a place of her own.

"I'm gonna walk Thurman," Lang said, pulling out their Saint Bernard's leash from one of the kitchen drawers. She needed air again. "Have the twins ready to go ice-skating by the time I get back."

Lang had taken her family to see *A Raisin in the Sun* later that week and called her best friend to make sure they were still on for Pretty Inside's Pamper Party. She'd refused to hibernate.

As they carefully slid their hands and feet under the nail driers, Lang and Aminah recapped their New Year's Eve. Aminah had spent hers at home with her family like always while Lang confessed to having spent hers on her knees.

"Excuse you?" Aminah asked, spitting out her Veuve.

"Get your dirty mind out the gutter." Lang laughed, mimicking a Salt-N-Pepa line. "I was on my knees praying in church seeking forgiveness, asking for clarity."

Aminah laughed. "For a minute I thought you were gonna tell me you were servicing Dante or something."

"Nah. I still think about him though. A lot."

Aminah rolled her eyes.

"It's just that we were more sexually compatible," Lang said, remembering the last time she'd sexed Dante, grinning slightly and then shaking the memory away. "There's this French classical author, François de la Rochefoucauld," Lang explained as Erika inspected her nails, "who said something to the effect of when love becomes labored, we welcome an act of infidelity to free us from fidelity."

Erika raised an eyebrow but said nothing.

"And loving Sean got to be too much work for you?" Aminah asked as Erika carefully dragged her finger across Aminah's shiny, dry pink nails, awaiting Lang's response.

"I think so," Lang said, shrugging her shoulders.

Erika nodded and released Aminah's hand.

"I've tried calling him, you know. He won't take my calls."

"It's too soon, Lang. He's hurting. It's still too raw."

"I miss him. I know you speak to him. Does he ask about me?"

Aminah hated answering that question. She closed her eyes,

shook her head, and then asked Richard to kindly pull her wallet out of her bag.

Lang released a long, heavy sigh. "'Heaven has no rage like love to hatred turned, nor hell a fury like a woman scorned,' or, in this case, a man."

"Shakespeare?"

"No, another William. William Congreve, from his play *The Mourning Bride*. So many people misappropriate and misquote. Well, I guess people paraphrase and then attribute 'Hell hath no fury like a woman scorned' to Billy Shakes." Lang chuckled at the memory.

Billy Shakes was Lang's and Sean's nickname for William Shakespeare. They both loved his work, admired his words.

"Do you have any regrets?" Aminah asked, carefully sliding out her new Centurion American Express, also known as the Black Card. Fame had received an invitation for the exclusive piece of plastic a few days after Thanksgiving. He was all too excited until he'd heard that Diddy carried the even more elite Beyond Black Card.

"Impressive," Lang said, pointing to the Black Card before answering. "Christmas present from Fame?"

Aminah giggled. "Sort of," she said, remembering how she'd jumped up and down like a Mega Million lottery winner when Fame had presented it to her in front of the Christmas tree. He'd recorded her uproarious reaction and took much pleasure replaying it over and over again for everyone who stopped by.

"Well, I don't do regrets," Lang said. "You know that. Guilt either. But I'm remorseful. I wish I hadn't hurt Sean. I wish he'd never found out. I wish there was a way for me to be me and enjoy what I enjoy and still have a committed relationship, still be married. Men seem to do it with no problem."

Aminah paid for their Sessions and four coconut pineapple Er'go candles. She thought they'd be a nice complement to the scrumptious coconut and papaya bath set Amir had given her for Christmas.

"You can be you and enjoy what you enjoy and be single, Lang," Aminah said, starting up her Range. "Why do you even want to be married?"

Lang stared out the window. Usher was singing something about it drivin' him crazy that he was missin' his baby.

"For the same reasons you do, Aminah," Lang answered, turning toward her best friend.

Aminah raised her eyebrow, doubtful.

"Seriously. I want to spend the rest of my life with Sean. I want to have children with Sean." Lang paused. "Someday. I want us to be a family."

"No, you don't, Lang, because you could've had all that. He was waiting on you."

Lang had no response. She sank down in the passenger seat, comparing Usher's confessions to her own.

Aminah drove over to Night of the Cookers. It was sure to be crowded for Sunday brunch, but neither of them minded. Aminah had a thing for their pan-fried catfish, and Lang for their blackened salmon.

"Hey, you ever see that episode of *Sex and the City* where they're disagreeing on the reasons men and women cheat?" Aminah asked, lucking up on a parking spot directly across the street from NOC.

"I'm pretty sure I have," Lang said. "Wait. Is that when Charlotte said the guy should have at least been faithful until the end of the date?"

"Yeah." Aminah laughed. "And Carrie said something like there's this cheating curve and she thought that how accepting someone was of cheating was in direct proportion to their own desire to cheat."

"Ah, the legendary Carrie Bradshaw. She may have been on to something," Lang said, holding the restaurant door open for Aminah.

"So you agree?" Aminah asked.

The hostess seated the two of them in the back of the eatery before Lang could answer. They both declined their menus, knowing exactly what they'd order off the prix-fixe menu.

"I guess I'd be a hypocrite if I didn't agree with Miss Bradswaw," Lang admitted, shrugging her shoulders. "So, yeah, I agree. I take it you don't?"

"Not one hundred percent. I mean, I think there's a whole lot more to it than that."

"Continue."

"Well, I think men of certain stature get an automatic pass, and I think women of a certain age more readily look the other way."

"Yeah, but I've witnessed broke men with no stature whatsoever get a pass and plenty of young girls who look the other way."

"I'm sure, but when there's a definite benefit, like money, fame, lifestyle, status, what have you, there's way more tolerance. Or if you're anything like me, you have this unrestricted, unconditional love."

Lang nodded in agreement at Aminah's point before taking a sip of her mimosa.

"Like when Chris Rock said, 'A man is only as faithful as his options'?" Lang asked, doing her toothy, squinty-eyed Chris Rock imitation.

Aminah laughed. "Yeah, there's definitely truth in jest."

"So I mean, if that's truly the case, I think women married to professional athletes, celebrities—hell, politicians—have to know that infidelity is par for the course, no? You don't marry men like that if monogamy is important to you."

"I think you're right," Aminah admitted. "I mean, I definitely think people are more forgiving of it privately than we may be publicly. And I do think that there is in fact a cheating curve, rules of fidelity that we bend depending on the caliber of the man, how much we have vested, and, quite frankly, exactly how much bullshit we're willing to put up with, amongst other things. I have to admit I was very accepting of it."

"*Was* accepting?" Lang questioned. "You mean you're not anymore?"

"No," Aminah stated firmly before blessing her food. "I'm not."

"Well, all right now," Lang said, raising her flute.

The happy pair leisurely enjoyed their meal and the live jazz band, tapping their feet to the music and laughing unabashedly. They reminisced on the highs and lows of the past year and made plans and predictions for the upcoming one.

"You think Fame will ever cheat again?" Lang asked.

Aminah didn't answer right away. The truth was she didn't know. How could she?

"I hope not," she said after sipping her lemon water. "He *better* not."

Lang squeezed her best friend's hand. "If you *choose* to stay, that's fine by me. But if you *have* to stay—I mean, if you feel obligated to stay—there's just something awful about that," Lang explained. "That's just not living to me."

Aminah smiled and kissed Lang's forehead.

"How about you, Lang?" Aminah asked. "Do you think you could ever be faithful to one man? Or are you still determined to have it all?"

Lang knew what Aminah wanted to hear. She knew the politically correct—no, the morally acceptable thing to say, but she couldn't lie. Hell, the year had just started. Lang saw no point in starting it by making false declarations.

"If I could have orchestrated this whole thing better or ideally, I guess . . ." She paused to gather her thoughts and finish off her mimosa. "I mean, if such a thing were even possible, I just never would've gotten caught," Lang admitted. "I never would've hurt Sean. I would've ended things with Dante smoothly. Got in and got out nobody hurt, nobody the wiser. But I cannot say I never would have had the affair. I mean, to keep it all the way real, I really enjoyed it. It was exciting, exhilarating. . . ."

"How, Lang?" Aminah questioned. "After all the pain you've caused yourself and him. How do you see not getting caught as the solution?"

"I didn't say it was the solution. Listen, Aminah, men aren't the only ones who get bored with the same ole, same ole, and it has nothing to do with my commitment to my marriage. And only part of it is the thrill of new dick. The other part is never wanting to feel like I'm settling or compromising my personal fulfillment for conventional standards of happiness, you know?"

"No, I don't know."

Lang shrugged her shoulders.

"I'm committed to my commitment," Aminah stated, making direct eye contact with Lang. "To my marriage, to my family."

"And I respect that," Lang responded, never batting an eyelash, nor breaking her stare. "I just don't see monogamy and commitment as one and the same. Okay, so maybe I can't have Sean back. Maybe I'm being selfish. 'Cause I know he's like you and most people in their conventional views of commitment. And maybe being with me isn't in his best interest," Lang reluctantly admitted. "But maybe my having it all means being in a marriage that can be open when it needs to be and exclusive when it wants to be—as long as the sex is mind-blowing, turn-me-out sex. I know I'm not alone in this. You know Ruby Dee and Ossie Davis did that for a while?"

"No, I didn't," Aminah admitted, surprised. They were her relationship idols. She trusted her best friend's knowledge, but she'd need to do her own research on that one.

"I know I can't say I won't ever find another man desirable besides my husband, whoever he may be. But, see, now, I'm the type of woman who if my husband's interested in a *ménage*, then let's go find that next chick together. Let's pick out someone we're both attracted to and enjoy ourselves together."

Aminah shuddered at the thought.

Lang laughed. "I know, I know, the idea alone grosses you out. I'm saying, though, you've never thought of a threesome with you, Fame, and someone new?"

"No!"

"You should come visit me in my head, Aminah. I've imagined a threesome with me, another chick, and Sean. Me, Sean and Dante—"

"Okay, Langston, damn. I'm still eating. . . ."

Lang winked at her best friend. They'd agree to disagree. It had worked for their friendship for almost thirty years. They worked around their differences and treasured their similarities. And while both were discovering new things about themselves, about each other, it was the familiar, the predictable, and, most importantly, their unconditional love for each other that kept them bonded.

Lang's gut told her Fame would probably cheat again. However, she just couldn't fathom Aminah ever really leaving him. Lang saw no point in sharing that thought with her girl though. And Aminah took comfort knowing Lang was finally starting to let the idea of Sean go. It would take Lang some time—not much though. Besides, Aminah also knew Sean could never trust Lang again. In fact he'd already started dating. But she spared her best friend that bit of info . . . for now.

"Can I get you ladies something else?" the waiter asked cheerfully. "Coffee? Dessert? More champagne?"

Tossing their heads back, laughing and raising their empty flutes simultaneously, they both opted for another glass of champagne.

THE CHEATING CURVE

Paula T. Renfroe

ABOUT THIS GUIDE

The questions and discussion topics that follow
are intended to enhance your group's
reading of this book.

DISCUSSION QUESTIONS

1. Lang supported Aminah and her marriage even though she didn't agree with her acceptance of Fame's infidelity. Was she being a true friend?

2. Lang states that she can separate sex from love, though women aren't socialized to do so. Is that possible?

3. Because Fame never lies to Aminah when she questions his behavior outside their marriage, is he therefore honest?

4. Is Aminah's acceptance of Fame's infidelity indicative of her insecurity, weakness, or love for her family?

5. Lang truly loves Sean, yet she finds Dante more sexually compatible. Does that diminish her love for Sean? How important is sexual compatibility in a relationship?

6. When does Lang first cheat on Sean?

7. Lang thinks monogamy and commitment are two different things. Do you agree or disagree?

8. What did you think of Sean's initial reaction to hearing his wife have phone sex? Was he weak for running away? Should he have immediately confronted Lang?

9. When Lang and Dante finally have sex, how did you feel for Sean?

10. Aminah cites Coretta Scott King, Jackie Kennedy, Hillary Clinton, and Camille Cosby as examples of beautiful, intelligent women who stayed with straying husbands. Is she wrong to use them as role models? Are there valid reasons to forgive and stay with a cheating spouse? Is it indicative of personal strength or weakness?

11. Ultimately, Sean does not forgive Lang. Why does it seem that men are less willing to forgive than women? How much does ego and pride play a part in that?

12. Do you think Fame will cheat again? If he does, do you think he'll "insulate" Aminah from it? Do you think Aminah will leave Fame if he cheats again?

13. Did Sean cheat on Lang when he kissed Aminah? Was he justified?

14. Did you feel any sympathy for Fame at the Thanksgiving dinner?

15. Do you agree or disagree with Miss Lenora's statement that there is no such thing as a powerful monogamous man?

16. Aminah asserts that cheating is simply a choice, not an uncontrollable urge; is she oversimplifying it?